A Triple Trilogy

Also By John Reseck Jr.

Nonfiction

Marine Biology

Marine Biology Lab Manual

SCUBA Safe and Simple

We Survived Yesterday

Kayak qualification and testing manual

(For the US Coast Guard - Not a public book)

Life According to Grandpa 1

Life According to Grandpa 1I

Fiction

(Amazon eBooks)

The Man Who Died Twice

The Invisible Assassins

The Cow Blood Case

Also published in

Skin Diver, National Geographic, Readers Digest,

Kayaker and The Voice Magazines

A Triple Trilogy

3

Murder Mysteries
Short Stories Very
Very Short Stories

John Reseck Jr

ISBN – 978-0-999-5622-4-8 printed
ISBN – 978-0-999-5620-5-5 eBook

Book formatting by Connie Shaw
Cover art by: Bruce Berglund

Dedication

To all of those that have touched my life and cause me to think.

With Thanks to those that have helped to guide me through the process of learning to be a writer.

To my wife, Sharon, who typed my ridiculous hand written writings.

To Ruth Caron, Marge Dieterich, Karin Crilly, Shelly McGrew, Diane Gnewuch, John Reseck III and Judy Wright - who read my various drafts over the years to help me along my journey to be the best I could be.

Yancy Sasan, my artist Son-in-Law that read the drafts and came up with the covers for the Trilogy stories.

To Bruce Berglund and Connie Shaw who designed the book layout and the covers for much of my work.

Table of Contents

JOHN RESECK JR.

The Man Who Died Twice

Prologue

Texas, December 23rd, 1910

The cold wind finally died down as the sun slowly disappeared behind the mountain ridge. The young man, now in his sleeping bag, stopped shivering and is resting comfortably leaning against his saddle looking at the stars. The moon was not yet visible and in the total darkness of the open range the stars were so thick in the sky it was hard to pick out the Big Dipper and almost impossible to find the North Star.

Jack knew no other life. His father had worked for the "W bar D" ranch as a range rider before he was born and when he was only eight years old he was riding herd with his father. He was tall and lean like his dad and most all the other open range cowboys in Texas at the turn of the century. Living the lone cowboy life since his father died of consumption five years earlier, he was now used to being alone.

Jack hardly remembered his mother; she had died when he was only six years old. He remembered she was pretty and that she loved him but not much more. He lived with the Wayne family at the "W bar D" ranch house for two years until he was eight; then his father said he was old enough and strong enough to ride herd with him.

His life with his dad had been a good one. They had ridden together for seven years before his dad got sick and died just six months later at the "W bar D" ranch house. The Wayne's told Jack he could ride for them as long as he wanted the job. Now five years later as he lay here looking at the stars all by himself, with the 80 head of cattle down in the draw his only family, he was thinking about the date, December 23.

Tomorrow is Christmas Eve. He and his father were on the range most every Christmas Eve they were together. He would miss him more than usual tomorrow night. He looked at his gun belt and the shiny big pistol that gleamed from its holster. He smiled and patted it like he was patting the shoulder of a good friend. The gun was the only thing he had of his father's. Harry White gave his son the gun on his death bed saying "This is all I have to leave you son. Treat it as your best friend, and it will keep you safe on the range."

Jack decides to celebrate Christmas Eve just like he and his father had for all those years they rode together. He looks at his gun and says out loud, "Well friend, it's just you and me tomorrow night at the camp fire. We'll cook us a rabbit over the fire and sing 'Silent Night' by our Christmas tree." He rolled over on his side and went to sleep just as the stars began disappearing in the increasing moonlight that filled the sky.

Chapter 1

The 911 call came in at 10:22; a man had jumped from the Elmore Building on 2nd Street. The call went to the Seattle police and the area fire department for the paramedics. A few minutes later it came to the attention of Detective Ron Steel via a shout from the inner office. "Hey Ron, we got a jumper at the Elmore Building on 2nd Street. Go check it out and don't forget to do the paperwork. We've got a busy week; let's get this one out of the way fast." The chief was a big man and looked as if he could have been a tackle on the Seahawks Pro football team. When he talked everyone listened, because he only said what he wanted you to hear. His comments were the 'don't ask questions just do it' type that expected and got action.

Steel put both hands on his head and shouted back, "Chief, I hate jumpers! There's nothing to the case except scrape up the remains and do three days of paperwork."

"Everyone gets their share of the mundane jobs Steel; you know that and you haven't had a jumper in over a year. Go on, get your butt out of here and I want your report on my desk tomorrow."

"Who do you want me to take along?" Steel asked.

"You're on your own – you don't need a backup on this one, even if you are just a farm boy. The only problem you're going to have is identifying what they scrape up off the sidewalk. It's a twenty-story building."

The scene was forty-five minutes old by the time Detective Steel got to it. There was no need to hurry to a jumper. The crime scene investigation people had been there and taken a roll of film and that was about it. "A cut and dried routine suicide," the officer that was keeping the public back said. "There are four witnesses that were on the roof when he jumped and the two officers over there in the doorway talked to them to get their statements."

"Thanks," Steel replied, and walked over to the two officers identifying himself as Detective Steel. "I understand you got statements from the witnesses."

"Yes sir, we did; they were very shook up, especially the girl. She couldn't talk through the crying, but what little we got from her matches with what the others said. They all work in the building and were either on break or working on the roof."

The next day, Steel spent until noon reading all the statements from those on the roof and some on the ground that had looked up. Being a man of few words, most farm boys are, his report was simple, to the point and short. It read:

Case #413416

At 1022 hours on December 13, 2006, a white male identified as Robert Blake, age 30 by the wallet in his pocket, jumped from the roof (20th floor) of the Elmore Building at 2nd and Marion Streets.

Papers were found that indicated he was deeply in debt to various loan sharks from gambling debts. He was single and had no family as yet identified.

There were four close proximity eyewitnesses to the jump. Their statements corroborate each other stating the man walked out on the roof, climbed out on the ledge, threw some papers down and said something like, "You can't get it out of me now" and jumped.

It appears to be a clear case of suicide brought on by the owed debts, the Christmas season and an unstable mental condition.

See copies of witness statements attached.

Respectfully submitted,

Detective Ron Steel

Steel was proud of himself for getting the whole thing out of his hair in just one a day.

The chief was happy to put it to bed and get back to the serious crimes that go on in the big city on a continuous basis. There were several suicides every day in the city, and the chief hated them. They took his men off the streets to do the paperwork. He didn't consider the time spent on suicides as "law enforcement," just record keeping. His officers felt the same way.

The newspaper article on the third page of Section B, the next day was short. "A man, Robert Blake, jumped from the Elmore Building at 10:22 a.m. Apparently, he was deeply in debt and depressed because of the holiday season coming up and decided to end his life. The suicide was verified by witnesses that saw him jump from the roof. No one else was injured when he hit the ground. He has no family as yet identified. The body has been remanded to the coroner's office. Anyone having information about family should contact their local police department."

The case was forgotten almost instantly until two days later when the phone rang on Steel's desk.

"Detective Steel?"

"Yes, this is Steel."

"This is Sally McKenzie at the County Coroner's office. How are you today?"

"I'm fine, what is this about?"

"You were on a suicide case, #413416 a few days ago. I read your report and I'm afraid it's missing a few rather important facts and comes to an erroneous conclusion." This was a blunt way of saying 'you screwed up,' in a polite and politically correct way.

Steel was on the defensive immediately. "What are you talking about, erroneous conclusion? Do you mean that jumper from the Elmore Building?"

"That's the one – your conclusion was a simple suicide wasn't it?"

"Yeah, that's what it was."

"Then how do you explain the bullet in his head, entering from the back, and him being dead already before he hit the pavement?"

Chapter 2

Steel sat down, his mind was spinning - he had to create a scenario that included a bullet in the head, that he now knew as fact. Then plan an investigation of this seemingly impossible situation that made it possible. Everything he thought he knew about the case made no sense if in fact the man was shot. This wasn't a suicide; it was a murder.

He had been a problem solver ever since he was a little boy on the farm. Some of his family used to kid him as a young man by saying "Ronnie, I think your mind must work in outline form, everything you do is so organized." It was true; he worked on paper by outlining any problem and putting down all the possible options and their probability of being correct. Then one by one he would eliminate them until he had the most probable answer. He said he had learned to do it that way in science class. He called it, *Ronnie's scientific method.* He was well known for his constant list making. His colleagues gave him a box of ballpoint pens for his birthday.

He was never good at multi-tasking. He always focused, some of his friends thought to excess, on one thing at a time. Steel thought the call from the coroner might be a joke his colleagues were playing on him. They called him the 'farm boy' because he came from a farm in the Midwest. His only experience when he was first hired on the Seattle Police force was as a policeman in the small town where he grew up. He would never have been accepted on the city's police department if they had not been in need of new officers in a bad way.

After ten years in the department he had become a highly respected detective but he was still often the blunt end of one joke or another. He understood and didn't mind at all. It was a male thing, the more they gave him a bad time the better friends they were. He had to go to the morgue and find out for sure if this was a prank or real. He thought it must be a prank.

Sally met him at the front desk when he arrived and took him into her lab area. They hadn't met before and his first thought was, she doesn't look like a coroner. The smell of the morgue area brought him back to most of it was in her report, but he was asking for more detailed information now. The bullet had been identified now as a 45-caliber, most likely from a handgun. It was an old hand gun because of the rifling, the groves in the gun barrel that spin the slug as it is fired to help the accuracy of the shot. This slug had almost no rifling marks. The gun was either manufactured without any, which was unlikely, or they had been worn down by a lot of shooting over the years.

This entire scenario was becoming more and more challenging. Such a gun with no rifling would be inaccurate and a normal 45-caliber should have had enough power to pass through the head, not lodge in it, if the gun had been close enough to be able to hit its target.

They finished dinner, had one more beer as they talked and Steel took Sally home. Their dinner meeting had finished with a lot of questions that didn't make any sense to either one of them. His focus was back on the case. He left her at the door, gave her a hug and a friendly kiss and said, "Sometime perhaps we could go on a real date. I really enjoyed myself tonight and you are so easy to talk to. It's like I've known you for a long time. It's been fun and a very helpful evening to the case. I hope you feel the same way and will forgive me for focusing so much on the case."

"Oh, I understand and I had a wonderful time. It's the first time I've been out with someone I was really relaxed with. I knew that you were interested in me for what I am and my ability to do my job well, not just the length of my skirt.

"On our next date I promise to be more interested in the length of your skirt." He smiled.

"Well, at least it will be the second date," she smiled back. She went inside, closed the door and said to herself, "I think I really like him."

Steel went home and couldn't sleep. There were just too many things that didn't make any sense. He stayed up most of the night making lists, then copying them so he could cut out each item and move it around on a wall board.

Each scenario started with a paper that read:

"Found dead on the sidewalk at 2nd and Marion –

Robert Blake, 30 years old, no known family, died of gunshot wound to the head, most likely from an old 45 caliber revolver." He went over all the information he had and none of it contradicted that statement. He would consider it true unless something else popped up later to change it.

The second paper read: "Pushed, dropped, or jumped from the 20th floor of the Elmore Building."

This too was a given true statement, but he had to determine which of the three options it was. It didn't seem possible at this point that he had voluntarily jumped. The answer wasn't the obvious one that he had been led to believe.

The third, fourth, fifth and sixth papers were the statements of Katie James, Conley the Chef,' Jerry Hall and Skip Johnson, the people on the roof. Their statements were where his options started. They either proved Blake was alive and jumped of his own accord or they were all lying, and killed him together. He would have to check them out individually to see if there was any connection with Robert Blake. It would make sense that the four of them planned the murder of Blake. It would almost have to be that way to make the pieces fit together. The other possibility was that Blake was murdered and the four on the roof were threatened and too scared to talk. That someone may have told them what to say or he would kill them too.

He decided to start there. He felt the four of them might be in cahoots. He had not actually talked to any of them because it didn't seem important, just cut and dried. He had accepted without question the statements they gave the officers at the time of the jump. He would now bring each one into the office individually and question them. He would start tomorrow with no warning to them so they couldn't talk to each other beforehand. If there was a conspiracy, he would continue to probe until he exposed it.

Chapter 4

Steel felt that there must have been some kind of conspiracy among the witnesses. These statements that he was going over for the fifth time were too close to the same story, and that is almost never the case with eyewitnesses. Everyone normally interprets what they see differently, and because they almost always see whatever it is from a different angle than the others, their stories generally differ quite a lot.

He had worked out a set of direct questions to ask each one of them. He wanted to see if he could find any discrepancies from their first statements in their answers.

Question #1 – Why were you on the roof at the time? This was a very important question. If it was unusual for them to be on the roof it would give him a reason to dig deeper. It would be consistent with a conspiracy. He was expecting at least one of them not to give a good reason to be there at that time.

Question #2 – Had you ever seen Robert Blake before or even had any dealing with anyone who might have known him? This was important because it was a 'trap' question. If they said 'no,' and his investigation proved otherwise, he had a possible hidden connection that he could pursue.

Question #3 – How long was he on the roof before he jumped off? This was just to check consistency of their statements. He expected the answers to be similar, but if they were exactly the same, it would spell conspiracy. Another trap question.

Question #4 – Did he yell or scream when he jumped? This was very important because it said he was alive when he jumped, which according to his evidence he could not have been.

Question #5 – Where were the other people on the roof, and what were they doing when Blake jumped? This was another consistency of statement question.

Question #6 – How well do you know the others that were on the roof when he jumped? If they were all connected it would be consistent with the conspiracy theory. If they lied about it, it would be even more positive for a conspiracy. If he could not prove a connection between them, he was back where he started – confused.

Question #7 – Did Robert say anything and if so, what, before he jumped? He knew he had said something from the statements, but he wanted to see if all of them would say they heard the same words. It was not likely that they did, so if they all say the same thing it would be very suspicious.

Question #8 – Did they hear anything that sounded like a shot? Plain and simple question; he knew there had been one. If they hadn't heard it, he would have to believe they were lying, or he would be even more confused.

He also had a complete check run on each one of them from the time they were born to the present. He was looking for a connection among the witnesses, Robert Blake, or the loan sharks that were identified from the notes Blake had left behind on the roof. Perhaps Blake was assassinated by a different loan shark who just had those letters left at the scene to throw the cops off his trail and on to someone else. More confusion.

He didn't know what these questions would prove, yet he knew Robert Blake had been shot. Still confused.

He didn't work on the street side witnesses because they really had no way, according his diagram, to have been involved. They were too far away and there were other people all around them. None of them had reported hearing a shot or a scream. The fact that no one reported hearing a scream was consistent with instant death from the gunshot to the head but the roof people did report him screaming. He thought most jumpers would scream all the way down; maybe not from 20 stories.

He made a drawing of the roof of the Elmore Building. Then he made five copies of it and put the name of each of the four witnesses on one and his name on the fifth one.

When he interviewed each one of them, he would give them their diagram and ask them to draw in the position of all four of the people on the roof. Then he could make a composite on his diagram and see what their accuracy was. He wasn't sure just what that would tell him except it was a chance for one of them to stumble on their story.

The interviews would not take long. The questions were simple and direct. He would have enough information to check their stories against each other and see how they compared.

If their stories were identical that would indicate that it had been a planned story and give him a reason to really probe into it. If they were similar, but not exact, they were probably telling the truth. If they were very different, then he had a different problem and would have to find out why. He didn't expect that. He was really expecting the first option, that they would be exact. That would match with Steel's theory of them either doing the killing, or being threatened by the one that did.

The interrogation room was a small room, only eight feet wide and ten feet long. The walls had nothing on them and were painted an off white. There was a small, plain table in the center that you might expect to find in a library and a folding chair on each side of it. The chairs were the folding metal chairs that might be used in a conference room to increase the seating. There was also a chair, folded, against the wall. It was an internal room and had no windows.

The lights were built into the ceiling and gave a strong, bright, but indirect light. Walking into the room was like opening the door to a desert on a bright day. It was barren, bright and the temperature was about 73 degrees, just enough to make you sweat a little. It was intentionally not a relaxing atmosphere.

He decided to have Katie Jones and Conley 'The Chef,' picked up very quietly at 0930 the next day by plain-clothes police and brought in. He would be all through questioning them by noon. He would have the two of them taken back to work and have the police bring in Jerry Hall and Skip Johnston to question in the afternoon. He figured he would have all the information he needed by 1600 and could start sifting through it, looking for some answers.

The police officers went directly to Katie and Conley's bosses and identified themselves. They told them that their employees were needed to give a statement at police headquarters to help clear up the case of the man who had jumped off the building the other day. It was just routine and they would be back to work by noon.

They were taken to headquarters in separate cars. Steel didn't want them to have any contact with each other. This entire interrogation was to be a surprise to all of them, and appear to be strictly routine.

When they arrived at police headquarters, they were taken into separate waiting rooms with comfortable chairs and a coffee maker and offered a cup of coffee, which they both accepted. Conley took out a cigarette and was told by an officer that he couldn't smoke in there. The door opened to Katie's room and Steel came in. He introduced himself as the lead investigator for the jumper case, and asked Katie to join him in the interview room.

Conley asked if he could step outside his room onto the small deck and have a smoke. The officer said, "Sure, that's okay as long as you're outside." "Thanks," Conley replied and stepped out on the deck.

Steel opened the door to the interview room for Katie.

Katie stepped in and immediately felt uncomfortable. The room reminded her of something out of a 1950 movie. Steel walked in behind her and shut the door. There were no windows, just the low hum of the ventilator fan.

Steel said, "Have a seat," and sat down across the table from her. He laid his notebook on the table and a tape recorder next to it.

"You don't mind if I record our interview?" he asked. It was more of a statement than a question. He already had it on the table and turned it on.

"My memory seems to be slipping a little lately."

"No, not at all," she replied, then added, "I told the officer the other day everything I saw and heard, what more can I tell you?" She was obviously very nervous but seemed to be ready to talk without any hesitation.

"Well, you know right after a terrible thing happens like that, we are kind of in shock and I just need to check all of the little loose end details to complete my report." That made sense to her and she relaxed a bit.

As soon as she relaxed, Steel hit her with the first question.

"Why were you up on the roof that morning?"

"Oh, I go up every day on my break. All I had to do that morning was a batch of filing. God knows I hate filing. Anyway, at 10 o'clock I grabbed my snack bar. It is one of those granola bars that gives you energy and lots of fiber and all. Anyway, I go up every day and eat my snack at the non-smoking patio. We have two patios; one is non-smoking and one is for the smokers that are trying to kill themselves. I can't stand to be around smokers." Steel broke in, to stop her rambling, making note in his tablet to check her habit of going to the roof every day at that time.

"Had you ever seen the jumper before?"

"Oh, goodness no! He came right by me on the running track, looked right at me, climbed up on the ledge and took some papers out of his pocket. I saw the policeman pick them up. I don't know what they were. Then he turned around and jumped. It is like a movie in my head. I can't shut it off. He just turned around and jumped."

"Did he say anything before he jumped?"

"Oh yes. I forget the exact words but he was telling someone to go to hell. I don't think it was me. I think he's the one that is going to hell."

"Why do you say that?"

"He committed suicide, that is a mortal sin."

"Oh yea," replied Steel. He remembered when he read her bio info that she was a regular church going Catholic.

"How long were you on the roof before he jumped?"

"I was just finishing my granola bar, so my break was about over, so about 15 minutes."

"Does the name Robert Blake mean anything to you?"

"No, should it?"

"No, actually it shouldn't," he replied. "Why do you go to the roof instead of one of the smoke free lounges?"

"The lounges are so crowded during break times. I don't have any friends here; anyway, I like to walk up the two flights of stairs, it helps me stay in shape. I'm single you know; I need to stay in shape unless I want to be single forever."

Steel smiled and so did she. He liked her and could find nothing yet to make him suspicious about her. She seemed genuine.

"Did he yell or scream when he jumped?"

"Oh God yes, I can still hear him. It sounded like 'Aaaaaa,' I jumped up and looked over the edge and his arms were flailing as he fell, like he was trying to fly.

"Did he yell all the way down?'

"I don't know, I guess he did, I couldn't watch. I sat back down and closed my eyes. I cried and cried for a long time."

"Were there others on the roof and did you know them?"

"Well, there was The Chef. I guess that's why he is sitting outside in the other room." She had noticed him when Steel took her into the interrogation room. "I don't know him at all; I just wave 'hi' to him because he is generally up in the smoking patio when I come up. Then there was the custodian, I don't know his name, I see him from time to time up there working on the machinery, for the air conditioning I think, and he was across the roof by the door. That's all."

"Wasn't there a window washer?"

"No, he wasn't on the roof. He was on the 'the thing' he hangs over the side. I could never get on that thing."

"Do you know him?"

"No, I've watched the window washers before on my break, but I don't know if he was one of the ones or not that I had seen before."

"Did you hear anything that sounded like a gunshot?"

"No, just his scream. Oh! I did hear the window washer say, 'Oh shit,' as the guy went by him."

"Thank you very much for your time and your assistance." Steel got up and opened the door and she went out into the waiting room.

'The Chef' was brought in and seated in the metal chair next and Steel asked the same questions.

"I was on the roof to have a smoke. I can't smoke in the kitchen. I go up about four times a day. I was there about 10 minutes before the guy jumped. No, I had never seen him before. He yelled like a banshee when he jumped. No, I didn't hear any shot, just him yelling. Yea, there were two others on the roof. A good-looking chick that comes up every day. That's one reason why I come up at 10. I like to look at her. The custodian was up there doing something across the other side and the window cleaner was working two floors down. No, I don't know any of them, but I'd like to know the gal. Tried to meet her once, but she would have nothing to do with me because I smoke and I'm not giving up smoking for any skirt."

Steel gave him the diagram and asked him to place the people on the roof and then the interview was over. Steel asked, "What is your full name? I can't just have 'The Chef' on the report."

"I go by Conley 'The Chef.'

"I realize that is your professional name but I need your real name for the report."

"Well, don't tell anyone, it's Conley Blake Jr."

Steel looked up. He had just heard something he could work with. "Did you know Robert Blake?"

"I had an uncle named Robert but he died a few years back. Why?"

"He was the jumper."

"No way! His name was Blake? No one I know in my family."

Steel made a note to thoroughly check out Conley's family and Robert's family, to see if there was a connection. He asked only if he could have a swab from his Conley's mouth to check DNA. The chef said "sure, if we are related, he'll be the only one in the family to ever make the newspapers."

Steel thanked Conley and had both Katie and Conley taken back to the Elmore Building by 11:30.

The same police officer that took Katie and Conley back to work picked up the custodian. The window washer, Skip, was on the 7th floor, out on his scaffold, so they decided to wait until he was finished and came in. They called Steel on their cell phone to check if that would be okay and he said, "Yes, but make sure the others don't talk to him." One policewoman stayed to watch him and make sure the first two didn't try to contact him. He didn't talk to anyone and had no phone calls.

Jerry Hall was 64 and had been on the job for about fifteen years. He loved his work and knew every screw and bolt in the building. He didn't know much about the people who worked there though. Most of them treated him like he was invisible anyway, and that was just fine with him.

He was hard of hearing because of all the years around noisy machinery and wore a hearing aid but still had a hard time carrying on a conversation in the busy building. There always seemed to be some kind of background noise, talking, music, or some copy or other machine running that made it difficult for him to hear.

Steel introduced himself and took Jerry into the interview room. Jerry sat down, looked around and said, "This is a good room. I can hear you, there's no background noise." Steel smiled, the room they had worked with the psychologist to make people uncomfortable, was making Jerry more relaxed.

Steel started through his questions and found out that Jerry had come up to the roof because of a drop in the pressure of the ventilation systems and was looking for a leak. He was not normally on the roof at that time of day. He was usually working his way up from the first floor checking all the bathrooms to make sure all the toilets were working. Generally, one or two were clogged from the morning rush as the people came into the building to go to work. He had been on the 11th floor when he got a call about the possible leak in the ventilator from the head of the maintenance department and was asked to check it out. (Steel made a note to check Jerry's boss about the call). Jerry had decided to go directly to the roof and check for the leak, because that was the most likely place for the problem to be. He would come back and finish the toilet check later. It was okay because it was the toilets in the lobby and the first few floors that gave him the most trouble. People would stop at the first bathroom they came to when they entered the building.

He had gone up to the roof, checked for leaks, found none, walked over to look down at Skip. He knew Skip; they talked every now and then. No, he didn't know the girl that was on the patio above where Skip was working, but she sure smelled good when he walked by her to look down and wave at Skip. The girl smiled at him; he didn't think she had said anything, he wasn't sure. He was just about back to the stairwell when the jumper came out and was face to face with him. He had never seen him before. The man hadn't hesitated, and had gone directly to the running track and hopped up on the wall. Jerry said he yelled, "Hey, get down from there," but the guy just turned and jumped off. He wasn't sure but he thinks he yelled as he jumped. Jerry said Skip should be able to tell him about that because he passed right by him as he fell.

Steel didn't ask about the gunshot; he knew with Jerry's hearing problem that would be useless. He had to laugh to himself about the room. It was designed to be totally bare and make the person being interrogated uneasy, but instead of making Jerry uneasy, it put him at ease. He thought different strokes for different folks. He liked the old man.

Only Skip was left. The first three had come out clean as far as he could tell. He had several things to check out, but didn't expect to find anything. Skip was not a real suspect because he could not have shot a falling man that suddenly fell past him in the back of the head, even if he had planned to, but Steel didn't want to leave any option open that he couldn't cross off his chart. He would get together with Sally and go over everything he found out. Perhaps she would see something he had missed.

Skip was brought in at 1700 after he got off work. Most of the questions didn't pertain to him. Steel wanted to know about the yelling, as Robert fell past Skip.

"I heard him scream as he passed me and I don't remember if he kept screaming after that or not. I think he did, but he got too far from me to hear him in just a few seconds."

"Did he know the other people on the roof?"

"I saw the guy and girl when the police were taking their statements, but I don't know who they were. I knew Jerry because we have coffee together every now and then when we happen to take lunch at the same time, which isn't very often. I generally just eat on the scaffold, less hassle." He liked Jerry and Said, "He is a good family man. Every conversation we had was about his grandchildren and my kids."

Steel thanked Skip for his help and made a note to himself. Skip Johnston (his real name) no longer seems to be a suspect.

Chapter 5

Steel called Sally at work. "Hi Sally, it's Steel."

"Steel, how are you doing on 'our' case?" With emphasis on the word 'our.'

"Oh, so now it's our case?"

"You just answered a question with a question, of course it is our case, but don't worry I'll let you have all the glory when 'we' solve it." The emphasis this time was on 'we.'

"Gee, you must really like me to be so good to me."

"No comment. Now, why did you call?"

"Two reasons; see how efficient I am? First, I want to ask you for a real date for dinner and a movie. But I get to pick the movie. Because we don't know each other well enough to go to a romantic movie, I've picked one that will fit with our lifestyle as police officers. It's the new Jackie Chan one, 'A Good Detective Never Dies.' I like the title."

"You're really lucky on this one mister because I happen to like Jackie Chan. He makes me laugh, and in my job, I don't find much to laugh about." She glanced at the body she had on her lab table. It was another drive by shooting, a young boy. "What is the second reason?"

"I need to sit down with you in my office and go over my chart on the case. I have a lot of pieces and I want your help to start eliminating some of them and creating new ones to check. I want you to go over them before I eliminate any of them, just to make sure I didn't miss something. I remember how my mother used to solve problems around the farm. She was sensitive to things my dad and I would miss. I've always approached a problem in a head on way and she seemed to come into the solution by the back door. She taught me to respect a woman's intuition."

"You mean a meeting to work on 'our' case so we won't have to have a working date?"

"You're very perceptive."

"Yes, I know, I'm a woman. I'll wear my short skirt."

They set the time for the meeting the next day at noon during both their lunch breaks in Steel's office. The date would start at 1830. He would pick her up.

Steel worked into the night on his chart. His chart had changed, because of the information he got from the interviews:

Man jumps from building yelling as he jumps

Three witnesses on roof

No connection between any of them or the jumper

All confirm scream

One witness on scaffold

No connection with roof witnesses or jumper

Jumper is dead when he hits the ground from a 45 slug in back of head, which killed him instantly.

Options:

One of the witnesses shot him

The man on scaffold shot him

He shot himself

Someone else on the roof shot him

Someone far away shot him

Sally arrived at Steel's office at noon. They both had a sack lunch and sat down at the table to look at the chart. "It isn't a very big chart." Sally said.

"I know. That's the problem. It seems to dead end no matter where I look. There must be another option that my logical brain can't see. That's why I needed your input to see if your anatomical brain might find some other option."

"So, you're saying that my brain isn't logical?"

"Women don't have logical brains; they have sensitive and sociological brains. They solve problems from a different direction than men do. You also have an anatomical brain to tell me all the possibilities that relate to the body. So, you see women have at least two types of brains and you have at least three types and I don't know, you might even squeak in a logical section. I only have one kind of brain. See how superior you are to me?"

"I wish you meant that," she said as she took a bite of her peanut butter sandwich. Steel noted the sandwich and thought to himself, she would make a good farm girl.

"How do you know I don't?" he said, as he poured her a cup of coffee and placed it on the table in front of her. "Just black is all we have here," he said.

"Black is fine on the coffee," and then added, "about if you mean it or not, only time will tell," and then looked directly into his eyes. "Are we going to have the time?"

"I think so," he said as he smiled, "but it might take years."

"I hope you're right," she said, "only time will tell. Now let's get down to work." They took each statement on the chart and checked it to make sure it was complete and correct.

'Man jumps from building yelling as he jumps.'

They could find nothing to question with that statement. They went over the interview of the four witnesses and found they could accept he was screaming as he went over the side and at least the first 100 feet. This statement was accepted as fact, and they moved to start a new chart.

The jumper is dead when he hits the ground from a 45-caliber slug in the back of the head, which destroyed a major section of the brain and killed him instantly. This too was taken as fact. Now they had to determine how he was shot.

Option #1 – Most reasonable – One of the people on the roof shot him.

The background checks, even Conley Blake's showed no connection with any of the others on the roof or with Robert Blake. They all lived in different areas of the city, came originally from different parts of the country, none of their work brought them together with the exception of Jerry and Skip, and that had only been casual over the years. None of them had a record of ever owning a gun.

Their families did not know each other; Steel had talked to them. It seemed inconceivable that they would cover for each other to commit a murder. Option #1 was crossed off.

Option #2 – Skip had shot him on the way down. They considered that impossible because Skip didn't know he was coming. Skip had no firearm that he could have concealed on his body. He was dressed in jeans and a T-shirt. He had no motive, and he could never have hit him as he fell anyway. Even if Skip shot him, it would have to have been at very close range and the bullet would have passed through the head. Option #2 crossed off.

Option #3 – He shot himself on the way down. Sally said, "It would have been impossible, because he could not have shot himself from behind, there were no powder marks, and at that close range, a 45 would have blown his head apart, and the gun would have been found in the street." Option #3 was eliminated.

Option #4 – Someone on the roof, that no one saw, shot him. This would have been a real possibility, except no one had heard a shot. Katie or Conley would have heard even a silencer on a 45 caliber. On top of that it was a bullet from an old gun. At least that is what the rifling, or lack of it, on the slug showed. Option #4 was eliminated.

Option #5 – Someone from far away shot him. The fact no one heard a shot was consistent with the option, as was the fact that the slug had lost a lot of power before it hit him and the fact that it was the only option left helped them to make their decision that they would pursue Option #5. But how?

All either one of them could think about the rest of the day was, how could this have happened? What are we missing? Not a good way to prepare for a non-working date.

He picked her up at 1830, and they went to a quiet little Italian restaurant and sat in a booth at the back. It was a little early for the dinner crowd and the place was only about half full.

She was dressed in a bright colored dress with flowers on it and an over the shoulder sweater. The dress wasn't a short one, but she looked really attractive and Steel certainly noticed. He wore a sport shirt, a casual jacket and a pair of well pressed pants. He was color coordinated she noticed, which was a first and he looked casual macho. She knew he had worked at picking out what he would wear. She was pleased - it was an unspoken compliment.

Neither of them had mentioned the case all through dinner. They ordered coffee, and there was a moment of silence at the table. She couldn't contain herself. She said, "It was an accidental shooting, wasn't it?"

"It had to be," he replied. The monster had raised its head and couldn't be shoved back into the box no matter how hard they tried. He took out his tablet and pen.

Statement – It had to be accidental. The bullet was fired from some remote location and in a 1/10,000,000-chance hit him in the back of the head as he fell.

She looked at it and said, "It's incredible, impossible and unbelievable, but it is the only thing left and I believe it."

"I hate to admit it, but I do too." He replied. "This is not going to look good on my report."

"There is no other explanation," she said.

"Well, then we start a new chart based on that statement. We'll look for the options that will make that a correct statement and help us prove it?" Steel started a new list and they both started talking at once. They had a new path to follow and both were excited.

Option #1 – Someone shooting a gun into the air.

Option #2 – Someone cleaning a gun and it goes off accidentally.

Option #3 – Someone on a shooting range ricocheting out of the range.

Option #4 – Someone hunting and shooting and missing his or her target.

Option #5 – Kids playing with guns and one was loaded.

Option #6 – A drive by shooing that went astray.

Option #7 – (Any new ideas)

They thought they were on the right track but were any of these options correct?

Suddenly, they realized they had to hurry to get to the movie. There was a brief moment when Jackie Chan almost took a back seat to Robert Blake, but Jackie won out, and they went to the movie.

The movie was a typical Jackie Chan movie. He and his partner decide to take in a play and during the play an actor is killed by an ax that another actor was supposed to bring down over his head, only this time it didn't stop short of his head. The shaft on the ax broke and the falling blade killed him right on stage. Jackie and his partner spring into action and find the shaft had been cut part way through with a saw. When the force to stop the axe's downward thrust, by hitting a cross bar was applied, it would break and the ax head would continue down. This was a murder!

The two heroes fight their way through all of the suspects with hilarious martial art fights and finally discover that the shaft was cut accidentally by a band saw in the stock room when it was pushed against the saw as someone walked by the shop table and bumped it. They had just pulled it back not realizing what had happened and what the consequence might be.

No one was charged, because it wasn't a murder. It was an accident with no knowledge or intent by the individuals involved, the actor who swung the ax, the person using the band saw, or the person that bumped the handle into the saw. "Pretty bizarre story," said Steel as they left the theater.

"Almost as bizarre as our case," she replied.

They arrived at her house and went inside. "Do you want a drink?" she asked. He didn't seem to hear her. She looked at him and could tell that his mind wasn't on her, it was on the case. She went into the kitchen and put on a pot of coffee. It was going to be a little different night than she had expected.

Coming back out of the kitchen with the coffee, she said, "Let's take another look at those options."

"Yea, that's a good idea. I've been thinking about them and I'd like to get my thoughts on paper before I lose them." She poured the coffee and they started going over the options on their list.

Option #1 – Someone shooting a gun into the air.

They discussed the angle of a bullet that was shot into the air, and it wasn't consistent with the angle of the bullet in Jack's head. It came straight in, not at an up or down angle. It would be possible if the body had been somersaulting down but he jumped feet first and he landed feet first. His arms 'flailing' as had been described by several witnesses, even those on the ground. The arms would have acted as a wind vane, like the feathers on an arrow and kept him in an upright position. This was consistent with the witnesses and the evidence in Sally's report that he landed feet first. Option #1 was used to start a most 'unlikely' pile.

Option #2 – Someone cleaning a gun and it goes off accidentally.

This had better probability because it could have come from any of the buildings in the area. It could have been fired from any height because all of the buildings in the area were ten to 39 floors, and the shot could have come through a window and straight into Jack's head at his level, thus the straight in point of entry into the skull. Option #2 starts a 'most likely' pile.

Option #3 – A bullet coming out of a shooting range

There were several ranges in the city but none were close enough that a stray bullet could travel that far. Option #3 was used to start a 'no way' pile.

Option #4 – Someone hunting and shooting in the air or just missing their target.

There was bird hunting nearby but not close enough and it wasn't buckshot they were looking for, it was a 45-cal handgun. There was no other hunting anywhere near them. Option #4 was placed on top of Option #3 in the 'no way' pile.

Option #5 – Kids playing with a loaded gun that went off.

This was very possible. They didn't need to discuss that one much. Steel had been on several such cases and Sally had done autopsies on children, as well as adults that had been killed that way. Option #5 goes on top of Option #2 on the 'Most likely' pile.

Option #6 – A drive by shooting that went astray.

They had a dozen "drive by shootings" a year in the area. They needed to take a close look at this one. 'Drive by's' were always directed at someone, not up in the air. Because the heart had been traumatized by the brain shock to the nervous system, it had stopped before Jack hit the street. That meant he was shot six or seven stories up at least, possibly even 15 stories up because that is about when everyone stopped hearing the screams. No one actually said that, but by looking at all the reports, it was likely that it happened between the 10th and 15th stories. The people on the ground did not hear any screams, and they probably would have if he had been screaming below the 10th floor. It didn't seem that it could have been a stray 'drive by.' Option #6 went into the 'most unlikely' pile.

There was no Option #7 – It was left open in case they thought of one.

"When does this become a non-working date?" she finally asked.

He looked at her and said, "Right now." He took her in his arms and they were strong, as she had anticipated, but his kiss was gentle; she hadn't expected that. He looked at her and asked, "Is this a good start?"

She smiled the smile that had caught his interest the first time he had met her and said, "Oh, yea." He kissed her again. She said, "I'll turn off the coffee pot, we can reheat it in the morning."

Chapter 6

The two options in the most likely pile, #2 and #5, someone cleaning a gun that goes off accidentally or kids playing with a gun were the two that made some sense. Either one of them could have happened in a room ten or fifteen stories up, which would allow for the observed entry angle of the bullet.

The place to start would be the police reports to see if anyone had reported hearing a shot at or about the time of the jumper.

Steel went to the report book and started searching through the reports for that day. They were supposed to be in chronological order, but he noted that some were out of order, so he went through the entire stack. It took him quite a while because he couldn't help himself; he had to take the ones that were out of order and put them in proper chronological order where they belonged in the book. There was no blatant report of a gun shot, but there was one of interest.

It read "1028, a 911 call reported hearing a shot in the apartment next door. Building is located at Marion and 4th street and is the 'Easy Way

Assisted Living' building. Officers sent. The woman calling lives in 1104 and her name is Mrs. Henderson."

The report read, 'Officers met the attendant at the desk on the main floor and asked about Mrs. Henderson and the 911 call. Officers were told she was 92 years old and complained about everything she could remember to complain about. She was, according to one of the attendants interviewed, 'a pain in the butt.' Officers went to the room with an attendant. When the attendant knocked, a voice cried out from inside, 'I don't want any, go away and leave me alone.' The attendant opened the door with his pass key and said, 'These officers would like a word with you.' The Officers were in plain clothes and when the attendant said they were officers. She said, 'Get them out of here. They're not cops; cops are in uniform. They're crooks trying to steal my china. Get them out of here.' She raised her cane and tried to hit one of the officers. The attendant said, 'she is pretty crazy'. Officers left; they could see no credence to the call. Attendant said that she didn't like the man next door and was just probably trying to get him in trouble. Officer Reno #949."

Steel read the report several times. Fourth and Marion, which was about two blocks from the Elmore Building. The distance was about right for a 45-cal bullet to lose most of its velocity. There were too many things that fit in the puzzle to ignore. He would go see Mrs. Henderson.

He called Sally. "Sally, I can use your help. This will definitely be work, not a date. I would like you to accompany me to see an old lady. I don't think she will talk to me. It has to do with *our* case and I need you to use those parts of the brain we talked about that I don't have."

"Sounds interesting, when?"

"As soon as you get off work. Do you want to go home first, or do you want me to pick you up at work?"

"Pick me up at home at 5:30."

"I'll be there and I'll fill you in on the way."

Sally met him at the curb and hopped in the car. "What's going on?" she asked. He showed her a copy of the report, and she agreed first that it needed to be investigated further and that her woman's approach might be better. "This old lady, Mrs. Henderson, obviously doesn't like men. I think I should go in alone and talk to her."

Steel didn't like that, but after thinking about it for about one minute he said, "Okay, but take this tape recorder with you so you have a record of what she says and we can have the police 'shrink' listen to it for their opinion on her credibility." Sally thought that would be a good idea also. She took the recorder. It was about 1/3 the size of a cigarette package. She put it in the outside pocket of her purse. If she set the purse in front of her, she would get a good recording. She asked, "Is it legal to tape our conversation and not tell her?"

"No," he said, but we won't be using it in court, it's just for our information so we won't miss anything."

She smiled and said. "Well, we will have the first secret in our relationship, a tape recording. Oh well, it's better than not having one at all."

They arrived at the building and found the front desk. After identifying themselves and why they were there, an attendant was assigned to take them up to 1104 and Mrs. Henderson. He mumbled all the way up about what a pain she was and all the trouble she was causing for them.

When they reached the door the attendant said, "She is going to be pissed." When he started to knock. Sally stopped him. "Let me do it and the two of you stay outside and be quiet so she doesn't know you are here."

She knocked, but not just a straight knock; she gave the old "Knock the Knock Knock – Knock Knock." It was quiet inside; she did it again only this time she left off the last two knocks. About a minute later there was a knock knock on the inside of the door. "Mrs. Henderson, It's me, Sally, may I come in?"

The door opened and Mrs. Henderson peeked out and looked at Sally. Sally smiled and said, "Why, Mrs. Henderson, how good you look this evening. I just thought I'd stop by and visit for a bit; it's been so long since I've seen you."

"Come in, I'd like to talk a spell," she replied. Sally went in, the door shut, Steel and the attendant waited.

The attendant said, "I didn't know she knew her."

"She doesn't," replied Steel.

"But Mrs. Henderson asked her right in, she never does that. She's always cantankerous as hell with all of us, even the female attendants."

Steel was smiling. "Well, they need to use another part of their brain." The attendant had no idea what he was talking about and decided he had to get back to work.

It was a half-hour before the door opened and Sally came out saying "Thanks you for the nice visit, Helen. "

"Come again soon, dear." Mrs. Henderson closed the door.

The attendant who had come back to check on them said, "Is Helen her first name? I never knew that."

Sally looked at Steel and said, "We can go now. I have something for you to listen to." They were escorted to the lobby by the attendant and got back into the car.

"You won't believe what I've got on tape. I think we've got our shooter. Let's go back to my place and listen to the tape and see if you come to the same conclusion that I did." They drove the short distance to her apartment.

Steel asked, "Is this a date?"

"Not on your life, this is work. I think I've just broken our case and I want your full recognition that I did before it will turn into a date."

He replied, "As long as I don't have to admit it to anyone else, we have a chance to have a date tonight."

"Men are all the same," she said. "They're real team players, just as long as they can be team captain."

"It's our heritage; it's genetics."

"It's genetics all right. No question about that." She put on the coffee while he started to listen to the tape.

They listened to the main parts several times before Steel got out his pen and pad to write down what he considered the important points. It was obvious that Helen was a complainer. She complained about the food, the security, the weather, the attendants and then the next-door neighbor. First, she complained that he had a better apartment than she did because it was a corner one. Steel wrote down on his pad. Corner apartment looks South and West.

Then she complained that he had no up-bringing at all. He was just a roughneck cowboy from Texas and that he was crazy as a squirrel. Steel wrote down, *Cowboy from Texas.* Then she said he should be arrested and taken to jail because he was dangerous.

"Why was he dangerous?" Sally had asked.

"Because he has a big gun on his hip all the time. He thinks he's still in Texas. The old idiot draws it and shoots everybody he sees."

Steel writes, *has a handgun – big, could be a 45 cal – draws it often and pretends to shoot people.*

The tape goes on. "He shot someone the other day. I heard him. I don't know why they haven't taken him to jail. I called and told them, but no cops came. He must have a friend from Texas at the police station, but I'll get rid of him yet. I want him gone. I hate him."

Steel wrote, *heard a shot – could be no one else heard it because he is in the corner apartment and she is his only neighbor against his wall.* There was nothing else on the tape he considered important. He turned to Sally, who had been quietly sitting next to him as he listened and wrote and said, "I think you have just found our shooter. I could never have gotten that information out of her. I admit you are a superior, covert interrogator. Can we have our date now?"

She turned off the coffee and said, "I'm glad you don't mind warmed up coffee, it saves a lot of time in the morning."

Chapter 7

Steel just sat down at his desk when his captain called him in. "You've had the time you asked for on the jumper case, what have you found out?"

"Well, Captain, I think we found the shooter. I'm going to find out for sure today. It looks like an accidental shooting and not a murder at all. I've been working with the coroner's office on it and we've narrowed it down to a single individual. I'm going to check him out today as soon as I can get out of here."

"Good." the Chief said. "I need you on another case as soon as you can pull that one together." The chief was a man of few words and when he spoke the answer was always the same. "Yes Sir." Steel went back to his desk and gathered together what he needed to interview 'the man next door.'

He drove back to the 'care home' and went to the desk. He said, "Hi, remember me?" showing his badge.

The clerk said, "Yes sir."

"I understand there is an old Texas cowboy living in the room next to Mrs. Henderson."

"That would be old Jack. Jack White is his name and you got it right, he is an old Texas cowboy without a doubt and lets you know it every time he opens his mouth."

"I'd like to see him. It's about the 911 call Mrs. Henderson placed the other day about hearing a gun shot."

"No problem, but I have to warn you. He carries his old pistol in a holster on his belt, draws it and pulls the trigger pointing it right at you. No need to worry; he has been doing it for years. Why, I've been shot forty to fifty times by now. He doesn't have any bullets; we made sure of that years ago and he hasn't left his room except to eat in two years. He has no visitors or family and can barely move around without the use of his walker. He couldn't have fired any shot."

"You're sure he has no bullets?" Steel asked.

"Oh, yes. We searched every nook and cranny of the room and totally went through his things before we let him keep his gun. That gun seems to be his only friend." Steel felt a knot in his stomach; perhaps they had not found their shooter.

The attendant knocked on 1102. There was no response, he knocked again. Still no response. "Sometimes he just ignores us and then shoots us when we come in." He opened the door and there stood Jack White. He had snow-white hair, thin, but still there, was about 5' 10" tall. He had been taller before he became stooped over from arthritis. He was looking right at them with cold dark eyes. His left hand was on his walker and in his right was a big handgun. He cocked the hammer with his thumb and pointed it directly at the attendant, then at Steel. Steel's heart skipped a beat. He was not used to having a gun pointed at him. The attendant took a step forward saying, "It's okay, Jack, we're friends."

"Stay back," shouted Jack, as he pulled the trigger. The attendant just ignored him but Steel started to reach for his gun. There was a loud 'click.'

Steel relaxed, and the attendant said, "We just want to talk with you."

"I don't know you, who are you?" Jack looked at Steel.

Steel, remembering a lesson learned from Sally with the interview last night with Mrs. Henderson, said, "It's been a lot of years since we talked, Jack. I think it was on that ranch in Texas. I can't remember the name right now." He put out his right hand.

Jack relaxed, put the gun in its holster that hung from his side, took Steel's hand and gave it a strong shake with a grip that had to have come from a hard life in the field. "I don't remember," he said. "It must have been the 'W bar D' brand up in the panhandle. I worked there long enough to wear out my britches. What was your handle again?"

"Steel," he replied. He was glad he liked to watch the old western movies so he recognized that Jack was asking his name.

"A good name," said Jack. "It speaks of strong character. Steel, Yea, I like that."

Steel told the attendant he wanted to visit a while with Jack alone.

The attendant went outside saying, "I'll be waiting in the hall if you need me."

Steel asked, "That's a fine-looking gun you got there. May I take a look at it?" Jack hesitated. Steel took out his automatic, dropped the clip out of it, and pulled back the barrel to make sure it was empty and offered it to Jack. "Nowadays they make these little things. I think they have forgotten what a real man's gun should look like."

Jack took the gun and tested its weight in his left hand. Then he took his gun out and tested its weight in his right hand. “This little thing is for shooting squirrels.”

Steel said, “Not much of a gun compared to yours. I’d sure like to see yours up close.”

Jack handed him the gun. “Handle a real man’s gun, but be careful. Don’t drop it. It’s been my best friend since my dad left it to me in ’05, and I hit the range as a single in the same year. He got her brand-new and she’s lived on my hip ever since my dad died. Everyone was getting the new double action guns, so this single action peacemaker was on special. Got a good buy on her. Best thing he ever bought. Just about the only thing he had to leave me and she never let me down.”

“Where do you get your ammo?” Steel asked, as he checked the caliber of the gun. It was a 45-cal and when he smelled it, he thought he could smell gunpowder. Jack leaned over close to him and said, “I loaded my own brass for years, but I don’t have any ammo anymore. They took it all away, but I fooled them, because I still had the most important bullet left. I fired the old girl just to see if she still loved me and to say ‘good-bye’ to her. The bad part is I don’t have anything to clean her with. I wiped her off with a towel, but I don’t have oil and a barrel rod to clean her proper.”

Steel took advantage of the opportunity. “Jack, if I can sneak old Betsy here out with me, I’ll clean her up like a new lady and bring her back to you tomorrow.” He hoped Jack would go for it. Jack was thinking it was obvious that he didn’t want to leave it with anyone else.

Steel said, “She has to be cleaned proper or she’ll rust and that would be awful.” Jack was still thinking. “I’ll leave my little pee shooter with you just in case you need it and have Betsy back tomorrow.”

Jack said, “Be really careful with her, and clean her good.”

Steel put the gun in his belt and pulled his shirt out of his pants so it would hang on the outside to cover the gun.

He winked at Jack as he stood up and said, “I’ll see you tomorrow old friend”. They shook hands and Steel left the room. The attendant had taken all this in from outside in the hall but had not acted like he had heard anything.

When they got outside, he said, "That was really slick, but how are you going to get your gun back?"

"I'll get it back tomorrow when I bring Jack's gun back all cleaned and shiny." The attendant didn't understand what was going on but kept quiet. He didn't want to seem stupid.

Steel took the gun directly to forensics to be tested to see if the slug matched. He told them when they were through with it to clean it and have it ready for him the next day. He was sure that this was the gun that killed Robert Blake but he needed positive proof. The ballistic check would do that. He then went back to the place where Blake had hit the pavement. He wanted to confirm that Jack White's window was in a direct line with the fall. He stood where Blake had ended his life and his heart sank. He couldn't see Jack White's building. There was another building in the way. "This can't be," he said out loud.

A man walking by gave him a funny look and hurried on his way. Steel thought for a minute and entered the Elmore Building. He went up four floors and entered an office that said, 'J.P. Brown Accountant.' The girl at the desk greeted him and asked, "What can I do for you?"

Steel showed his badge and said, "You can let me look out your window."

"What? Look out my window?"

"That's all I need today." He walked over to the window and looked towards Jack White's building and sure enough he could see Jack's floor and his corner window. "Thank you very much, you just made my day," he said to the woman at the desk as he walked by her and out the door.

He breathed a sigh of relief. Now he knows two new facts. Jack White was probably the shooter and Blake was shot somewhere from the fourth floor up. Screams were heard down to about the 15th floor, so between the 15th and the 4th was where he had been hit. His report was going to sound okay. What he needed now was to get a positive ballistic report on the gun and to find out where Jack White got the bullet everyone was sure he didn't have. If he had any more, he could accidentally kill someone.

He gave Sally a call when he got back to his desk. "Hello, pretty lady, how is all my competition doing today?"

"They're not very lively," she replied, "they're all just lying around."

"That's the way I want them," Said Steel, "anything of interest?"

Not really, two drive-buys and a stabbing came in but nothing like our case."

"Well, I've got more info on our case and it all falls into place. Do you want to hear it now over the phone or over coffee at 5? I've got some errands to run, but I'm free between 5 and 7."

"Coffee sounds good. How about the Starbucks on the corner of 2nd and Marion?" she suggested.

"Great, I'll see you about 5:15."

"I'll be there."

Steel realized now that he was going to have to find out where the shell came from that Jack had fired and one other problem had raised its head. Now that he was 98% sure that Jack had fired the shot that killed Blake, he had to know:

Where's the bullet case?

How and why he fired it out of the room?

Why no one but Mrs. Henderson reported hearing a gun shot. He went back to Forensics to see what they found out.

"You have no idea how big of a problem you gave us," was the greeting when he walked in.

"What problem?" he asked.

"We had to call every gun shop in the city to find the right shell and bullet for that old gun. We finally found a shop that hand loads special shells for gun collectors and he had some casings. We should have the results for you in the morning; we'll do it first thing as soon as we pick up the shell. One thing I can tell you is that no one just walked into a store and bought the bullet we found in the jumper. We were told that particular style of slug hadn't been commercially manufactured. The gunsmith said it was probably molded by the owner a long time ago."

Steel met Sally at 5:15 at Starbucks. “I’ll have a latte,” she said, “I can’t take their coffee straight, it’s way too strong for me.”

“You mean I have a wimp for a partner?” he said.

“Be careful, macho boy, unless you want to see a full-page ad in the newspaper about a woman solving your **case** for you.”

“Oh, so now it’s my case is it?”

“Not on your life, it’s our case and don’t you forget it.”

She found a small table in the corner with two chairs and sat down. He went to the counter and ordered one latte and one drip coffee, medium size. The large was too much even for ‘macho boy.’ He joined her in the corner and started filling her in.

Yes, Jack Whites’ window was in line with the trajectory of the bullet that killed Blake. That piece fit into the puzzle perfectly. He told her it had to have been above the 4th floor.

She said, “That’s a lock with my coroner’s report that he was dead before he hit the street.”

“Without your report, two bad things would have happened,” he said.

“And what are those?” she asked.

“First, the Case 413416 would have been closed improperly as a suicide instead of a murder or accidental shooting, still up to the DA to figure that out and second, you and I would not be here having coffee.”

“That number 2 is really a bad thing,” she said. Then she asked him what he was up to after 7.

He told her the late seating for dinner at the rest home was at 7 and Jack White was in that seating. He wanted to check out the apartment without Jack there so he could give it a thorough check for more shells or the empty casing from the shot that hit Blake.

She asked if she could come along, but he said no, he wanted to move fast and this was work for his logical brain working like a man’s and figuring where Jack would hide shells.

She said, "Well, okay, but if I were there, I bet I could help you."

"If you were there," he said, "I couldn't focus on what I was doing; you have that effect on me and I need to focus."

"That's about the only acceptable answer you could have given," she said.

He reached over and took her hand and kissed it. "Do you have enough coffee, or should I stop and get some?"

"You don't think we're drinking too much coffee, do you?"

"I'm beginning to wonder if we're drinking enough," he said.

"Another good answer," she said, with a smile.

The search warrant Steel had was to look for shells in Jack's apartment. He knew he needed to get some answers about where the bullet came from that Jack fired.

Steel was at the home by 6:30 and explained what he wanted to do. An attendant was assigned to go with him - not to help look, but to be a witness to whatever he did, and to relieve the administration at the home of any liability.

They entered the room as soon as Jack was taken to the dining room. Steel first had to find out how the bullet got out of the room. He checked the windows and none of them opened but there was a small sliding panel on the top of each of them that did open for ventilation. He asked the attendant if Jack could open and close them.

"No" said the man. "If it's going to be a warm day, we open them when we check the patients in the morning."

"Have they been opened this last week?" Steel asked.

"Yes, every morning for the last two weeks, I've opened all the ones on this side of the building."

"But it's closed now." Steel replied.

"The attendants close them in every room when they come and take the patients to the dining hall," was the reply.

The small window was about one foot high and two feet long. There was one above each of the four windows. Two of the windows faced the Elmore Building. The windows had drapes and they were partially drawn. Steel remembered they were drawn when he was here before. He got a chair and inspected the drape up at the height of the window that would open on the Elmore Building side. Nothing. He moved the chair and looked at the second one. He pulled the drape out straight between his hands and, voila! There was a hole that matched up with the sliding window and looked out to the Elmore Building. He was positive now what the ballistics test would show.

He only had 20 minutes left, but he hit every nook and cranny looking for more shells. He found none. At least one of the questions was answered. Jack had fired his gun and it did go out the window on the Elmore side of the building. He took pictures of the room from all angles to look at later to see if there was something he had missed.

They got a call on the attendant's radio from the attendant that had taken Jack to the dining room. "We're starting back."

"Roger," said Steel's attendant and they got out and on to the elevator before Jack saw them as he came shuffling back from dinner. He didn't want Jack to see him because he didn't have his gun to return. He would bring it back tomorrow.

He left the rest home and drove to Sally's. He told her what he did and what he had found out. There was still a missing piece. If the ballistic report said, 'yes' it was Jack's gun that killed Blake and they were sure it would, the question remained, where did he get a bullet for it? He didn't seem to have any now. The attendants searched for bullets long ago because they knew that he would be pointing the gun at them and pulling the trigger, and found none. He knew they had really looked carefully because that's about the best motivation to do a good job that he could think of.

"I hadn't thought about that, but you're right." She said.

Steel said, "We need to base our thinking on the fact that the bullet had to have come in from outside some way."

"Let's start another chart," said Sally. "I love your charts."

"Is that all you love about me?" He said with a grin.

"When we're working, yes," was her answer.

"Fair enough, let's hurry up and get this work over with."

Question – Where did the bullet come from?

Option #1 – He had it hidden in the room.

Option #2 – He had it hidden outside the room.

Option #3 – Someone brought it to him.

Option #4 – He received it through the mail.

Option #5 -?

"Before I spend too much time on these options, I need to have some more information."

"What do you need?" she asked.

"First, confirmation that it was his bullet that killed Blake. I'll get that first thing in the morning. Then I want to talk to the gunsmith about the bullet and how hard it would be for him, Jack that is, to get the bullet. Next, I'll check with the rest home on his mail. How much does he get and where does it come from? Does he ever leave his room and wander around the building, especially in the last month? Does he have any regular visitors and if so, who? That's the information I need to evaluate the options."

"Your mind does work in outlines and charts doesn't it?" she said.

"That's where you come in - to write the paragraphs from the outline," he said, and gave her a kiss. "I think it's time for you to turn off the coffee so we can go to bed. "

"And think about the case?" she said.

"Are you kidding, I'm tired. I was planning on going right to sleep."

She kicked him and said, "Over my dead body."

"You coroners always talk about dead bodies, but that's okay, I love you anyway."

Sally turned down the bed with a smile on her face; it was the first time Steel had ever said he 'loved her.' It made her feel good to hear it even though it was said in a joking way, or was it? She couldn't tell.

In the morning they drank the warmed-up coffee and Sally made some oatmeal in the microwave. "Oatmeal," Steel said, "I haven't had oatmeal in 30 years."

"Yes, and you probably have high cholesterol too," she replied. "Just stop complaining and eat your oatmeal."

All he could think of to say was, "Yes dear."

Chapter 8

At the office he got the report on the bullet. It was Jack's gun that killed Blake. There was no question that Jack was the one that fired the gun because he never had it out of his sight. Steel would take it back to him this morning. The chief would be really upset if he knew Steel had left his gun with Jack.

He got the name of the gunsmith the forensic people were using. It was on the way to the rest home. He got Jack's gun out of the evidence department and had to fill out a lot of paperwork. He even called out a few favors to get it back so he could return it to Jack. It was now a murder weapon and was needed for evidence.

He had turned it into the evidence department, which was required, then checked it out as the investigating officer. He would return it to Jack and figure out how to get it back if he ever needed to. He didn't think he would because it was an open and shut case of accidental shooting.

The gunsmith was a cool looking man in his late 50's or early 60's, Steel thought. He was tall, 6 foot one or two inches, had long gray hair tied in a ponytail and was slim. He talked with a slight Texas accent like he was from Texas a long time ago, much the same as Jack. Steel showed him Jack's gun.

"My God, that's a beauty. Why, I haven't seen one of these in years, and it's in pristine condition. It's worth a lot of stars if he wants to sell it."

"No, he definitely doesn't want to sell it. It's been in the family since it was new," Steel said.

"The owner of this gun bought it new?" the gunsmith asked.

"His dad did," answered Steel. "This is a true Texas cowboy."

The gunsmith asked, "You said he was a range rider when he was young?"

Steel says, "Yes, he was, somewhere in the panhandle. He rode for the W bar D Ranch."

"God! That is barren country. I've been there, done that, wouldn't want to do it now. That ground would seem awful hard to me. I hate to admit it, but I've become a city boy. I still dress and act like the old days on the range, but the truth is I'm faking it now, it's good for business. I keep my spurs and my cowboy Christmas tree in the office to remind me who I used to be. Then I check my e-mail to remind me who I am." They both laughed and Steel said goodbye and thanked him for his help.

He hadn't gotten much information from the gunsmith, but he had a better feel of who the real Jack was, because he had spent his entire life on the range until he had been thrown from a horse that stepped on a rattle snake. Jack had broken his leg and hip. He had not recovered well from it because he tried to walk on it before it was healed, and it broke again. The wound got infected with a staph infection, then catching pneumonia he almost died.

He had recovered, but not got well enough to work on a horse anymore. He needed work and he didn't really have any 'city skills' to get a job. He was 35 years old and looking for work when he came across an ad for a job he was sure he could handle.

The Wrigley Company needed a security guard on their Catalina Island ranch off the coast of California. The job meant living in a ranch house that was in the center of the island away from the town of Avalon. He liked that; he didn't like towns.

He would patrol the island's interior in a jeep, instead of on horseback and look for poachers instead of rustlers. He would be on his own and his job was just to take care of the island animals. The job description was perfect for a cowboy that couldn't sit on a horse any more. He moved to the Black Jack Ranch house and took over the security of the island.

For forty years he drove the trails on the island chasing the poachers off by shooting at them from the ridge tops where he patrolled in his jeep along the fire breaks. He never hit anyone but the people in town were never sure if it was because he didn't want to, or because he was too drunk. He was known to drink quite a bit in his later years, but he was a major part of the history of the island and nobody cared.

He finally became unable to do the job and was forced to retire; he needed a walker to get around.

Steel was getting a picture of who Jack used to be; he liked Jack even more. He now thought of him as a lean, mean, riding machine. That young man is still inside Jack, but the fence of old age has him locked inside.

He had no family and he had outlived all of his old friends from the range and the island, so he ended up in a small room, in a high rise, in the middle of the city. His position in life right now was the true meaning of purgatory.

When he got to the rest home, he asked to talk to the several attendants that worked on Jack's floor and with Jack. One of them delivered the mail to all the patients on Jack's floor.

"He's only gotten five or six things in the mail in the last year," said the attendant. "And, I don't remember, but I don't think they were anything but junk mail. Jack can't read very well. We have to help him with menus and stuff like that." Well, so much for Option #4, he didn't send or get it by the mail system. It was illegal to send shells in the mail anyway, but he felt sure now Option #4 was no longer an option. Option #1, he had all but totally eliminated also. The room had been searched over and over by many people over a period of several years, and no shells had been found.

Option #2 was still in the picture. He could have hidden the bullet outside his room somewhere, but it didn't make any sense to hide just one bullet somewhere. He would check the hallway when he went up to see Jack just to make sure there were no hiding places where he could have hidden a box of shells years ago and where they would not have been found by the cleaning people or the maintenance people in the last five years. He doubted it, but he would look.

Option #3 didn't seem likely because he had no visitors, not even the others on the floor. They all had changed many times over the last few years because most of the residents didn't come there until they were very ill and most died within a year or two. Jack and Helen were the two that had been there the longest, Helen even longer than Jack.

Neither had any family and were both 'wards of the State,' which meant they had no funds at all. Everything they had was turned over to the State and from then on, the state payed the bills. Neither of them had family, friends, or money. Steel hadn't realized how lonely life could be at the end. He wondered why Helen had been so emphatic on the topic. "I hate him," she had said. He would have thought they would have befriended each other. They had no one else. Oh well, people are strange and we can never figure what we will be like when we pass 90 years old.

He asked the attendant if Jack and Helen had ever been friendly.

"Yeah, they would talk every so often and Jack would go to her room and visit about every week or so until about a month ago. Mrs. Henderson told us to keep that SOB away from her. Who knows, maybe he made a pass at her or something." Everyone laughed, but Steel made note of the change in attitude between them. He didn't believe in coincidences. He was more than just curious about what had happened.

He went up to see Jack. Jack asked him when he walked into the room, "Did you get my gun cleaned?" He didn't say 'hello,' or anything, just did you get my gun cleaned?" He didn't seem to realize that an extra day had passed. Steel was glad because he didn't know how he was going to explain it.

Steel said, "I sure did and it's nice and shiny now." He handed the gun to Jack. "Won't need cleaning now, 'till you fire it again."

Jack took a deep breath and said, as if to himself instead of Steel, "That ain't ever gonna happen now."

"Why is that Jack?"

"No more ammo son, used up my 'safety bullet.' It's the end of the track for me. When you shoot your 'safety bullet' it means a man's ready to close the gate and walk out onto the range for the last time. I'm ready now."

"Can I have my gun back Jack?"

"Sure, it isn't worth much anyway." Jack reached under his loose shirt and took the gun from under his belt. He handed it to Steel and said, "Thanks for cleaning Betsy for me. She should be clean when she's laid to rest."

"It's not your time yet, Jack," said Steel.

"It's close enough and if I don't die natural like that old tumble weed next door will probably poison me."

"Why do you say that, Jack?" Steel thought he was about to find out what the problem between them was.

"Isn't important, I don't blame her. I was mean to her, but I couldn't help it. It was their fault." He pointed to the attendant. "If it weren't for them, I wouldn't have had to do it." Now Steel was even more confused – how could it have been the attendant's fault they had a fight?

They chatted for a few more minutes; Steel said goodbye and left. He needed to know what went on between Helen and Jack and he wasn't having any luck doing it. He needed Sally. He called her and asked if she could get away. He said, "I need you to talk to Helen Henderson for me again, it's important." Sally said she would work through lunch and meet him at 2 p.m. at the rest home.

He called the station and asked for Ted. Ted had the desk next to Steel, and they were friends. "Ted, is the Chief at his desk right now? I can't seem to find him."

"No, he's in a meeting down in Vice. Can I give him a message?" That was just what Steel had hoped for.

"No, it isn't important. I'll catch him later. Thanks." Steel dialed the Chiefs phone and when the answering machine came on, he said, "Chief, this is Steel. Sorry I missed you, but I wanted to bring you up to date on the jumper case. All is going well, only a few loose ends to make it tight, and I should be through with it by tomorrow."

That should get the Chief off his back without any questions, that he didn't have the answer to yet. He felt he would have all the answers soon. He could hardly wait the half-hour till 2 o'clock. He wondered if it was because he was anxious for Sally to find out about Helen and Jack's fight, or just because he wanted to see her. It didn't really make any difference he decided; it wouldn't change the clock. It was still a half-hour away. He got a cup of coffee. He liked the things it reminded him of.

At 2 o'clock Sally drove into the parking lot. Steel told her about his talk with Jack and that he needed to find out what happened between them a month or two before. Sally had to get Helen to open up and tell her. Sally said she would do her best. Steel gave her the recorder and she went to see Helen Henderson. She thought to herself on the way up. I really like this old lady. If she had a bullet for Jack's gun, she probably would have put it in the gun hoping he would shoot himself or someone else and be gone from next door. That was a ridiculous thought because she wouldn't even know how to load the gun if she had a bullet. She was a city girl. Why did she hate Jack so much after the years they had seemed to be so friendly and good friends?

She knocked on the door with the secret code knock. Knock, the knock knock – knock knock. She said "Helen, it's Sally, I've come to visit with you for a while like I said I would." The door opened and Helen was in her robe with a quizzical look on her face. It was obvious that she didn't remember Sally, but the knock was entrenched since she was a child. Sally knew that people with dementia try to cover up the fact that they don't know you, so they won't be embarrassed and you won't know they can't remember. Sally gave Helen an escape route. "I'm sorry I'm here so early." She said. "I know I told you it would be after dinner, but I have an appointment this evening with a fine young man and I didn't want to miss our visit. I don't mind at all that you are in your robe, and a very pretty robe it is, too."

Helen bit on it and said, "Well, I had planned on being all tidied up for you when you came, but it is a pretty robe isn't it?"

The robe was silk with a dragon on it. It was very pretty and very expensive. "Yes, it is, where did you get it?"

"A gentleman friend gave it to me as a present many, many years ago. It's the last present anyone ever gave to me, (she hesitated), that I was allowed to keep." Sally wondered what she meant by that. "Some people are mean and no good, they give you a present and then they take it back," she said.

Sally asked, "Who would do something like that?"

"That stupid old cowboy next door. He gave me a present when I first met him, and I liked it a lot. No one gives me any presents anymore and I thought he was my friend. He came calling, you know, and I was nice to him and we talked about everything."

"What did you talk mostly about?" Sally asked.

"Oh, you know, just everything." Sally didn't push it. It was obvious she didn't remember what they talked about, but it was also obvious that she had liked Jack and thought of him as one of her suitors.

"What did he give you that he took back?"

"Nothing of any value, he's a nobody, and doesn't have any money anyway. I don't know what I ever saw in him." Sally had to find out what it was that after several years Jack wanted back.

"Maybe it was something that was very important to him, and as he got older it brought back memories, and that is why he took it back," Sally said thinking out loud.

"He gave it to me and he had no right to take it back. It wasn't even Christmas," she said. "It sat right there on my mantle for all that time. It was the last gift I ever got. It was mine and he took it. I don't want to talk about it."

Sally stayed about 10 minutes more but couldn't get Helen back in the subject of the gift. She gave the tape to Steel and went back to the coroner's office.

It wasn't much help. There was a gift, it was 'nothing of value,' whatever that meant and Jack took it back after a long time. Jack didn't seem to remember anything for a long time let alone a gift that was 'nothing of value.' Her statement, "and it wasn't even Christmas" didn't make sense either. Would it have been okay to take it back if it was Christmas? She said she kept it on the mantle. One of the attendants might remember what it was. He was in his car listening to the tape. He got out and went back to the desk.

"You again," said the receptionist. "Don't the police have more important things to do then harass a bunch of old people?"

"Well, I'm trying very hard not to harass them, but loose ends drive me crazy and there are a couple of them walking around up there on the 11th floor by the names of Jack and Helen. Who works in Helen's area as the maid?"

"That would be Mary, most of the time. She covers all the rooms on that floor."

"Is she here now, I'd like to speak with her for just a couple of minutes."

"I'll check housekeeping and see where she is."

Mary was in Room 1112; Steel went up to talk to her. He introduced himself and she said, "I know who you are. You're the cop that's checking out Jack and his gun. He scares me every time I clean his room. He points that cannon at me and pulls the trigger. You can hear the click when he shoots you."

Steel said, "It's Helen's room I want to ask you about?"

"Helen? Who is Helen?"

"Mrs. Henderson." Steel was surprised no one even knew her first name. Growing old is even tougher than he thought.

"Oh! Mrs. Henderson. She is nice to me, but she hates the men attendants."

"She claims that Jack gave her a gift and then took it back. What can you tell me about that?" Steel asked.

"I don't know anything about a gift," Mary replied.

"She said she kept it on the mantle for a long time, not really sure how long, but I think four or so years and then Jack came over and took it back."

"There was an old dead twig sticking in a Styrofoam base. I used to have to clean around it. It disappeared a month or so ago. I asked her what she did with it and she just said, 'I don't want to talk about it?" I said okay, it was just a dead twig anyway."

"How big was it?" asked Steel.

“About a foot high. It had a bunch of branches that had been trimmed into a ball shape. It was kind of pretty in a strange way. She called it her ‘Christmas Tree.’ I always thought that was really dumb.”

“Are you sure she called it a Christmas tree?” he asked.

“Oh, yes. When I cleaned the mantel she often said, *be careful of the Christmas tree.*” He asked her if she had seen it in Jack’s room after it disappeared from Helen’s.

“No.” She thought for a moment, “I did find what could have been the foam base in Jack’s trash a while back. I remember because I wondered at the time where he got the styrofoam.” I don’t check on the trash, I just tie up the plastic bag and toss it in the dumpster.”

“Was that before or after it disappeared from Mrs. Henderson’s room?” Steel knew he was on to something important, if he could just figure out what it was.

“I can’t remember when it was, but I wondered about it at the time.” Mary replied.

He thanked her and went back to the car. Something was buried deep in his head and he couldn’t pull it to the surface. Why would she call an old twig a Christmas tree? He thought that at least he could account for the empty shell casing. If Jack tossed it in the trash, Mary would not have seen it.

Chapter 9

He called Sally on his cellphone and told her he found out what the gift was, but he couldn’t figure out what it meant. She said they could work on it after dinner. She would make spaghetti and then she would solve their case for him. He responded, “At this point, I’ll even accept that as an option.”

She made good spaghetti. He brought a bottle of red wine from the wine country of Argentina. Bottled in Mendoza. She remarked what a good wine it was. She put the dishes in the dishwasher and said “Not enough to turn it on yet.”

She came back to the table and they listened to the tape again. Steel told her what the maid, Mary, had told him about the 'Christmas tree' and that she found what could have been the base of it in Jack's trash. Question? Why would Jack give Helen an old twig? Why would he then take back an old twig and then destroy it? Why would he take it back and make Helen hate him if he was just going to destroy it? Steel kept saying, "I know that I know something that I don't know I know."

Sally said, "Well, if you figure out what you know that you don't know you know, will it solve our case?"

"I don't know," he said.

She laughed and said, "Well, you take notes on everything just to make sure that you can remember what you know. Get them out and maybe you'll find out what you don't know you know."

He said, "You have a great way with words, but you're right. What I'm looking for is probably in my notes and I didn't realize it was important at the time." He kept two notebooks. One was his field notes that were sometimes hen scratches and incomplete, and the more heavy-duty book where he transcribed the field notes into thought notes derived from the field notes.

He gave the thought notes to Sally, and took the field notebook for himself. "You've heard the tapes and all, look for something that might fit into the puzzle that we have missed." They spent several hours discussing various statements, ideas, etc. that they found in the notes but nothing clicked until Sally said," "What's a cowboy Christmas tree?"

"That's it!" Steel said. "The gunsmith said he kept his spurs and his cowboy Christmas tree to remind him of the old days."

Sally said, "Close, but no cigar. It says here It was to remind him of who he used to be."

"That's it! That's what I knew I knew but couldn't remember."

"Once again the fairer of the two sexes saves the day," said Sally.

He didn't even hear her. "I've got to talk to the gunsmith again, first thing in the morning, right after we have our coffee."

"I'm not sure if it's me you like or just my coffee." She had a frown on her face.

"As long as you keep making good coffee, it's unimportant," he said.

She hit him on the shoulder and said, "Sometimes I need a cannon to blast a compliment out of you."

"Well, your coffee maker's really good powder for that cannon, but it's just the powder – you're the bullet."

She looked up at the ceiling, screwed her mouth to one side and said, "I think that was a compliment wasn't it?"

"You're damn right it was." He kissed her and said, "Is the coffee turned off yet?"

She reached across the sink, pulled the plug and said, "It is now."

He was at the gunsmiths at 8 a.m. The sign on the door said hours 9 – 5 Mon. – Sat. "Crap," he said out loud and went to the coffee shop on the corner and ordered a Grande black coffee and blueberry muffin. He poured over his notes while he waited. He was excited; he could feel that he was close.

At 9 a.m. the door to the shop opened. The gunsmith must have come in the back way through the alley. He recognized Steel at once and said, "What historical point can I help you with. You don't want to sell that gun, do you?"

"Like I said before, the gun isn't mine to sell, but you said something when we talked last about how you kept your old spurs and your cowboy Christmas tree to remind you who you used to be. Am I correct on that?"

"You are," he said. "Don't go spreading that around or people will think I'm riding a three-legged horse."

"I know what spurs are and why they would be a reminder of the, 'good old days."

The gunsmith broke in and said, "I didn't say they were *good* old days just that they reminded me of who I was for so many years."

Steel was anxious to find out about the Christmas tree but he let the gunsmith go on with his story.

"The open range cowboy was about as lonely a life you could think of living. He generally worked on spreads that had no boundaries. The cattle roamed the open range for miles and the man that rode herd on any given brand just kept track of where they were and moved along with them. He lived right with the herd. There were rustlers in those days, and a man's gun was his only buddy when trouble hit. Sometimes it was rustlers, sometimes wolves, or maybe even a Grizzly bear. His gun was his friend and his protector. That old gun you had was an original Colt 'peacemaker.' They called several of the old guns 'peacemakers,' but Colt made the best one. When there was trouble of any kind, the peacemakers would solve it. There was many a rustler that was caught, tried, judged and executed, by 'Judge Colt.'"

"What about the Christmas tree?" Steel reminded him why he was there.

"I'm getting to that, but you have to understand a few things first before the Christmas tree will make any sense to ya."

"Sorry," Steel said. He was finding out that old cowboys talked in stories. As much as he liked and learned from the stories, it was important to get to the Christmas tree. It's a great thing I'm a farm boy he thought, a city feller couldn't hold out this long.

The gunsmith went on. "The worst thing that could happen to a range cowboy was to run out of shells. If that happened, he had no friend, and no protection. The only time he would let himself run dry on shells was when he was at the end of his rope, and he knew the end was either there or near. Only then would he shoot his last bullet, his 'Safety Bullet.'"

Steel pounded his fist on the counter. "Jack said he had fired his 'Safety Bullet,'" he said out loud.

"Well, the old cowhand figures his days are over and he's ready to go. That's what that means."

"I need to know where he got the shell to shoot," said Steel.

"You came here asking about the Cowboy Christmas tree, didn't you?"

"Yes, I did."

"Did the old boy have one?"

"I think so," Steel said. "What does it look like?"

The gunsmith smiled with a melancholy look on his face. "Want to see one? I'll show you mine. It's about 70 years old. It was given to me by my father. He shot his safety bullet just before he died of cancer four years ago. I redecorated it, and it's in the back room on my desk." He led Steel through the lathes, saws, and other machinery a good smithy needs for his trade, to a small room with a desk in it. Amongst the papers was a dry branch from a tree. It was a small branch only about 18" high and quite bushy with little twigs all over it. "Here it is, in all of its glory – The Cowboy Christmas tree."

Chapter 10

Steel looked at it and wondered how in the world this could have anything to do with the case. "No offense, but it sure doesn't look like much," he said.

"It's the cowboys' gift to himself," said the Smithy. "Remember what I said about when he fired his last bullet?"

"Just before he thought he was going to die?" said Steel.

"Right, well there's the last bullet, the 'safety bullet,' the last one you think you'll ever shoot."

"What do you mean?" Steel was confused again.

"Take a good look at the tree. Go on, get close and take a good look." Steel did, and tucked down in a crevasse between two of the inside branches was a bullet tied in with hemp string so it was nearly invisible.

"My God," said Steel, "that's why the search never turned up anything. He was keeping it in Helen's room." It was obvious now. "When he decided he was ready to die, he went and got it from her. The old coot was using her all those years to hide his 'safety bullet' from the bad guys, AKA, the attendants. He destroyed his tree after he fired his bullet," said Steel.

"That tells you that he was a very lonely man - no friends, relatives, or sidekicks to pass it on to. He saw himself as being totally alone." They talked some more about the Christmas tree, why it was important, why it was called a Christmas tree and Steel could see the entire picture now.

Steel was so excited; all the loose ends were tied in somewhere. He thanked the Smithy and called Sally from the cell phone. "We've got it; I know where the bullet came from."

"Where?" she asked.

"I'll tell you at dinner, only this time I cook. Meet me at the Mexican restaurant up on the hill. I can't remember the name, but I remember it's good food."

"Come on, tell me."

"Nope, you gotta wait. That's just to prove that I'm in control."

"That will be the day when any man controls me, but I'll be there because this is our case remember?"

"See you at six." He went to his desk to write a final report. He would make it brief and to the point.

REPORT Case #413416

Robert Blake jumped from the top of Elmore Building to commit suicide because of large debts he had incurred from loan sharks. Four witnesses verify the jump was voluntary. On the way down he was hit in the back of the head by a 45-caliber side arm bullet. The gun was accidentally fired from an old hand gun owned by Jack White, a resident of a rest home. Mr. White has dementia and did not know the gun was loaded. Mr. White gave us the gun to be tested and ballistics verified it was the gun that fired the shot that killed Blake. He had hidden his last bullet in his room. He stumbled on to it years later and put it in the gun. He fired it out the window from across the room. Everything points to a completely accidental firing of the gun. There was certainly no intent to hit Blake falling from a building two blocks away. The old man, Jack White, does not remember the gunshot.

My recommendation is it is recorded as a suicide, involving an accidental shooting. I recommend that no action or charges be made against Jack White. He does not remember the shooting and the man he accidentally killed was only several seconds from death by his own hand. Think of Jack White as the chosen Samurai to cut the head off of a warrior friend when he had been ordered to commit seppuku, (Hara-kiri) in the old Japanese kingdom. His bullet relieved Blake the pain of the final smash on the sidewalk.

End of report Detective Ron Steel

Attachment 1:

This case could not have been solved without the diligent and consistent attention given to it by the coroner's office. I commend Sally McKenzie for her persistence and thorough work.

Attachment 2:

Various notes, etc. relating to the case. Nothing of major concern to waste time on. Just included to make the report complete.

He knew no one could ever read his hen scratch notes, but if something did come up, he was doing a CYA (covering his ass) so no one could say he withheld evidence.

Steel was immediately assigned to another case and Case #413416 was filed as solved and complete. No action was taken against Jack White.

Epilogue

Steel and Sally visited Jack and Helen a couple of times in the next few months. They enjoyed their stories and appreciated their loneliness. They would go up together and Sally would see Helen and Steel would see Jack. The two of them never got back together. There was too much dementia in each of them to understand what went on. Steel got a phone call from the rest home several months later. Jack had died in his sleep the night before. "You're the closest thing to a friend he had," the attendant said, "So I thought you should know."

"What will you do with him?" Steel asked

"He will be cremated and his ashes spread at sea."

"No, I want his ashes and his gun." Steel said. The attendant didn't argue; it was just less work for them at the home.

They visited Helen. She cried for a week; then died three days later. Steel asked for her ashes too.

Later that month, Sally and Steel took vacation time and flew to the Texas Panhandle. Steel had found where the W bar D Ranch had been in the early 1900's. It had been broken up into smaller units and sold in the 1950's. Most of those had been subdivided or broken up into small ranchettes of only 60 to 100 acres. His research had revealed one portion, about ten sections that were still totally wild. That is where he and Sally were headed.

Their plane landed at a small airport and they were able to rent a jeep. The 4 x 4 was needed to get into the backcountry. There were dirt roads, but they were very rough and full of potholes. On their drive they saw no tracks in front of them as they made their way deeper and deeper into the old W bar D wilderness.

Driving up a canyon with no road as far as they could get the jeep and then walking another mile through the brush, they found a good spot at the base of a large rock outcropping. Steel dug a hole with a U.S. Army pack shovel he bought in a surplus store near the airport.

Helen and Jack's ashes were in their boxes, placed side by side in the hole. Steel said, "I know you each want your own space, but you will not be alone anymore."

"Helen," Steel said, "this may not be your territory, but I'm sure that jack would want the two of you together. Don't worry, Jack will take care of you." He laid Jack's gun, secured in a baggie, in the hole on top of the boxes. He then filled up the hole and picked a branch from a close shrub bush. He tied a cartridge in it that he had the gunsmith load for him and stuck it in the ground over them.

"I wonder why they call that a Christmas tree?" Sally asked, on the drive back to the airport.

"The gunsmith told me. It makes perfect sense" Steel replied.

"Well?" She looked at him.

"The range riders were the lonesome cowboys that started young and spent most of their life on the range. They had very little, if any, schooling, and many, if not most, couldn't read very well if at all. Being alone, they only had the cows and God to talk to. The smithy told me they would have long conversations with God by the campfire at night. Because they couldn't read well, they didn't have books, including the Bible, but they were quite religious. They knew what Christmas was and a Christmas tree was their 'religious symbol.' Having it there made it easier for them to talk to God."

Sally was listening. She asked again, "That's very interesting, but how did they get a Christmas tree out of an old dead branch?"

"Well," Steel said, "There's not much else out here and after all, it is, a *'Cartridge in a Bare Tree.'*

She just shook her head, kissed him on the cheek and they drove along the lonely dirt road back to the airport.

The Invisible
Assassins
The Steel Mysteries Book 2
John Reseck Jr

The Invisible Assassin

"Something Worthwhile to Do"

A Steel Mystery

This story is a work of fiction, or at least a distortion of events that have, or might have taken place in the past or may take place even in the future.

Believe in your heart they are real, Even though your head may tell you they are not: Who knows what good, or evil can be conceived by men,

That have time on their hands, And problems to solve?

Dedicated to those that were silent–swift–deadly

You may have never existed **But** you are not forgotten

Prologue

Early February 1959

Somewhere on the mainland coast north of Japan

It was new moon, which means, the moon was hiding in the shadow of the earth, as if it were hoarding its light; the highest high tide and the darkest night of the month occur at this stage of the moon. The waves that originated in some unknown spot across the dark sea washed up on the featureless sand beach and disappeared as if by magic, into the sand.

The black rubber suited figure, deposited on the beach by one of the waves, slithered on his belly and like the water that transported him from sea to land, melted into the environment. Staying flat on his chest for 100 yards until he came to a large bush he could crawl under, he sat up. His swim fins made a drag mark along the sand under the bushes like those of the seals which were at random, scattered along the beach.

Removing his fins and rubber suit he buried them under a bush, then opened one of the bags he had towed ashore. It was a waterproof bag that rolled down tight and then strapped shut to ensure a good seal. Inside the bag he had dry clothes, a map, a compass, and three small bags containing food, along with four KA-BAR knives. He buried the bag under a different bush than the swim gear, in case one was discovered, hopefully the other one would be missed.

The second dry bag he brought to shore had straps that were part of the bag so it could be carried as a backpack. It contained 30 pounds of plastic explosive and ten small sodium magnesium incendiary devices and their electronic detonators.

The knives in the pack he skillfully and almost lovingly, strapped to his body. One on the inside of each calf, one on the inside of his pants under his belly button, and one in a sheath that was strapped tightly to his back, behind his head under his shirt. He carefully removed and checked each knife, to be sure that it was accessible with either hand.

There was something inscribed on the blades of the knives. The left calf read, 'Silent,' the right calf read, 'Swift,' the one under his built read, 'Deadly' and the one behind his head read, 'No Fear.'

He chose not to carry a gun because to fire a gun would mean instant detection and a quick death. Even worse than that, he was told, it would mean a failed mission.

Checking the map and his compass with a red beamed penlight, he jogged away from the beach and disappeared in the direction of his target.

Mid-February 1959
Several Hundred Miles Inland

According to his map the lake in front of him was two miles long but only one-half mile wide. There were ice patches along the edges but it had been a very mild winter and the lake had not frozen over. The small island at the north end was round and looked like a pancake sitting in the water.

The five wooden buildings that rose from the island were arranged in a circle around a large centrally located tank. All of the structures were on raised foundations four feet off the ground, to insure if the lake should rise, they would always be above the overflow height of the dam. In the spring when the rains came the water was channeled off the island by cement drainage ditches that ran from the large tank in the center out under the buildings into the lake. It was a good system and kept the island free of any standing water that could freeze.

The most impressive structure on the island was the center tank; it was huge, an impressive twenty feet in diameter and about that high. It held enough fuel oil to last the complex an entire year. Everything on the island was totally dependent on having fuel to run the generators. The complete isolation of the lake and the severity of the weather at times made it mandatory they had a large reserve. Running out was not an option; if the power went down and the incubator units dropped to freezing, years of work would be lost.

The closest point on the island to shore was 50 yards. There was a floating foot bridge connecting the two. At the shore end of the bridge was a small guard house. The uniformed guard there was in contact with his command unit, over fifty miles away by radio and had to report in every four hours.

The buildings on the island were very plain on the outside but were well insulated and state of the art lab technology on the inside. One building was living quarters for six people, two of which were medical microbiologists; three were lab technicians and a maintenance engineer. There were six guards that rotated eight-hour shifts around the clock and lived in a separate military building at the island end of the bridge. The other three buildings were high tech labs, each specializing in a particular deadly pathogen. They had been biologically engineered, cultured and were just waiting to be spread over some unsuspecting population to prove a political point. The potential human death was in the millions.

It was 1210 in the morning. The sky was obscured by a layer of low hanging clouds. The only sound was the never-ending low hum of the generators. The shoreside guard stood up and stretched, uttering in Russian, "I don't know why they even have a guard out here," *which had become his favorite comment since he was assigned to this post.* Contacting the control center on his radio, he called in his standard report, "Island lab, operations normal, out." He sat back down, picked up his book and went back to reading before the reply came back. "Good copy - out."

****

The explosion was so great that it broke the windows out of most of the buildings and collapsed two of them. The central diesel tank now had a huge hole in the bottom. The fuel oil gushed into the drainage canals that ran under the buildings filling them to overflowing. Fifteen seconds later ten incendiary bombs simultaneously exploded at various well-placed locations to create fires that within minutes had the entire island a raging inferno.

The fuel oil, which now saturated the island and was running into the lake, formed a ring of fire around the island. There was no escape for anything living on the island.

The sentry in the guard house at the land end of the bridge ran out staring in horror not believing what he was seeing. It was as if his mind had turned to mush, nothing was computing. Reality finally came to him, he turned to run back to the radio and call it into the command center. He never saw the knife that cut through his carotid artery, his jugular vein and his wind pipe; he fell to the ground in total silence, dead in only four seconds.

When the ops normal report didn't come into the command center at 0400, the radio operator reported to his superiors that he was having radio trouble. They periodically had loss of communication due to weather or heavy freezes that affected the sending units. If there was still no contact by 0800, they would dispatch a unit to fix whatever was wrong.

By the time the attack was discovered the next day when the team that was sent arrived, the ashes were cold. The only evidence of what might have happened was a dead guard with his throat cut.

Mid-March 1959

There was no public report of the incident; it was as though it had never happened. However, only two weeks later, thousands of miles across the Pacific Ocean in a room with a long oak table, five men with note pads and coffee cups in front of them sat in leather padded chairs looking at a large screen.

The men were intently studying the projections of photos taken by a U2 photo recon plane four weeks before and comparing them with one taken just a week ago. The man at the head of the table stood, leaned forward to get a better look at the images and said "It would appear that operation 'Wee Beasty' was a success".

"Yes sir, as you can see the island is clear, no structures at all are left."

"Just how did he manage that?" the newest member of the group asked.

"More important than that, did he get out?" asked the man at the end of the table, as he sat back down and added, "We can't afford to have him captured."

The oldest man at the far end of the table had been sitting with his hands folded in his lap and had said nothing up to this point. He leaned forward, placing both elbows on the table, looked directly at the man in the big chair at the other end of the table and said, "Sir, we don't call him the 'Salamander' for nothing. We've had no word but it has only been a short time. My bet is he's dug in under a rock somewhere waiting for a storm, so he can move undetected through the country side. He'll get out, I'll bet on it. It may take a while, but he'll get out. Salamanders are survivors, they were here before the dinosaurs, but the real reason I'm so sure, is the fact that I personally trained him."

He stood to leave, "If I may be excused sir, I believe we have covered all that concerns me at this session."

"We'll see you at the briefing tomorrow morning. Notify me if you hear anything about the Salamander," was the reply, as the old man left the room.

After he was gone, one of the men at the table said, "I've heard talk that he is the best handler the agency has ever had."

The man in the big chair nodded his head and said, "He was in the OSS for a long time. He has more experience than anyone else in his agency, we are fortunate that he decided to stay active and come with us."

The meeting went on to other matters.

Chapter 1
June 2005
In a Village in the Woods by the Bay

Jim got out of bed, looked at the clock and said, "Crap, its 8:30." He looked out the window at the sky and decided to drive to the coffee shop instead of walking. It was only one mile but the sky looked like rain and in the northwest, especially in Washington State, that generally meant rain. He thought, "No reason to chance getting wet."

Running the electric shaver over his face, not taking a shower, just putting on clean clothes he goes to the garage. It was big enough for four cars but was instead full of his "stuff." He proclaimed that if anyone else owned all this "stuff" it would just be crap, but to him, it was his important "stuff."

The accumulation represented a lifetime of past activities. He had three pairs of skis, one for powder, one for racing and one for cruising, four kayaks (one single and one double sea kayak, one folding for taking on trips and one for whitewater), two bicycles, snow shoes, two bows with arrows for each, various tools, three anchors from past boats, a SCUBA tank that was seven years out of hydro, four spear guns with rotten rubber slings on them and yes, there was even a car. It was a 20 years old Ford Aero Star but still in good shape for an old van and ran perfectly. He liked it because it was all-wheel drive. He always said old Betsy would take him anywhere he wanted to go; he started her up, pushed the button on the door opener and rolled out onto his gravel drive.

He met his two friends every Monday morning at the local coffee corner located in the small store that served his rural community. They referred to themselves as the "Old Farts of Distinction."

The "OFD's" had started their routine when Jim's wife, Betty, was killed in an auto accident five years earlier. His two best friends had lost their wives some time before that, one to cancer and the other to a better looking, younger and richer man. All of their losses were traumatic emotional times for each of them.

They found themselves not only being alone, but realizing that they were really alone. The perception of being alone is bad but the realization after a while that they were really alone was a hard reality to face.

When they first got together it was kind of a therapeutic help group for them, although they never thought of it that way – now after five years they looked forward to Monday mornings. It had become about 80% of their social life. Jim wondered what they still had to talk about. He decided that they just got together to insult each other – that's what men friends do. Their wives had never understood how they could be such good friends and call each other names like "dim bulb," "brainless" and a dozen others. Betty had told him,"If I treated my friends like you do, I wouldn't have any friends." He just told her it was a man thing and let it go at that. He knew that if he didn't have friends, he could treat like that, he didn't have any real friends.

He parked in the lot at the village store and looked out through the woods at the bay. The marina was full of boats; they reminded him of his past boats. He had many, both big boats and small ones; wood boats, glass boats, rubber boats, and kayaks, he was a water person.

His first boat was 12 feet long and made out of Masonite. His father bought it when he was eight years old, and he ran it all around the harbor in Newport Beach, California. It had a five horsepower Neptune outboard on it and with that outfit he learned to be a boater. His biggest boat was a converted Coast Guard buoy tender. It was made of wood, he loved wood boats. He said they had a soul that metal and glass boats just didn't have.

He walked into the coffee room at the side of the small store and joined his two friends. They chastised him for being late. "Where the hell have you been, it's 0902, this meeting starts at 0900."

"Robbie, you're so full of shit I can't believe it." He said with a grin.

Robbie was about three inches shorter than Jim. He had his coffee cup in his hand and a big frown on his face.

"Didn't your mother ever tell you that if you made a face like that it would freeze that way and make you even uglier then you are, as if that were possible."

Robbie said, "That would be the day. I know you can't change the way you look Jim, but at least you could stay out of public places."

Jim just ignored Robbie, looked across the table and said, "Take Lem here, he's 85 and still got his hair. That means he was saintly his whole life. Now you and me, the only hair we have comes out of our nose or ears, and by the way – you forgot to trim yours this morning. Don't let them get in your coffee." They laughed and Jim walked over and filled his cup from the thermos on the counter that said "Dark Roast."

Robbie looked over at Lem and said, "You're awful quiet this morning."

"I'm kind of bummed out. I saw my doctor last Friday."

Jim asked, "Bad news?"

"It depends on who you are," Lem said, "For me it's not so bad. The doc said I was in good health, for my kids and their family it's very bad." Lem was obviously serious and not joking.

Robbie had a puzzled look on his face and the mood wasn't the same as it had been one minute before. "What do you mean?"

"How can having a long life be bad," asked Jim.

"Well, he also said I had plaque in my brain, some new 'Pet Scan' that indicated I will have severe dementia in a few years. He said I won't be able to live by myself for more than a few more years and I need to start thinking about making arrangements for a care home."

"Wow," said Robbie. "What are you going to do?"

"I don't want my kids to have to take care of me. It would totally disrupt their lives. I'm going to need total care the doc says and I could live to be a hundred years old. I don't have any money. At eight thousand a month, I checked around and that's what it costs, my money would be gone in six months.

No one spoke for a couple of minutes; they didn't know what to say. Finally, Jim said, "Don't worry Lem, it will work out, I'm sure it will." He didn't sound sure.

Lem said, "Well, the only good thing for me is I won't know how much trouble I'm causing everyone around me. I wish I didn't know now."

To change the subject Jim picked up the newspaper that had been left on their table by someone and said, "It looks like Mongo is at it again." The picture on the front page was of detective Ron Steel of the Seattle police department watching a limo drive away from the country court house. The caption under the picture read, "Mongo's cartel beats the rap again." Detective Ron Steel of the Seattle Department of Drug Enforcement, was quoted as saying, "Someday Mongo will make a mistake and we'll nail him."

Lem says, "It sounds like old Mongo has a few problems of his own."

Robbie added, "That Steel cop has the big problem of what to do to get rid of the Mongo cartel."

"That's his problem." Lem replied, "I'm just going to worry about mine."

Lem got up to leave, "See you next Monday." He left, and the mood was not good.

Jim shared his thoughts, "Ron, you know I have wondered about this same problem with my kids. My dad lived with Betty and me for fifteen years and had Alzheimer's the last ten. We were stuck at home taking care of him. I didn't mind, because he was such a great person. He never complained about anything, but he had no idea who Betty and I were, we were just the people that took care of him. The trouble was Betty and I didn't get to do a lot of the trips we had planned on. When Betty died, we still had a full 'Bucket List.

I'm like Lem; I don't want my kids to have to put their lives on hold for me. I've been worrying about it a lot lately, even enough to keep me awake sometimes at night. It never occurred to me that the day would come when I'd be old. I don't think I'm old now but when I look in the mirror it scares the hell out of me. I'm just three years behind Lem."

Ron was quiet for a minute or two then said, "Don't complain, you're a year younger than me. The problem that's been bugging me has been that I don't have something worthwhile to do. I can't seem to come up with anything an 'old fart' can do that means a dam thing to anybody. Long term care is the second problem. If you find the answer to those two questions, I'll stop calling you a "dim bulb."

They laughed and stood to leave, "See you Monday, Dim Bulb."

"You just wait; you may not be able to call me that anymore."

"That'll be the day - I won't hold my breath." They waved a Rose Queen wave at each other and went to their cars. Neither of them smiled much the rest of the week. They tried to think it was Lem they were concerned about and they were, but they knew Lem was just a mirror that they were both being forced to look into.

Chapter 2
Problem Solving

The next Monday, Jim was the first one to coffee. He had been thinking about their last meeting all week. The mirror Lem had put in front of him exposed images that he had suppressed and denied in his own life. He, like all of his friends who were in the eightyish category, plus or minus a couple of years and that was most of them, hurt somewhere in their bodies every day.

Some had bad feet, some bad knees, some bad backs, but all had reminders that they were in the biodegrading process. They all joked about it saying, "We have to hurt somewhere so we are sure we are still alive." They couldn't deny they hurt but they did their best to ignore it and go on with their lives. It didn't do any good to complain.

Robbie stated what he saw as the problem at their last meeting. "I've wanted to have something worthwhile to do," he said. Jim thought about that and realized that was why he was so listless and felt so empty all the time. He didn't have anything worthwhile to do either. Lem's problem was different, but could also soon become their problem, and none of them wanted their kids tied down with them.

Jim was a problem solver. He had always told people that there was no such thing as a problem, just a new project. His approach to solutions was a step by step process. It had worked for him all of his life.

Realize there is a problem.

Identify the problem and box it in so as not to be distracted by things that were not essential to solving it.

List the possible options that would lead to a useable resolution.

Prioritize the options as to the most realistic to do and the probability of success.

Set in motion the steps to make it happen.

He now had two problems to solve. He was excited to talk to Robbie and Lem about what they might do to define them better and then, to work on them. If nothing else, it would give them all something worthwhile to think about.

****

Jim had finished his first cup of coffee before the others got there; he had been a half hour early. He was excited. He wasn't sure why, but he knew it had to do with the three of them working on a project together. Now they had to determine what the project would be.

"Yo, Jim, did you sleep here last night?" Robbie asked as he filled his coffee cup from the pump thermos on the counter.

Lem cut in, "No he didn't sleep here, because if he had slept anywhere, he would look a lot better than he does."

Jim put on a long face and said "You guys don't appreciate a true friend with only your well-being at heart. Last week we said we had two problems, one was finding something to do that would make a positive difference in the world, or at least for us, and how not to live off our kids and make a negative difference in their lives. Do you remember that?"

Lem agreed, "Even I remember that and I don't remember much anymore."

Robbie jumped up and said, "You've got it all figured out. Quick, tell us the answer so we can rest easy and not worry about it."

Jim laughed, "Sit down, Dumbo, I'm serious. I think we can figure some way to mitigate our problem. Look at it this way, if we try to come up with a plan, we will at least be doing something worthwhile. Lem sits around all day and builds boat models; you sit in your closet with your radio, talking to other HAMS. Personally, I think you're both turkeys, you've just lost your feathers."

"And what do you do all day; spend it at a Mensa meeting? The last I heard, you spent your time sitting on your boat trying to figure out why it wouldn't start, or crawling through the underbrush in the hills seeing how close you can come to some poor deer. Don't throw any stones at my glass house, yours isn't exactly made out of Lexan, it will break too."

"You're right," said Jim. "That's why we need to work on this together. Three heads are always better than one, even if they're all ugly."

"Speak for yourself," said Lem, "I've noticed that since I broke my glasses last week I look a lot better in my mirror than I used to, even you two idiots have lost a lot of the wrinkles you used to have. I think we may all age next week though."

"Why is that, Lem?" Robbie asked.

"I'll get my new glasses," was Lem's reply.

They all laughed and took a drink of their coffee. Lem opened up the paper and looked at the headlines. *Mongo Ebo walks free after witness fails to appear in court. Ebo, head of the Nagaza Cartel, one of the most violent drug cartels in the world, once again, 'beats the rap.' This is the third time that the leader of the Nagaza Cartel has walked free due to the disappearance of witnesses.'* The article went on to say, that the body of one of the witnesses from the first failed trial, washed up on shore years ago. They never found any of the others.

"Now there is a bad dude," said Robbie. "He must get up every morning and pour olive oil all over his body because he always seems to slip out of the grip of the police."

Lem added, "Now, there's something worthwhile to do."

Jim looked up, "What do you mean Lem?"

"I know what he means," said Robbie. "He means this Mongo Dude knows how to beat the system. We could take old Mongo out; all we would need is a 1,000-man army and a gun off an old battleship that could reach him in Mexico; maybe we could snatch one off the one in the Bremerton Naval Yard. There are a lot of old moth ballers there that might have a big gun we could liberate some night when the guards were sleeping on the job."

They all laughed and more coffee was downed as they sat in the warmth of the sun coming through the window.

Jim looked out the window as a gentle breeze moved the trees. The local kids were getting on the school bus in the parking lot. He looked up and said, "Why not?"

Robbie looked at Jim dumb founded, "Why not what?"

"Why don't we take him out?" was the reply.

"Because the naval guards never sleep on the job and we couldn't get the big gun we would need to reach him in Mexico," said Lem.

Both Robbie and Lem broke up. Lem said "How, with what, where and when? Think we could get it done by next Monday?" They laughed again.

Jim looked right at them and said, "He doesn't spend all his time in Mexico. He has a boat right here in the Hood Canal. I'm not kidding. What do we have to lose? We get killed, so what, we're all on the down slope anyway with no breaks. We get caught. Two possibilities; the cartel catches us or our own police catch us if we are successful. The cartel will shoot us, big deal. Our guys will put us in jail and we have assisted living, and free health care for the rest of our lives. It's a win, win situation. The best part is we will have something worthwhile to do.

They suddenly realized Jim was serious. "You're not kidding, are you?" asked Robbie.

"No, I'm not," was the reply.

"Good God man, do you realize what you are proposing? You're saying we should kill someone."

"That's exactly what I'm saying."

"Well," said Lem, "That would sure be something different."

Jim thought to himself, 'no, not really'. Then said, "There is a time to live and a time to die, we have had our time to live, now perhaps it is time to help slime ball Mongo find his time to die and give those kids on the school bus out there more time to live."

Robbie and Lem just looked at each other. "He's dead serious," said Lem.

"Good God. "Was all Robbie could come up with.

"Even a good God needs help sometimes to shovel the shit out of his house." Jim responded, "First we must decide if this Mongo is truly a problem. Then, if his billions of dollars put him outside the 'rule of law. Would our country be better off if he were eliminated? If we go back in history, the 'Scottish Realism' of common sense and the Frontier Code of people like Davie Crockett was, 'Be sure you are right, then just do it.' Makes a lot of sense to me. What we have to do is decide the answers to those questions, then discuss if we want to commit to the project."

They were silent as they finished their coffee. Jim broke the silence, "Think about it, read what papers are saying. They're all talking about him now and we'll see where we come out next Monday."

They forgot their Rose Queen wave, or even to put their coffee cups in the trash when they left. They had other things to think about.

Chapter 3
Is There a Problem?

Robbie went home after their meeting and couldn't think of anything else but their conversation. Had they really talked about killing someone? Yes, they had. "Wow," he thought, "A hit man at 83." It was so impossible that he could actually consider it. He knew it could never happen, but he was intrigued with planning it. "Something to do," he thought as he looked at his radio display on the office desk.

There was a marine VHF radio for talking to the local boats and monitoring for distress calls to the Coast Guard for help. He had an HF for monitoring some of the Ham friends he had made over the years and even a backup set in case the main one developed a problem. The UHF radio also had some Ham channels as well as some channels enabling him to listen in on planes and law enforcement units. There wasn't much on the air-ways that he couldn't hack into.

He spent many hours a day checking into one 'net' or another and logging all his activities. He had a dozen log books full on his desk; most of which had enough dust on them to attest to the fact that he never opened them. He looked at his reflection in the old style 16-inch TV screen, which was on his desk. "Well, look at the old man on TV," he said out loud. "If we could pull this off you might get on TV when it's actually turned on." He laughed. He was in.

****

Lem was thinking what the doctor had told him when he asked if there was anything he could do to stop or slow down his dementia. "The more you do to use your brain, the better. Do crossword puzzles, word games, math problems; anything that takes calculation or planning; building the model boats you build, is good; watching TV all day is not."

Lem had tried to think of something to challenge his brain but hadn't come up with anything but word games. It would be great fun to play assassin, especially with his two best friends. He was in.

****

Jim went home with a totally different frame of mind than his buddies. He was going to plan a 'sanction' on an enemy of the people. He wasn't playing a game; he was reliving his youth and planning a new project. He hadn't focused on a project of any importance for many years, but he had never failed on one and he didn't intend to start now.

He asked the question "Is there really a problem?" In the news they had talked about how Mango and his cartel were responsible for an unknown, but suspected high number of murders, both in Mexico and the United States and how he always was able to have enough distance from them, that his team of lawyers could keep him in the clear.

When asked about the murders by a TV reporter, Mongo just laughed at the press, threw his hands up and said, "I know nothing" mimicking the TV show of the past, 'Hogan's Heroes'.

The reporter asked, "If you know nothing and aren't involved in any way, why do the police keep bringing you in for questioning?"

"You know the police," he replied, "They like to talk to someone intelligent once in a while so they bring me in for a chat." He and his four attorneys got in a big shiny, black limo laughing and drove off. Jim watched them all laughing as they left and thought, there was no question, they were the enemy of the people.

The answer to the first question on Jim's project list was answered, as far as Jim was concerned. Yes, there was a problem.

In Jim's world the drug cartel was at war with the rule of law and that made them an enemy of the people and the country. War only had three rules with Jim's background; identify the enemy, kill the enemy and escape if you can. Mongo was without a doubt the enemy; that just left rules two and three to work out.

Robbie and Lem had also paid attention to the news channels, and the newspapers. They listened to TV news and read everything in the papers about Mongo's walking on all charges, due to 'insufficient' evidence. They too had decided there was a problem, but they were still looking at it as an interesting exercise to have fun with. Jim would soon change that.

Chapter 4
The Assignments

Their discussion the fallowing Monday was not as frivolous as usual; each had spent time thinking about Mongo. The more they read and heard about him on the news and in the papers, the more they realized what a really bad slime ball this guy was.

Jim began the discussion, "Did you come to any decision about our project?"

Lem was quick with his answer. "I think we ought to plan his demise. If we have a good enough plan maybe we can publish it on You-Tube and someone will use it to rid us of this 'fungus among us."

"We could always hire a hit man," was Robbie's suggestion.

Jim looked at them, smiled and said, "Don't worry. If we have a good plan, we'll find a way to make it work." He brought out his pen and pad and told Robbie, "Your chore is to find out what kind of communication do the cartels use? What type of radios and their frequencies? Do you think any of your 'wire buddies' can help you run that down?"

"I can try. If they use radios, I should be able to figure that out, but they probably don't. Cell phones are about the only thing used now days. I hate to say it but the radios are almost out of date for any important communications, but I'll give it a shot."

"Lem, you know more about boats than the rest of us. You build models of all kinds. Mongo has a boat he spends a lot of time on. I have a feeling he feels comfortable and safe on it; he believes he can secure it well. You get on line and find out what you can about his boat, make, model and interior layout, everything you can. Is that a reasonable request? Is information like that available?"

Lem thought for a moment and said, "Sure, all I need is the make and model, the manufacturer will have all the details. I'll contact them and say I want to build a model and talk them out of pictures of the interior and the outside as well. We can get all the specifications we want."

Jim was thinking out loud, "The boat for us, is the weakest part of his life. He thinks he is safe on it due to the security around it and the fact that it is in the United States. I think it's the one place where we might have a chance to get him. I'll see what I can come up with. Do you both feel you have something worthwhile to do now?"

They all laughed – Robbie threw up his hands and said, "I know nothing."

Lem said, "We already know that, Dim Bulb, but thanks for reminding us."

They were in a good mood as they finished their coffee and got ready to leave. Tossing their paper cups in the trash and giving their Rose Queen wave to each other, they were all smiling as they walked out to their cars

"Why are we so happy?" asked Robbie.

"Because we have something worthwhile to do," said Jim. They gave each other the Rose Queen wave again and were off to investigate their assignments

Chapter 5
Backgrounds Count

When Jim arrived home after the meeting, he parked the car in the garage, got out and looked around at all of his stuff. He didn't know what he might need because he had no plan yet, but he was confident most of it would be somewhere in his garage.

He entered his house, filled an electric tea kettle from the sink and plugged it in. He got out a peppermint teabag, put the bag in an empty cup, sat down at his desk and waited for the water to start to boil, never letting the water bubble, he said that changes the taste of the tea, making it bitter.

His desk was neat, with only a few stacks of paper on it. When the water began to steam, he poured it into his cup. Then he set it aside to let it steep for a while. He drank tea during the day and coffee only in the morning; both were good antioxidants, but it wasn't good to overdue either one. He was very health conscious and worked out with his exercise equipment every day; keeping a daily record to make sure his workouts used all the muscles in the body evenly. He laughed about it, saying, he didn't want to be lopsided, like an old listing boat.

They had identified their two problems and they were real problems, in each of their lives. They had come up with a possible solution for at least one of them, killing Mongo; that would be something worthwhile to do. There was a high probability that they would get killed themselves in the process, but that would serve to solve the second problem of long-term care. Perhaps there was a better solution to the second problem; they would have to work on that. He leaned back in his chair and started to work out a plan. Mongo had a lot of security around him all the time. They needed to become invisible to get close to him.

****

Jim had led an interesting life. He was an only child, born in southern California on a 160-acre dry farm in San Diego County just out of the town of Escondido. His father tried to make a living dry farming wheat. His crops were totally dependent on the rain fall. When it didn't rain for a couple of years, causing him to lose his crops, he had to sell the farm to a rancher that could use it to graze his cattle.

When he was seven years old the family moved to Los Angeles and his father found work as a truck mechanic at Blue Diamond Building Materials. His parents used the money from the sale of the farm to buy a house in South Gate. It was in Los Angeles County and close to his father's work. Jim didn't like the city at first because he was used to being a loner and wandering about in the brush on the farm. He had his own 22 rifle and was a good shot by the time he was six years old; his mother would send him out to get dinner and he would come back with a cotton tail rabbit every time.

The farm was a great life for a young boy, but a very hard life for his parents. The family was poor, but Jim didn't know what poor was. He was a happy, much loved, little boy.

In the city he had many other kids to play with, but he had to learn to play in the street and look out for the cars. By the time he was ten he had become a city kid. He was active in sports at school and doing well in his classes. He was a happy camper again. He tried all the sports and found three he was good at and a dozen that he wasn't. He settled into football, skin diving and Judo. The football would be left behind when he left school but the diving and the martial arts would be with him the rest of his life.

1953 was a good year for him, having placed third in the national judo championship and third in the national spear fishing championship. When his friends gave him a hard time for placing only third, he would say, "Anyone can finish first, but it takes great skill, to always finish third."

In the next couple of years, he became interested in many new hobbies. He took up archery, knife throwing and bicycle riding, working in 50 to 80 miles three times a week. He also started running to work which was an eight-mile round trip several times a week. His only explanation was, he enjoyed it. His philosophy was, 'You have to open every door in life, because you might find something behind it that you do better than anyone else'.

He married, had five children, a bunch of grandkids, even seven great grandkids. He and his wife were very close and when she was killed in an auto accident he went into hibernation. His friends finally got him to come for coffee with them and the 'Old Farts of Distinction',(OFD), was formed, which now was a very important part of his life. He kept contact with his family but none of them lived nearby so his two friends became his second family.

****

He was sure his fellow OFDers would do their assignment and come back on Monday with some ideas for the 'Mongo' project. He needed to do his homework too. He knew the location and the name of the boat from the newspaper information he had collected on Mongo. Jim was familiar with Pleasant Harbor Marina, where it was berthed and had been there several times. It was a nice drive of about 25 miles down the Hood Canal; he decided he could use a scenic drive. He got his camera, went out to his car, and turned onto the main highway headed for Quilcene and then on to Pleasant Harbor Marina, where he would become just one more invisible tourist.

Chapter 6
Robbie Becomes a Player

His garage being full, Robbie parked in his driveway. It was a collection of his past, like Jim's. He didn't have as much 'stuff' as Jim but he also had less room in his single car garage. His workshop was separate from the house and he spent a lot of time in it doing various wood working projects. His present endeavor was a small jewelry box for one of his grandchildren. The project had been delayed when he needed some rosewood to do an inlay on the cover and couldn't find any locally. He was planning on driving to Bremerton where he had located some. He liked to go to Bremerton where there were a number of old navy ships tied up. He served in the Navy as a radio man for eight years; seeing the old ships brought back many memories.

****

Robbie was born in Panama, Central America, but was a U.S. citizen because both of his parents were citizens, and he was born in the American Canal Zone, which was U.S. territory at that time. His father worked at the canal as an engineer on one of the Donkeys.

Donkeys are small train engines that control the speed of the huge ships as they pass through the locks taking the canal from one ocean to the other. The huge freighters just fit in the canal locks and must be controlled, so as not to touch the lock gates. The slightest damage to a lock gate could shut the canal down for a month while it was being repaired. That would mean many of the ships would have to make the trip around South America to get to the Pacific Ocean, or back to the Atlantic.

His father's job was one of the most important in the area, and also one of the most boring. He spent most of his life tied to some huge ship by a steel cable, never moving more than two miles an hour for more than a few hundred yards, controlling the position of the ship in the locks.

The family had a nice house in Puerto Balboa which was where all the ships dropped anchor and waited for their clearance to proceed to the Locks from the Pacific to the Atlantic. When it was their time, a Canal Pilot would board the ship and be in charge as it entered and exited the Locks.

The back patio of Ron's house looked down on all of the ships as they waited their turn and he spent a lot of time doing his school homework on the patio under the big umbrella that covered the table. The sun is hot most of the time in Panama and when he took breaks from his studies, he did a lot of day dreaming.

He learned what countries each flag represented by the time he was fifteen and had visualized himself on ships from most every one of them, cruising off to some far away land on an adventure.

One of his school projects was to build a crystal set for his science class. Wrapping some copper wire around the center from a used roll of toilet paper, he was able to create a radio receiver and could hear voices. Radios became his passion; he never stopped building them, becoming a real 'radio guru'. When he enlisted in the Navy, his radio skills were recognized and he spent the next eight years in his favorite spot, in front of a communication center.

Over the years he had logged contacts with other Hams in all of those countries that he once dreamed of. He even talked to some of the scientists at MacMurdo Sound station in the Antarctic. He caught them on the air one night and had a good chat with an Ichthyologist on the ice. He recorded the call sign, KC4USV, but was never able to get through to them again. He had to look up what an ichthyologist was. It turned out to be a fancy name for a man that studies fish, he wrote that in his log.

After the navy he married, moved to Port Ludlow, Washington and was finally able to buy his own boat. It was a Cal 24 sail boat. He loved it and whenever he had time off from work, he would take his wife on week long trips north to the San Juan Islands. After a few years his wife told him she was tired of floating around the local islands at three miles an hour taking all day long to get to somewhere she could drive to in 45 minutes. He was unsympathetic when she said "I want a bigger boat so we can take off and really go somewhere".

His lack of concern was a big mistake. A couple of years later she met a younger man, that had a 50-foot Ocean Alexander; she packed her clothes, jumped aboard and motored off to that, 'somewhere,' she always wanted to explore.

The divorce papers came in the mail from an attorney in Hawaii. He signed them.

****

Robbie entered his house and went directly to what he called his 'Com Center'; everyone else called it his office. He sat down, looked at his collection of radios and thought out loud, "Now how am I going to find out what Mongo has on his boat"? He knew from the newspaper that the boat was a 79-foot historical tugboat that had been converted on the inside to have state of the art technology in all areas, but on the outside, it still looked like an old wooden, working tug. Robbie knew the boat had been bought right in the slip it was in now, in Pleasant Harbor. The Name had been changed to, '*Induced Dreams*', a fitting name for a drug dealer's boat.

The newspaper had carried the story of the boat being refitted by local cabinet makers on the inside and what a financial help the entire refit was to the local economy of the small town. There had been criticism of making money from a crook but the local stores didn't care. Money was hard to come by in a logging town where there was no longer any logging going on. Robbie knew the local electronic technician and he was well known for being the best one on the Olympic Peninsula. He would be the logical choice to install any electronics. Robbie decided to drop by and have a friendly chat with his friend.

Chapter 7
Lem Had Expertise

Lem pulled into his drive, pushed the garage door opener and drove into what looked like a hardware store. Every piece of equipment and tool was perfectly placed in its special location on the wall. These were the tools of his life's work; he wasn't a hobbyist; he was a professional.

Getting out of the car took a little more work than it used to. He swung his body around so both feet were on the floor and then reached out with his left hand and took hold of the top of the open door. His right hand grabbed the door frame on his right as he hauled himself to a standing position. He pulled his shoulders back, pushed his chest out and thought;" at least I can stand up straight", and walked into the house. Standing up was always the hardest part.

****

Lem was a Washingtonian through and through. He was born in Port Angeles which is the main USA port as you enter the Straits of Juan De Fuca from the Pacific Ocean. It is the only water way too many Canadian ports, as well as Seattle, Tacoma, and Olympia, which are located in Washington's Puget Sound.

As a young man he worked as a helper to various tradesmen in the boat yards and harbors in the area. He had gained many skills related to boat maintenance by the time he was 20 years old, when he joined the Navy. He spent the next 20 years doing ship repair and then retired as a Chief.

He married his high school sweetheart while in the service. When he retired, they started a ship repair and refitting business in Port Angeles. They did very well for the next 23 years when his wife one day complained of severe stomach pains. He felt her stomach and it was hard as a rock.

She said she had been having pains and didn't want to bother him about them, but they were so bad now she couldn't go on and needed to see a doctor. He rushed her to the emergency room and they admitted her immediately. The next few hours were horrible. The doctor came with a bunch of papers for him to sign, so they could take his wife to surgery; she had a tumor and they thought it was ovarian cancer.

More hours passed, he couldn't remember how many, finally the doctor came back and sat down beside him. "We've finished the operation," he said, "I'm afraid the news is not good. The cancer has spread all around the abdominal cavity and there is nothing we can do. Your wife is going to expire, I'm sorry."

Lem was so upset along with being hard of hearing he didn't at first understand. He choked out," She going to do what?"

“She is going to die,” answered the doctor. Lem hung his head and with tears running down his face asked, “How long does she have?”

“My best guess is about six months. We will send her home and give you drugs that will relieve her pain but there is nothing we can do to help heal her, I’m so sorry.” Lem was devastated.

Lem put his business up for sale and it sold within a week. The shop had such a good reputation and he priced it so low that it was a true bargain. A local friend bought it and Lem knew he would continue the good work his shop was known for. Lem then became a full-time care giver. He gave his wife his full and undivided attention until she died five months later.

After his wife’s funeral he told his local friends he was going to sell the house and move. His reason was that he had to go to some place new so he wouldn’t expect his wife in every room he entered; it was just too hard staying in the same house they had shared together for so many years; he decided to move to Port Ludlow.

Port Ludlow, only 45 miles from his old house, was a good choice, he said, because it was still in his AOR. That is what he called his ‘Area of Responsibility’, even though he didn’t have any more responsibility. It was also close to his two daughters. One lived in Port Townsend and the other one in Silverdale. They each had two children and there were also a couple of great grandchildren, or ‘Bilge Rats’, as he called them. He loved them dearly and he was happy when they came to visit and happy when they went home; they wore him out, they were perpetual motion machines.

He didn’t want to own a boat anymore, but he missed working on them. He thought about starting a new business, but he just didn’t have the needed fire in his belly to pull it off. Besides, he wouldn’t know how to keep the books anyway, his wife had done that.

He found the perfect answer. He would build model boats from scratch, not one of those kits from the hobby store, but from memory, just like a real boat is built. He was working on his tenth one now, a sail boat. It was 36 inches long and a replica of the copra carrying ships of the late 1800’s in the South Pacific.

He picked up the same newspaper article that Ron had read. His plan to go to the manufacturer to get plans and photos wasn't going to work. This boat was built in 1890. Like Ron he also knew everyone in his line of work within 50 miles, it would to be easy to find out which company had remodeled the inside of the "Induced Dreams" and gather whatever information the "OFDs" needed to know.

Chapter 8
What Do We Need to Do?

It was a raining hard Monday morning, with a steady 15 knot wind. People in the northwest know there is no such thing as bad weather, just improper clothing. The OFD's all had proper clothing and were in the coffee shop with a full cup in their hand at 0900.

"Another day in Paradise" said Robbie as he pulled his chair up to their table and took off his Gortex jacket.

Jim just laughed and crawled out from under his poncho. Lem said, "The rain is my fault. I can't stand to be seen with a man that has a dirty car and Robbie's was a mess. I had to pray for rain to clean it off, so I wouldn't be embarrassed being seen with him."

"Talk about being embarrassed," Robbie snorted, every time it rains, we have to be seen with you in that oil cloth yellow bib overhaul you just happen to have on right now."

Lem looked down at his outfit. "Well! It's a lot better than that high tech Gortex thing you wear; at least I stay dry, (he emphasized dry), when I get lost in the woods, they can find me from a helicopter that's 5,000 feet up. That camo poncho Jim is wearing makes him invisible."

The mood was set, they were all in good spirits and it was time to think about Mongo.

Jim asked Lem, "What did you find out about the boat?"

"I have a good friend that has been on it. He worked for the company that did the remodel of the inside and did some of the work himself.

It's a real tug hull, made of two-inch-thick iron-wood the whole length of the hull, and is really tough, probably bullet proof. The bow section has been converted into a Captain's suite. He has a king-size bed, clothes locker and a complete head. Before he bought it, the previous owner had taken it to the yard and took the old Atlas engine out and put in two 160 hp Perkin engines in line so they turned a single shaft. They installed a new prop with a lower pitch to turn faster with the new engines. The old engine had a four-foot prop that only turned 300 rpm at cruise. Now it cruises at 12 knots instead of 8.

The upper cabin was not changed as far as arrangement. The salon and galley are still in one area in the aft cabin. There are four bunks in two separate cabins forward. The cabins have been made to look like a new yacht inside, really fancy paneling and a big TV set connected to a satellite dish that is self-adjusting on the wheel house.

The wheel house was left to look original but all the controls are electronic, and the boat is steered with a joy stick. He had bow and stern thrusters installed at his last haul out.

I don't know why he did all that, they say the boat never leaves the dock. It's being used as his getaway place; kind of a safe haven that everyone knows about, but can't get close to, because of the guards."

Jim had a big smile on his face, "You did a great job Lem. Did your friend have any idea why you wanted to know about the boat?"

"No, not at all, I just dropped by and told him about my new life style since my wife died and I moved to Port Ludlow. In the process we drank a six pack of Matutu Lager that I bought, which by the way is a great beer. It's imported from Raratonga down in the South Pacific Island country of the Cook Islands. It's really hard to find here but I found a source."

Robbie interrupted, "We don't care about your beer. Go on with your meeting."

"Well, the beer is important. By the time we had finished the six pack he was really in a talkative mood. When I asked him if he had worked on any interesting vessels lately; I used the term vessel instead of yacht, to make sure he would think of Mongo's tug; he talked for an hour all about it. I missed my calling; I should have been a spy."

"You are a spy now," said Jim. "What you just told us is real Intel and we couldn't go forward without it."

Robbie spoke up, "I've got information on the electronics. I got it pretty much the same way Lem got his. My friend's son installed all of the electronic on the boat; he has it all. On the port side of the pilot house there is what used to be a chart table and is now an electronic console."

"I was right about the radios being used for coms. I don't think he used them much at all. His communication seems to be an encrypted satellite phone. He also has wireless internet through a Verizon Hot Spot. My friend's son helped him set up an e-mail account and answered his questions about putting messages in his draft box. He asked if someone that had his password could they open his account and read what was in his draft box without it ever being sent. What a clever way of sending messages. By not sending them you keep them private."

"The other gear on the boat is regular navigation type gear, chart plotting GPS, Fathometer. The only off the wall item is a side scan sonar unit that can detect anything approaching his boat from under water. He has an alarm that goes off if so-much as a big salmon swim by. My guess is that it's turned on 24/7 whenever he is aboard. There's no way anything can approach from under water without being seen on the screen. When the alarm goes off everyone will look at the screen."

Jim said, "That means no SCUBA or limpet mines. Nothing would stick to a wood hull anyway. They more than likely, if they went to the trouble of the side scan unit, have a few grenades handy to drop over the side and kill anything in the water from the shock wave. I guess my SCUBA equipment will just have to stay out of date."

Lem spoke up, "What do we do now, Jim? Did you find out anything or are you leaving all the work to the two old Navy guys?"

"Well, old Navy guys; I wasn't in the Navy floating around in the Pacific visiting south sea islands and watching the girls dance like you two were. I worked for; let's call it, 'another government agency'. We did something. In fact, what we did was so important that no one even knows about it."

Robbie laughed, "What did you do sleep with the Admirals wife?" They all broke up.

"Well, while you two were socializing and drinking beer, I became a covert field agent. I visited the marina at Pleasant Harbor. Here's what I found out while eating a hamburger in the marina coffee shop. The boat has a live aboard bodyguard and a general maintenance man. They are there all the time. Both are well armed.

When Mongo is aboard, they have three more body guards that travel with him everywhere. There is always one at the head of the finger dock to the boat. The boat is on an end tie at the end of A Dock. Two of them stay on the boat and one stays on land where he can watch the entrance to the harbor. Mongo would be notified instantly of anything unusual happening anywhere around the marina. He has an inflatable tied next to his boat with a 150 hp engine on it that can probably go 40 or more knots for a quick getaway if attacked from land.

They say he arrives at the marina in a big black limo that is bullet proof and it stays in the parking lot. I think that if the attack came from the water side, his escape path would be up the ramp while the guard on land brought the car to the head of the ramp for him.

He would have three guards with him on the way from the boat to the car. He would be moving fast so a sniper would have trouble from any distance making a good shot.

"The other thing they say about him is he comes up every seven or eight weeks like clockwork. He must be on some kind of a schedule. Oh, and one more thing. He is probably under surveillance from our people, whoever they may be, local, FBI, or some other agency.

Let me work on it for a week and you two see if you can come up with any angle that might give us a chance at him."

They had a lot to think about now, not just a silly project, but rather a heavy mission to plan. Each week their meetings were getting more and more interesting.

****

Their next meeting was one of substance not just ideas. Jim said, "We now have enough info for some solid planning; there are separate events that have to happen if we are to be successful; I have them identified. What we need to do now is figure out how to make each one happen in sequence. There's an old saying, *'Don't wish your enemy harm, arrange it.'* That's what we need to do now, arrange it."

Robbie asked, "What are these events we need to arrange?"

Lem chimed in, "Yeah, and what exactly do you mean by events?"

Jim placed a list on the table. "These are the segments of the mission as I see it." He started to go over each item.

1. Mongo must leave the boat. The boat is not a good place for an attack. Too many people in too small a space.

2. How can we get to him in the short distance between the bulletproof boat and the bulletproof car with the guards all around him?

3. What would be the best weapon to use?

4. How do we get away with our lives?

The OFD's were all focused now on the details of what was ahead. Their meeting lasted three hours, which was two hours more than normal. When they were finished Lem said, "I feel I'm back in the Navy only now I'm going to be the captain of the ship."

Robbie pointed his index finger on his right hand at Jim and said, "Bang."

Jim smiled pushing his chair back and said, "We can polish it up as we set it up, but now we have a plan. It's time to become invisible, so we can verify that it will work. They walked out to the parking lot.

"If you think of any way, we can streamline anything, we will work it in. Lem start working on your new project. Ron, you got the electronics and the coms we will need. I'll become invisible and start practicing, in a month or so we will have a better idea of what we are capable of."

The ever-present Rose Queen wave was their parting jester. Life was good, they had a plan.

Chapter 9
Five Months Later

February in the Northwest is either rainy and stormy, or dead calm. It had been calm for a week with temperatures in the mid-forties. This was ideal winter weather, Mongo was on his boat with the heater going, enjoying the quiet seclusion of Pleasant Harbor.

Winter was not considered to be boating season. Opening day of boating season, was in May, and the yachters made it a day of celebration, with parties at the yacht clubs and special cruises, to start the new season. It's always a big deal because the Northwest with all of its Sounds, Straits, Islands and harbors is the perfect place to go boating. A boater can go someplace new, every day for the entire five-month season, if they choose.

Mongo spent more time in the winter on his boat when there was no one around. He felt safe with his bodyguards on the boat and on the dock 24/7. He felt he had the perfect security; no one could get close to him without being detected.

The bodyguards got complacent standing watch on a dock with no one on it. They spent their shifts sitting in a chair at their designated location reading books. This was thought to be sufficient because they could see anyone approaching from several hundred feet away. They used hand held VHF radios to check in, every thirty minutes.

Mongo's boat was at the far southern end of all the docks. The ramp from the parking lot at that end of the marina, was not used much by anyone. The ramp down to the dock in the center of the marina was where the main stairs were located from the parking lot on the hill above; they came down to the marina office, snack shop and restrooms.

Those that lived aboard their boats were the only people on the docks with any regularity in the winter. There was a dozen or so boats in the marina that were home to the people that owned them. In the winter the live aboards were all hunkered down in their cabins come nightfall with the heaters going; it was just too cold to be outside.

As the sun set, the temperature dropped below forty into the thirties. The guard on the dock wondered why he was even there; then he remembered his pay check and went back to reading under the dock lights that came on automatically at dusk. He would be relieved in two hours, go down the ramp to the boat and hop in his bunk to get warm. Looking around the harbor he saw no movement of any kind. Even the dock cat was tucked away keeping warm in a box, with a blanket in it, that one of the live-aboards had put out for him.

The guard glanced at his watch; only an hour to go. He looked up again to check the harbor and was startled by an explosion. Jumping up and getting his gun out, he saw nothing, but the explosion, although not huge, was definitely in the marina somewhere. His radio came alive; "Our boat has been attacked. There is a hole in the hull and we are taking on water. Escape plan alfa is in effect – Get the limo, over."

He replied as he was running up to the parking lot to get the car, "Good copy, Wilco, out."

The explosion caught the attention of the live aboards and they all came out of their cabins to see if there was a fire in the harbor. Harbor fires are one of the biggest fears for a live-aboard, they will spread from boat to boat, and have been known to destroy entire marinas. They usually start when a propane tank blows up. There was no sign of fire, but at the southern end of the marina there were men running off the dock. By now there were a half dozen people on the phone to 911 to report an explosion in the Pleasant Harbor Marina.

When the officers arrived, they found no fire but a frantic guard and maintenance engineer that had been told to stay with the boat, trying to caulk a hole at the waterline of the hull of the 'Induced Dreams'. It wasn't a big hole, but the water was coming in at a good rate. They had stuffed a blanket and a sheet into the hole slowing the flow for a while, but it wasn't going to hold. They would have to nail a patch of plywood over it on the outside, and on the inside, to give them time to get the boat into a boatyard, to repair it.

When asked what happened, the guard said something had blown up against their hull. He had no idea of what, or how it got there. The sheriff asked about the other people on the boat, and was told they ran off the boat and left in their car. No one was hurt by the explosion; someone was trying to sink their boat.

The sheriff's men then took statements from all of the live aboards. One said that he had seen the whole thing from the fly bridge on his boat. He identified himself as the part time security guard hired by the marina.

The statement read:

"When I got to my flying bridge I saw two men running from the tug, 'Induced Dreams', one stopped half way up the dock, the other ran to the top of the ramp and stopped where the regular guard, that was normally at the top of the ramp had been, but now he was running to the parking lot

to get the car I guess. When the second man got to the top of the ramp he talked into his radio and held his position. A third man came off the boat carrying a brief case and walked up the ramp. When he reached the first guard, that guard ran in front of him up the ramp and joined the one that was already there. The man with the briefcase walked up the ramp. He slowed down because he had a bad limp and the ramp was very steep; it was the lowest tide of the month.

When the man with the briefcase was halfway up the ramp a gunshot rang out. It seemed to be far away up in the trees, but the man on the ramp dropped the brief case he was carrying, and took a few more steps, before he fell to his knees. The two guards ran back to his aid just as the big black limo slid to a halt at the top of the ramp. The guards took the man on the ramp under his arms and carried him to the limo. They got in and sped away. They went north towards Quilcene, as best I could tell from the sound of the car.

I called 911 and told them that a man had been shot and was being carried away in a black limo towards Quilcene. When the sheriff arrived, he sealed off the ramp where the man had been shot. I could see a trail of blood on the ramp where the man was carried up to the limo, he was really bleeding badly."

End of statement.

The firemen that arrived had no fire to put out, but did help seal the hole in the boat with a temporary rubber seal held in place by some scrap wood they nailed to the hull, and then left.

The Sheriff called on the phone to his headquarters and had the road that lead north blocked off. They were to check all cars, but watch especially for a black limo transporting a man that had been shot. The car was said to have three other men in it all assumed armed. It was not known if they would be hostile or not.

Chapter 10
Something Doesn't Make Sense

The Sheriffs at the road block saw the black limo barreling down on them and had guns drawn ready for anything that might happen, when the limo driver saw he was going to be stopped. They were relieved when the limo slowed to a stop and three men got out with their hands up when the megaphone asked them to. They were told to lie down on the ground, and complied.

The Sheriff had info from the scene of the shooting that a man was wounded and asked, "Where is the man that was shot?"

"He's in the back seat, dead" was the reply.

The limo, the three live men and one dead one were taken into custody and transported to Port Townsend. The men identified themselves as bodyguards for Mongo. They said they were in great trouble because they had failed to protect him. They gave their statements of what happened. Mongo was fleeing the boat because of a bomb that went off. On the way off the boat Mongo was shot by a sniper from somewhere up in the woods. There was nothing they could have done to save him. They got him out of there before they were shot too.

They were on the way to find a doctor in Port Townsend. They knew where the hospital was and that is where they were headed. Mongo died in the car about fifteen minutes before they were stopped by the police. They didn't know what to do when he died. They considered dumping him off the road somewhere and just disappearing, because when the cartel found out he was dead under their watch they were dead men too.

The news that Mongo was dead hit the papers and TV the next day. It made headlines due to all the press he had received during his career laughing at the cops and their incompetence.

The body was sent to the Seattle coroner's office because of the ongoing cases the Seattle department had that involved him. It arrived with a note from the Jefferson County Coroner to the Seattle Coroner saying, *"This should be an interesting case. I just took a quick look at the body to confirm identification before we sent it to you. I also read all the eye witness and police accounts and statements. One thing they all agree on is that he was shot by a sniper. It was obvious to me that he wasn't shot at all. Have fun."*

Sally Steel, one of the Seattle coroners, signed for the body when it arrived, and read the note. "Wait 'til Ron reads this," she said under her breath and started to examine the body.

Sally Steel had been a coroner for many years and was married to Detective Ron Steel of the Seattle Police Department. They had met during a case they referred to as 'The Man Who Died Twice'. It was an intriguing case because the dead man did not die by the obvious way everyone thought he had.

Ron was now the lead detective on the drug task force and had worked cases that involved Mongo's cartel but had not been able to pin Mongo directly enough to anything to put him in jail.

As Sally examined the body, she immediately saw what the Jefferson County coroner saw. There was a hole in his chest and one in his back where something had passed through the body, but it wasn't a bullet. She wiped the skin clean and looked at the entry wound, then at the exit wound; they were exactly the same odd shape. She studied them for about five seconds before she smiled."

Sally called Ron at police headquarters. "Hi Sally, I was expecting your call. The body of Mongo must have arrived."

"You're right on that, but that's not why I called. Have you read the reports they emailed to you from Port Townsend about the murder?"

"Yes, I have. They did a good job of getting five statements from eye witnesses and the three bodyguards. It's not very often you have that many statements that all basically agree on what happened. Looks like a sniper finally got our boy when we couldn't."

"Well, don't write any reports yet. Remember when we first met? I called you and said you had filed a report that was wrong about the man that died twice."

"Of course, I do. That was an interesting case and it got us together, how could I forget?"

"Well Ron, you just told me that according to five eye witnesses Mongo was killed by a sniper somewhere from a great distance, right?"

"Yeah, that's right. Don't tell me he has powder burns and was plugged by one of his guards."

"Okay, I won't tell you that, but I will tell you that he was killed with a bow and arrow, not a sniper. That means the killer was close, probably thirty yards, plus or minus five. The arrow passed through the body and is most likely still out there somewhere in the brush or floating around the harbor in the water depending on the angle of the shot. Bring copies of the reports home and we can go over them tonight and start one of your Farm Boy Charts."

"I'll do that. Does anyone else know about the arrow?"

"Just the Port Townsend coroner."

"Good, let's keep it that way; no leaks to the press. He was killed by a sniper just like they have been reporting. That will give us a lead no one knows we are following. Maybe we will find the shooter. I was thinking that if it was a drug killing by a sniper, we would never find him, but the Cartel doesn't normally kill with bow and arrow. We may solve this one."

"I'll see you at dinner – love you – bye." Sally put the phone down and looked again at the wounds. This case would be her first death by arrow.

Chapter 11
Making Sense of What They Know

Ron arrived home at 6:00 p.m. They lived in a two-bedroom condo in a gated complex near Lake Stevens, north of Seattle. It was quiet and gave them relief from the hectic jobs they both had during the day. One bedroom was upstairs with its own bath and was their personal cave. The second bedroom was for guests. It was downstairs with its own bath. Ron told Sally that when they were too old to climb the stairs, they could move downstairs, and make the guests climb the stairs. Sally suggested they would need a sign on the door saying, 'No guests over seventy allowed'.

Sally usually had dinner ready when he got home because she got off work at 5 p.m. and was home by 5:30. They were both very health conscious, their dinners were simple. Generally, stir-fry veggies, and a piece of fish. They normally ate about 6:00. Their friends asked them why do you eat so early? Ron's reply was," Because we're hungry."

Sally asked if he had the statements and reports from the Mongo case and he said he did, but he wanted to have dinner and relax with a glass of wine first. His favorite saying was, 'Life is good, but only if you work at it'. He made sure he and Sally worked at it.

Their normal routine was to clear the table and wash the dishes. She would wash, he would dry, they only had a few dishes and they used the time to chat together about their day at work. This time Sally rinsed the dishes and put them in the dishwasher, while Ron spread out his papers on the table. He often brought home cases that were, he used the word, 'mushy', to get Sally's opinion on them. He always said, 'women solve problems from back to front and men solve them front to back'. Sally had been invaluable in a number of cases by seeing things and motivations he didn't think of. They made a good team.

Ron had marked a few places in the statements with a yellow highlighter. Sally asked, as she sat down at the table, "What does the marked stuff represent?"

"The ones in yellow are the points that the witnesses all seem to agree on. The orange ones are things that only one or two of them saw. It's the only real place we have to start."

"Well, let's start there then," Sally sat down and looked at the list he had created.

Ron had one column that was captioned 'All Agree'. There were seven statements: three from the guards that were in the car, one from the guard that was left on the boat and three from live-aboards that came out to see what was going on when they heard the explosion. The maintenance man had been asleep and knew nothing except there was a hole in the hull and that he was told to fix it as the others ran off the boat. One guard had stayed to help him and protect the boat from anyone that might try to get on it.

	The list read: Yes or No There was an explosion	Yes	?
1	The boat was taking on water	3	4
2	The guard at the head of the ramp left to get the car	4	3
3	There were three men on the ramp leaving the boat	7	
4	There was a gun shot from somewhere up the hill	6	1
5	One of the men on the ramp fell when the shot was fired	5	2

6	The man that was shot (an assumption) was carrying a briefcase	3	4
7	Two men on the dock carried the wounded man to the car	6	1
8	The car left and went north	4	3
9	There were no other people on the dock or on shore.	6	1
10	The police and fire department came and sealed off the area	4	3
11	The man was shot – they all were sure of that	6	1

Sally said, "We know that he wasn't shot when the gun went off up the hill. I don't see any way it would be coincidence that he was shot with the arrow, when the shot up the hill went off. The shot had to be a 'red herring' and it worked. The real shooter had to be right there to hit him with the arrow dead center like that, and should have been caught and killed by the guards."

"I had the same idea. It also gave the guards a reason to get out of there as fast as possible, because they thought the shooter was still there, and could have them in his sight," Ron pointed out.

"This was well planned and needed more than one person to pull it off, "Sally emphasized.

Ron was thinking and finally said, "I don't think this was a Cartel hit. They don't plan that way; they're just in your face. They would have just shot the guards and Mongo with a hundred rounds of automatic rifle fire."

"Perhaps the Cartel hired professional hit men to take him out because he was in the USA.

"Possible," said Ron, "but most hit men work alone. If it had really been a sniper that got him, I would be more inclined to believe that, but this took at least two and perhaps more to pull off."

Sally had a confused look on her face. Ron asked, "What?"

"If not the Cartel, who?" Sally asked.

"I guess that's what we have to find out. Whoever it was, did us all a favor. We need to search for someone that has a motive."

"That must be a list with 1,000 names on it," said Sally. "Maybe it was a project by a family that lost a member to drugs."

"Not a bad thought. They could have military types in the family that could have put this together. There is a team going over the scene looking for anything they can find. I contacted them and told them they were looking for an arrow with a broad head on it. It must still be there somewhere. I also told them that there was a brief case that was reported to be at the scene that seems to have disappeared. It wasn't in the limo when they stopped it. I want to know what was in it, and what happened to it."

Sally made up the coffee pot so all they had to do was push the button in the morning. "It's almost midnight, time to go to bed. You have a lot to do tomorrow."

Chapter 12
It Doesn't Make Any Sense

The next several weeks were frustrating for Ron. The crime scene investigation team had found the arrow. It was floating in the bay just fifty feet from the ramp. The broad head was heavy enough for it to float straight up and down with the plastic veins about four inches out of the water. It was tangled in some seaweed growing on the side of the dock and was hard to see, it was right against the dock and was all black, even the plastic veins. The shaft was carbon fiber. No sign of the briefcase was found.

The field forensic team also found the spot from which the arrow had been shot. They confirmed that Mongo had been on the dock when shot, from the blood on the ramp, and the statements that confirmed it. They knew that the arrow had gone through Mongo's body and fell into the water. There was only a narrow strip of water between the dock and the land at that spot. It wasn't difficult to draw a line the arrow must have taken. It had been fired from between two waste bins that were right next to the ramp. It was only about a thirty-five-foot shot.

That explains the gun shot up the hill. Without that shot to throw the guards into full panic mode, it would have been easy to find the shooter. It also explains how such an accurate shot could have been made. There was one odd thing about the arrow; it had the letters RED hand written on it.

The missing brief case was still a mystery. What could have happened to it?

The other unanswered question was what caused the explosion? The boat had such good detection gear aboard that nothing could have come to it under water without setting off the alarms.

It was a wood boat so no magnetic type bomb could have been attached. Why not make it a big bomb, if the idea was to kill Mongo? It was a small charge, just big enough to make the boat take on water. It didn't make any sense to go to all the trouble to figure out how to do it, and then just put a small charge there when it could have done the entire job, without all the other planning that seemed to be done. It just didn't make any sense.

Ron and Sally talked a lot about the case over the next few weeks. They could not figure out why anyone would make such an involved plan to kill Mongo, when they had already figured out a way to blow up his boat with him on it.

Other cases came up for Ron, and life went on without the answers in the Mongo case. He had a hard time having any enthusiasm to find Mongo's killers anyway, but he really wanted to know who had planned such an involved hit, and what kind of a professional team had pulled it off so smoothly.

Chapter 13
Three Years Later

Ron was sitting at his desk going over one of his 'Farm Boy Lists', when the mail was delivered to the office. A hand written envelope addressed to 'Ron Steel, Homicide Detective', was in his box.

A hand addressed letter was very unusual in itself and addressed to Ron Steel, 'Homicide Detective', was even more unusual; no one had called him that for years. He held the envelope up to the light and saw there was just one piece of paper in it. He opened it wondering if it was a joke. He and his colleagues played jokes on each other all the time. There was no return address on it. He took out the paper and read the hand written message.

Dear Detective Steel,

We have an interest in one of your cases of several years ago. Perhaps you will remember it, the assassination of Mongo the drug dealer. It seems you have had no luck in finding the people responsible.

Ron's mind fixed on the words, *'people' responsible.* This person knows there was more than one shooter. That information had never been released to the press. He read on with more attention than he had when he started the letter.

I would like to invite you to join me, and my friends, for lunch. I do hope you can make it. We are writing a short story, and would like to get your input as to its believability.

We understand you are married to the coroner. We would be honored by her presents also, to get the women's point of view on our story.

Please join us at:

Seaport Landing
1201 Hancock St.
Port Townsend, WA

They serve lunch at 12:00 sharp. It's not fancy, but it is a nutritious lunch. Please arrive at 11:45.

We will see you Saturday.

Jim, Robbie, Lem – REDs all

Ron's mind was spinning, he couldn't believe what he had just read; he looked up the, 'Seaport Landing', in Port Townsend. It was an assisted living facility.

Ron called Sally. "Sally, I have a surprise for you, we're having a lunch date next Saturday," he blurted out even before she could say hello.

"Who is it with?" She asked.

"I have no idea, but I assure you it is going to the most interesting lunch date you have ever had. We have never had lunch with anyone like these people before."

Chapter 14
What's A RED?

Ron and Sally caught the 10 a.m. ferry from Edmonds to Kingston on the Olympic Peninsula. The ferry took thirty minutes to cross Puget Sound and then there was a one-hour drive to Port Townsend. Sally had never been to Port Townsend so she was looking forward to it.

Ron had not told her about the letter; he was going to let her read it just before their lunch. She pretended to be very unhappy with him for keeping her in the dark, but she was having fun trying to guess. She asked, "Is this lunch with someone really important?"

Ron answered after pretending to think about it, "I don't know."

Sally said, "Well that rules out any sports figures, you'd know they were important. Do I know them?"

"That I know," said Ron. "No, you don't."

"Do you know them?" she asked.

"No, I don't, but I think I want to."

"Does this have anything to do with business?"

"I hope so," was his answer.

"Are you looking for another job?" she asked.

"I may be after our lunch," he said.

As they drove across the Hood Canal Bridge, Sally was fascinated by the calm water on the north side, and the white capping rough water on the south side of the bridge. Ron explained it was because the wind was pushing waves from the south and when they hit the floating bridge they bounced back, and collided with the wind waves and that caused what the boaters called, 'confused seas.'

Sally said, "How do you know all that?"

"I used to do a lot of kayaking, and that was important to know." They drove on for about 30 minutes through the agricultural area and even passed a herd of buffalo a farmer had on his land. It was a welcomed and pleasant change from the hustle and bustle of the Seattle side of Puget Sound. All too soon, for Sally, their country drive was over and they entered Port Townsend via the two round-a bouts.

"What a fine-looking old town." Sally said as they came down the hill and looked out over the waterfront.

"It has a real history," explained Ron. "If the railroad had come up the peninsula to it, a much bigger town would be here, but when it went up the mainland side, Tacoma and Seattle became the big towns and the major seaports. Port Townsend is now more of an artist type community."

"Will we have time to go shopping?"

Ron said, "We'll see after we have lunch, which brings me to finally tell you what the surprise is, and who I think we are going to meet for lunch." He reached in his pocket and took out the letter and handed it to her.

She started reading the letter and said, "O My God!" When she finished, she looked at Ron and said, "I can't believe what I just read. Are we going to have lunch with a group of assassins, and if so, why are we doing that? Are you going without a backup? I don't understand what we're doing."

"Well," Ron said, "I checked on the place we're going for lunch. It's an assisted living home for old folks; they serve lunch to their resident's right at 12 sharp. I also checked if they had three residents by the name Jim, Robbie and Lem. They said they couldn't release that information. I identified myself and said my wife and I had been invited to lunch with them, and wanted to make sure we were coming to the right place.

The lady told me that they did live there, and had for over two years, and yes, they said they were having guests for lunch today. I thanked her for confirming I had the right address. I don't think we are in any danger.

You will notice that in the letter there is nothing that is even close to an admission of guilt, just enough information to let me know who they are, so I would be sure to come to see them. They knew about you too obviously, so this should be like I promised, a most unforgettable lunch. We're going to find out what, and who, the REDs are.

****

They found the Seaport and parked in the parking lot at 11:42, so they would walk into the lobby at exactly 11:45 a.m.

They were met by an old man using a walker. "Hello, Mr. Steel, it is truly an honor to meet you in person. My name is Jim. Mrs. Steel, it is a pleasure indeed to have you join us for lunch. Oh, by the way, the two gentlemen standing directly behind you are Robbie and Lem." Ron and Sally turned around to see there were two more old men that came up behind them while they were meeting Jim.

"You guys are sneaky," said Ron, and shook their hands as they all laughed.

"There are times in life, when being invisible is an advantage," said Jim. "One thing about being old, is that you become invisible to everyone; they never even know you're there. Follow me; I have a table for us over in the corner. It is quieter there and I can hear a little better. Please excuse my walker. I got over zealous on one of our exercise machines, and my knee is making me pay for it. I'll be better in a month or two."

They sat at a round table. The waiter brought them all water.

Jim said, "I hope you like salmon. We order in advance here and I figured you being from the Northwest, you must like salmon. I ordered meat loaf for me in case one of you didn't like salmon. I will be happy to trade with you." Both Ron and Sally said, they loved salmon, and thanked Jim for ordering it for them.

Jim continued, "There is nothing like reading a story that has loose ends, especially one that has no ending. Len, Robbie and I, are in the process of writing a story about the death of Mongo a few years back. You were the investigator in charge of the case according to the papers. Is that true?"

"Yes, it is. It's not my best case. I never solved it and now it is listed as a 'cold case.'"

Lem said, "We're going to write a story, based on it." Then turning to Jim said excitedly, "Do I get to make another boat Jim?"

Jim smiled, "Lem has some memory problems, so he may sound like he isn't quite all there; of course, he isn't, but that's okay, because here, (he looks around the dining hall) almost no one is." They all laugh, even Lem. "Lem, you are working on a boat now, the one with two sails."

"Oh yeah, it's going to be a good one too. I'd still like to build another one with a motor though, so I can run it in the pool."

"Finish the sail boat first, then you can do another one with a motor." Jim said. Then turning to Ron, he said, "In this story we want to write, we need your help to get some of the details. Let me tell you the plot, and you can help us fill in the details the story needs to make it plausible. How does that sound?"

Ron played along, "Sounds like it might work, Sally and I would be glad to help." Then he turned and asked Robbie, "What did you do in your younger days?"

"I was a radio man in the Navy, and a ham all my life."

"And what did Lem do?" he said looking at Lem.

Lem told him proudly, "I repaired boats. I was good at it too."

"Jim, what did you do?'

"I had many jobs. I taught school mostly; on occasion I even worked for the government."

Ron glanced at Sally and said, "I thought perhaps one of you had worked for the government."

"Everybody has to do something. It doesn't matter much what you do as long as you are good at it." Jim pointed out.

The waiter brought their food and they started eating their lunch. Ron was more interested in talking than eating, but he held himself back. He asked, "Why did you get in touch with me and why now?"

Jim replied, "Well, we know more about you and Mrs. Steel than you are aware of. We talked about it and decided you deserved to have lunch with us."

"What is the information you have about us and where did you get it?"

Jim responded, "We were having lunch just like today a month or so ago and one of our managers sat down and visited with us. I mentioned your name as the detective on the Mongo case, which Lem, Robbie and I were following. He said he knew you, and your girlfriend. (Sally's ears perked up). It was years ago when he was an attendant at a home in Seattle. He told us how you and then girlfriend (he assumed) Sally had befriended two of their patients that had no friends. He thought both of you were very special for doing that. You seemed to really care about people, not just the law."

"The three of us discussed your situation and decided that an unsolved case would haunt you forever and because you seemed like a friendly person, we decided to ease your frustration a little if we could. We know nothing of course, but perhaps the writing of our story might help."

They continued to finish their lunch, as the dining room emptied. Most of the people in the dining room left and went somewhere to do something. According to the bulletin board there were at least a dozen activities going on all the time.

Jim asked, "What are some of the questions you would have to address if you were writing the story?"

Sally asked, "What would your motivation be in your story, to kill Mongo?"

Lem said emotionally, "He was a bad man and he hurt people, even little kids."

Jim broke in saying, "That's right Lem, he was a bad man. Let me think why we would want to kill him. Well, it could be because we were bored. Perhaps we had nothing to do that was important to anyone anymore. We were the invisible men in society. Perhaps, we just wanted to do one more thing that would make a positive difference in the lives of a lot of kids, perhaps even our own grandchildren."

Sally asked again, "wouldn't you be afraid that you would be caught?'

Jim answered again, "Well, none of our characters have any money to speak of and they didn't want to live with their kids and mess up their lives, so what did they have to lose? If they screwed up and got caught by Mongo's guards, you would have found them floating face down in the Hood Canal. Their problems would be solved."

"If they successfully snuffed Mongo and got caught by you – they would be put in jail for the rest of their lives, which would only be a few years anyway, getting assisted living and health care, for free. Our characters planned that if they got old Mongo and didn't get caught, they would have at least solved one of their problems and done something worthwhile."

Ron looked around the now empty upscale dining room and said, "Let's say they didn't get caught, and pulled it off. How would they have solved the problem of long-term care?"

"Well, we didn't have an answer for that one for a while, but in our story, we decided to put in an unpredicted turn of events. Their plan was to take place at New Moon, so it would be as dark as possible, and they had a better chance of escaping. We also knew Mongo had a bad leg from an old gunshot wound, and he always had to slow down when he came up the ramp. He had to pull himself up the ramp by the rail when the tide was down to a real low level like it always is at new moon. We got that information by putting an invisible old man on the bench at the top of the ramp to make observations during the months before we started to write our story".

"In our story we planned on it being an easy shot with a bow and arrow from the dumpster. It was only about ten yards. We would have a person up in the trees by the road with a 306 rifle. When Mongo started up the ramp we would have said 'now' into the radio, and the person with the 306 would fire it out toward the bay, so as not to hit anybody by accident. As soon as the sound of the gun was heard the arrow would have been let go. By shooting at the soft tissue just below the breast bone the arrow would pass through the body and being all black, would not be seen by anyone. It would have been hardly felt by Mongo. A razor-sharp broad head traveling at 300 feet a second would pass through the body in 1/100 of a second with no impact and not even be felt if it didn't hit a bone. The internal bleeding would be massive, and he would collapse in just a few seconds. All of this would have been part of the plan in our story."

"It would be unexpected for him to be carrying a small suitcase, but we decided to write it in. Of course, he would drop it when he was shot, and it would have to slide down the steep ramp and fall off over the side near the bottom into the mud. We could write that in too. As our shooter slipped over the side of the ten-foot cliff to the exposed muddy beach and rocks below it would have been a natural thing to pick up the suitcase and take it to his escape car at the boat ramp, which, due to the low tide was accessible from the beach."

"Of course, to make the story more interesting, we would have to write something important to be in the suitcase, like a half a million dollars. That would solve the long-term care problem. In our story the three characters could stay in a nice place, even like this, for the rest of their short lives."

Ron said, "What a fascinating story, but there are a few things that need to be explained when you write it. How would you know when Mongo was going to leave the boat?"

"When there is an explosion that blows a hole in your boat, and you're a man of Mongos background, I think I would get out very quickly," said Jim.

"How would you arrange to blow a hole in his boat on demand, with all the detection equipment he had on board?" asked Ron.

"That would present a problem. You would need someone that could build a model boat that was radio controlled, and then someone that understood radios well enough to control it. It would need to be a special design able to carry a small shape-charge on its bow. If you had all those things it would be simple. An electric motor in a three-foot model boat, could easily do that. You would just put the bow of the model boat, with a small shape charge on it against the hull and BOOM – a perfect hole is blown in it."

Ron sat back in his chair, stunned by the old men in front of him. They were confessing to a brilliant crime in such a way he had no evidence against them. He finally said, "You're right, that would work, and the model boat would be completely destroyed. One last question to finish up all the loose ends. Why go to all that intricate planning when you could have just used a big bomb and killed Mongo on his boat?"

Jim said, "In our story we are the good guys. Lem could never bring himself to destroy a beautiful old boat like that one. He spent his entire life caring for classic boats like that old tug. That one was built in 1890; it is a one of a kind survivor and you just can't destroy a piece of history like that, it just wouldn't be right.

There were other reasons of course. Mongo was a bad man (Lem repeated – Mongo was a bad man) but the body guards, were not the kind of bad that in our story the characters wanted to kill. That seemed a little extreme to the fictional characters in our story. They also did not want to do anything that would cause a fire to break out at the marina. Fires are horrible and someone could have gotten hurt. They didn't want to take any chances on any of that happening."

Sally said, "It sounds like you have a tight story without any loose ends. When do you plan to write it?"

Robbie spoke up for the first time. "We'll probably never get it down on paper. It is best told as oral history. In a few generations of telling it, our characters will become heroes instead of murderers and will have wiped out the entire Cartel. I like it better that way."

Ron told Sally that they had to get going. They had to catch a ferry. He shook hands with the three old men and said, "I think you're right. It is best told as oral history. By the way, what is a RED?"

Jim answered, "You should go to more movies, 'Retired, and Extremely Dangerous.'"

Ron said, "Well, I think you're right; you three are all REDs. Oh, one more thing before I take off to catch that ferry."

"What's that," asked Jim.

"Promise me that this is the only story you're going to work on. No more stories."

Jim laughed, "I'm afraid we are all storied out." The three men gave Ron and Sally the Rose Queen wave as they drove off and went back in to have another cup of coffee, which was now the only important thing they had to do.

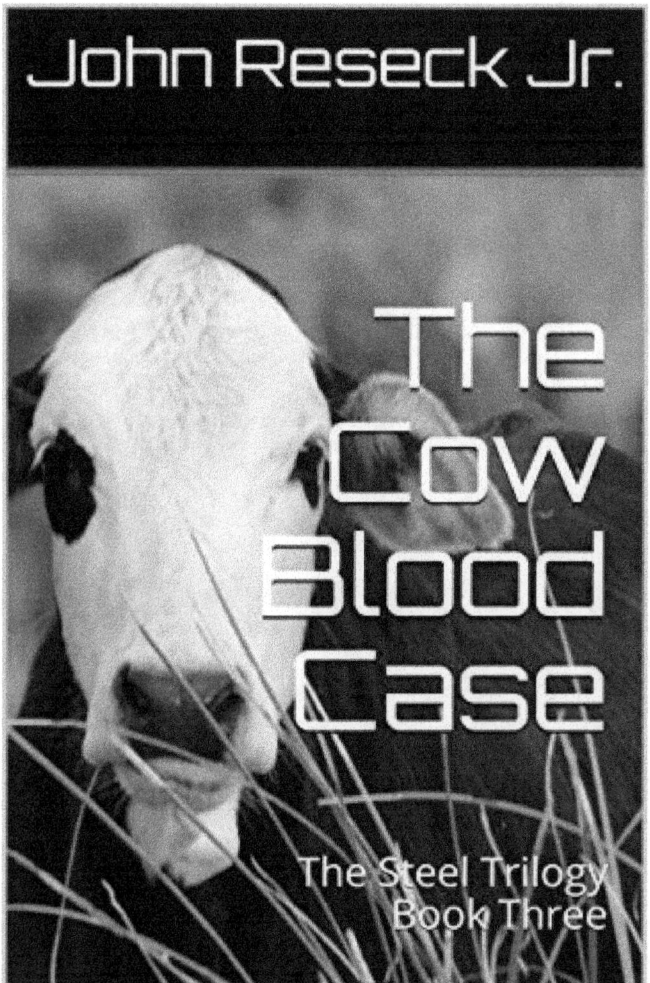
John Reseck Jr.
The Cow Blood Case
The Steel Trilogy
Book Three

It is my belief that
What we call
Life,

Is a journey across
A giant stage.

Each scene played
On that stage
Affects
All of us

The Cow Blood Case

A Steel Mystery
Scene 1

Karbosky joined the organization at the age of 16 and worked on the street dealing drugs for a while until he was promoted to being a product currier. Now at 19 he was known only as Karbo and had just been promoted again to money currier, which was a real step up in the power pyramid of the organization; he was elated.

The aluminum briefcase he was given was locked and heavy. He didn't know money could be this heavy, there must be a lot in it. His instructions were simple and clear, and because he was new at the job, they even wrote them out for him so he couldn't make a mistake. "Go to the marina around 3am, walk out about half way on F dock to the boat, 'Pops Float', place the case in the storage boat box on the dock. The box would not be locked. Put the case under all the other stuff in the box then use the padlock he was handed and lock it." He wasn't in possession of a key; the pick-up man would have one.

When he got to the marina at three am it was dark and cold with a heavy mist in the air. He almost slipped on the wet metal section that ran down the middle of the dock. He slowed down and nervously, very carefully, walked the rest of the way out, giving most of his attention to where he stepped so his leather soled shoes would not slip again. "If I fall in the water and drop this heavy case it will sink, and I'll get a shot to the head." He didn't know how to swim and was afraid of the water, but he was even more afraid of the people that gave him the money to deliver

Scene 2

Art came down to the boat at the marina after he and Karen moved off of it, deciding they were not going to live on it, to pick up the few things left behind. He was depressed because without living on the boat they couldn't afford to buy it. They couldn't afford both a house and a boat, so they rented a boat to give it a try, and it hadn't work for them.

He gathered all the little things they had left, tooth paste, several towels, a vase with artificial flowers in it, two jackets and some charts he had bought to plan the trips he wanted to take. Then he remembered his battery charger in the dock box.

He loaded the things he had collected in the boat into a dock cart he had wheeled down with him, then went to the dock box to get his charger. It had a lock on it. "Where the hell did that come from?" He was already depressed, now he was angry, too. He went up to the marina office to complain that they had no business putting a lock on his box.

The harbor master said, "Not us, we didn't do it. Perhaps the people that still own the boat did it. I have their phone number right here in my book, I'll give them a call." He called the probate officer and the son that was handling the sale of the boat for the estate, and they both said they knew nothing of the boat now it was in the hands of the broker and they both thought Art was going to buy it.

The harbor master told Art that it must have been some of the kids that live on their boats in the marina. We have a lot of live aboards in the marina and enough kids that the school bus has to make a stop here. Every once in a while, the kids do something stupid like that thinking it is funny. It is never funny to the person that has to take care of it. "I'll loan you my bolt cutters to cut it off. If there is anything missing let me know. A joke I can overlook, but not a theft."

Art took the cutters down to his dock box, and cut the lock off. He looked inside and everything looked like it was still there. He could see his charger under the coil of line. He took the cutters back to the office and thanked them. "Just a bad joke, they didn't take anything." He went back to the boat to finish up and go home to have supper.

He opened the dock box again and reached in to get his charger. As he lifted the big coil of line off the charger to get it out, he thought how did this line get on top of my charger? He was almost certain he had set the charger on top of the line. When he lifted the charger out, he saw the aluminum briefcase. "What in the world is in this?" he said, and lifted it out.

He tried to open it, and couldn't, so he put it in his dock cart to take up to the car. He figured the case belonged to the previous owner of the boat, and was missed by the family when they stripped it to sell. They were a very rich family and seemed bothered that they had to deal with the procedure of closing out the estate of the old man. They were always in a hurry.

None of them were boaters, and may not have realized the structure on the dock belonged to the owner of the boat in that slip. He should have just left it where it was, but his curiosity got the best of him. He had to see what was in it.

The case was heavy and the only thing he could think of that would be that heavy were a set of zincs for the boat. They were expensive and easy to steal but he wouldn't have though they were expensive enough to lock up like that. Why would they be bought before they were needed for the boat anyway? They were readily available in any marine hardware store all the time. It had been dark when he put the charger in the box and he figured he just hadn't seen it.

When he got home, he took the case to his shop and opened it with a small crowbar unhappy that he had to ruin the case to do it. Lifting the lid, he said, "Holly shit!" He sat down in the chair by the work bench and just stared at the case. Finally, he got on the intercom he had to his wife in the house and said, "Karen, come out to the shop."

Scene 3

A week later after his drop, when Karbo read about the murder at the marina, he was sure the pick-up man had tried to skim the money. "What an idiot." Karbo knew that no one could get away from the enforcers if they screwed up; they would follow you to the ends of the earth, they never gave up. He was feeling good about the fact he was a strong team player; he had a future in the organization.

He was munching on a hot dog with sauerkraut, mustard, catsup and relish on it, standing relaxed, next to his preferred street vender, eating his favorite lunch. He was there every day; he was habitual. A black Cadillac sedan pulled up to the curb next to him and he recognized the two men inside as members of his organization but he didn't know them personally. He said, "Hi, you guys here for a dog?"

"No, not right now, but we would like to talk to you if you have the time. Hop in."

"My time is your time." Karbo knew that, 'If you have the time', with these guys meant, do it now. He got in the back seat, thinking that they were going to give him a new delivery or something else important to do. It turned out to be, something else.

One of the men got in the back seat with him banging his head as sat down because he was so tall, and casually asked, "What did you do with the case you were supposed to deliver to the marina?"

Karbo was stunned. What he had just heard was the same as a judge saying, 'Hang by the neck until dead.' "What do you mean, what did I do with it. I did exactly what I was told to do with it. I put it in the dock box on F dock."

Well the owner of that box said you didn't, and we are inclined to believe him, because it was his last dying statement. We were wondering what your last dying statement will be."

Karbo realized who these two men were, the enforcers he had heard stories about, he couldn't speak for a moment, he was so scared. Finally, he shouted, I'll show you right where I put it. I locked the box and everything just like I was told to. The pick-up man was lying." He was visibly shaking now and wet his pants.

The men said nothing, but started driving. When they got to the marina it was raining, they parked right next to the ramp down to the dock, in a handicap spot. The driver put up a handicap placard on the mirror. Karbo wondered who they killed to get it. All three of them walked out on F dock, and Karbo pointed to the dock box behind 'Pops Float'. "That's the one, right there; I put it in just like I was told."

The box did not have a lock on it, the tall man opened the box. There were only three life jackets in it. "Someone took all the other stuff out. There was a lot of stuff it, and I put the case under it all, just like I was told." Karbo was crying now.

"We know, that you know, what happens in circumstances like this, that's why we wanted to talk to you. We're good guys, said the shorter of the enforcers, we wanted to give you a chance to return the money or tell us where we can find it, and save your life."

"I left it right here I tell you." He sobbed. He knew he was going to die and he didn't even know why.

Karbos' body was found two days later floating with the tide just outside the harbor by a group of kayakers that were out for a paddle.

Scene 4

"Not right now Art, I've got dinner on the stove." Karen said over the intercom."

"Turn off the stove, dinner isn't important, and get out here right now."

"Art are you hurt?"

"Karen, come out here right now, and no I'm not hurt, at least not yet."

Karen ran out to the shop totally confused; Art had never talked to her like that before. She found him standing and staring into the case. She looks at it and said, "OH My God, did you steal that. Art, what have you done?"

"No, I didn't steal it but I think we may be in big trouble anyway. It was in our dock box and I thought it had been left there by the owner that died but now I think it may have been someone else. I think it may be connected with the murder on the boat two slips pasted ours. I think it may be drug money that got left in the wrong dock box.

You know how we always laughed at how close the name of our boat was, to the boat of the druggy in the slip two down from us, the one that got beat to death?"

"What does that have to do with a suitcase full of money and gold bars?"

"Everything, if this was left in our box by mistake instead of his. They killed him because they thought he took their money. How long will it be before they realize what happened and kill us?"

"Art, what are we going to do? We have to give it back."

"Karen, we can't just call them, even if we knew who 'them' were which we don't, and say we would like to return you're million or so dollars. They would kill us anyway so we couldn't talk about it to the police."

"We can't just keep it"

"Why not? They obviously don't know we have it yet, or we would be dead. If it is drug money, we're not stealing it from anyone but crooks. I'm going to put a tarp over the stern of the boat we were on, so the name is covered. Hopefully if they don't see the name, they won't make the connection. Karen, we can buy the boat and motor off and they will never find us, even if they figure it out. We can disappear, just like we dreamed about would be so wonderful to do."

"What about the kids? We can't leave the kids."

"They're not kids anymore, they're in their fifties, they don't need us for anything, in fact I think that when they come to see us now it's just an obligation, they feel that they have to. We can't tell them anything about this now; maybe later we will be able to contact them. Now we have to plan what we are going to do, and do it fast I think, if we want to live. We really don't have a choice."

Scene 5

Ron and Sally were looking at the water in the Port Townsend marina, as they sat on the fly bridge of their new boat, enjoying a glass of Opolo Vineyards' Merlot. The water was dead calm inside the breakwater, but white capping with a vengeance on the outside. Sally said, "It's too bad the water in all of the oceans isn't as calm as the water in the marina."

Ron's response was, "If that were the case everyone would be living on boats. Then, where would we go for a vacation to get away? Now we have the entire inland passage clear to Alaska to explore, just as long you don't get seasick."

Sally looked out at the white caps and told Ron that, she didn't get seasick, but she did get scared and he had better be careful where he took her if he wanted to do a lot of cruising. Ron just laughed and said, "Don't worry about that I'm no hero when it comes to rough water. I don't know enough about boats to take on bad weather. We'll always check weather before we go anywhere."

They bought their boat used when they retired, a month ago. Living in the northwest it just didn't seem right to not own a boat in one of the prime cruising environments on the planet, where there is water everywhere, and hundreds of islands to explore.

Wanting a boat for years, it was finally time, they were retired. Their jobs with the police department were too demanding to break away for cruises, and if you couldn't do that, a boat didn't make much sense. Now, they had the time to learn to be boaters. They looked at a lot of boats before they found one, they both could agree on. It was a 42-foot tri-cabin, twin diesel and had the room and the striking interior that Sally wanted and the safety elements Ron wanted, like two engines and big enough that it should be safe in the waters that they would be boating.

Sally insisted on taking the safe boating course from the local Coast Guard Auxiliary, so that they would be confident that they could take on the San Juan, as well as the Canadian Gulf Islands safely. Their plan was to take one cruise before launching their new detective agency, 'Steel and Steel'. Ron said, "First things first, and pleasure is now first on our agenda.

When they first retired, they tried the night club scene; after a few nights the decision was jointly made that wasn't who they were. Ron's only comment was, "The places were full of drunks or people that looked like they should be having fun but weren't." He said to Sally, "As a policeman I always wondered where all the DUIs came from, now I know, I think we should concentrate on the boat."

They were taking on enough provisions to last them four days, going as far north in the San Juan Islands as they could in that length of time, on their first cruise. It would depend on the weather and whatever just felt good, as to how far they got. It was great to have a general schedule, not a specific one. Sally said, "When I look at our non-schedule, I feel we really are retired and not just on a tour." They were both very excited and ready to get underway for a relaxing, and hopefully, not too exciting trip.

It took them several weeks to decide the area they wanted to explore, and then to put the various clothing, food and equipment they thought they would need aboard. Sally realized, as she was storing the food they had bought away, that she was going to be preparing all the meals for them; that would be a change for Sally, they normally ate out often. She turned to Ron and said, "It looks like I'm going to be the galley slave for the trip. I hadn't thought about that."

Ron laughed saying, "I wondered when that would dawn on you. Not to worry, there are restaurants on most all the islands and we can go ashore whenever you think you are being over worked and I'll even help with the dishes when we stay aboard."

Sally's face lit up with a big smile, "I'm getting to like cruising more and more every day and we haven't even left the dock yet."

Ron laughed out loud at that. "Hopefully we will discover a few more reasons so you will love, not just like, cruising." Then he handed her more cans of corn beef hash to store under the sink.

She was sitting on the floor, stuffing supplies in the storage area under the sink. With a smirk on her face she looked up at him. "You keep looking for those reasons, just in case I happen to miss them." They both laughed at that.

The boat was well equipped when they bought it, with radios both on the fly bridge and below in the main cabin; the radar, fathometer, and chart plotter GPS were all on the fly bridge. The only things they bought extra in the way of equipment were two inflatable life vests. In their boating class the instructor emphasized to wear a life vest, which she called a PFD, at all times when on the boat. She told them of all the people that drown 85% of them were not wearing a Personal Flotation Device. Sally told Ron that was good enough for her, she wanted a life vest.

They both wanted the inflatable type. That type was comfortable enough that they would be more likely to wear them all of the time, like they should.

The fly bridge was completely enclosed with a canvas top and clear plastic windows all around to give a 360-degree view of their surroundings. They would be protected from the rain and even the occasional hot sunny day. It was also the safest place to operate the boat, because they could see any other boat traffic, as well as drifting logs that could appear in front of them. The logs were very hard to see from down below, and very common in the water they would be traveling in. They could do great damage to their boat if they happened to hit one.

Ron stood on the dock thinking, what have I forgotten? Sally was on the boat in the cabin putting things away that might fall and break, if they were to hit some rough water.

Scene 6

Ron finally came aboard with the yellow electrical cable in his hands, coiled it under the seats on the bridge, and started the engines. He turned on all of their electronic gear and checked it out. "Everything seems to be working." He told Sally.

She was perspiring from carrying stuff to the boat and then securing everything in the cabin. "Well I know I'm working." was her reply.

"Time to throw off the lines and get underway. Do it just like we practiced it," said Ron. They had worked out a procedure the two of them could use to untie, and then retie up the boat when they went into a marina. The boat backed out, made a right turn and slowly left the marina behind. Ron brought the RPMs up to 1800, the boat increased in speed to eight knots, and he looked at Sally, smiled and said, "I can't believe it, we are finally actually on our first cruise."

Sally responded with, "I hope it will just be a good cruise and not an adventure." She reached over and gave him a kiss.

"Why? Since when don't you like adventure?"

"Well you always say that an adventure is a near death experience that you survive and I don't think I am ready for one of those on our first trip out of the slip."

"Game on." Was all Ron could think to say.

Their planned first day was to cross the Strait of Juan de Fuca on a course that would take them just to the east of Smith Island. Smith Island was nearly half way across the strait and had a weather station on it, so they could get current weather on their VHF radio and not get caught in rough water. Their destination was Sucia Island.

On the south west end of Sucia was Fox cove. In checking the chart during the planning, it looked like a well-protected place to spend the night and he figured it was an easy trip of only about five or six hours.

They had a pleasant, uneventful crossing and found Sucia Island as planned, carefully entering the entrance between Little Sucia and the big Sucia into Fox cove. Sally was looking around as Ron slowly navigated through the pass with rocks on both sides. "We're the only ones here, I can't believe it, this is nature in all its elegance, the water is so calm and with the reflection of the trees in the water, it looks like we're entering an upside-down world. I think I could spend our entire trip right here and be happy."

"I don't know about the whole trip, but it looks like we won't encounter any problems in a place like this."

Being new to the art of anchoring, they followed all the steps given in their class to the letter. The cove was tight; they had to be careful.

When they were secured, Ron was still a little uneasy about going to sleep for the night. What if a wind came up? Were they truly in deep enough water to still be ok if they were to swing around to a different position at low tide and not bottom out? He checked the anchor one more time and then went to bed. All these 'what ifs' were in the back of his head making for a restless night.

Ron got up after an hour in bed, went to the 'head', and checked the anchor once more, just to be sure they were holding tight. A wind had come up, causing the boat to drift to a new position, and the chain on the anchor made some noise as it adjusted to the new position. Everything was as it should be and he was more relaxed now and went back to bed, and finally got to sleep.

There was a knock on the hull, then two more, harder. Ron and Sally both sat up with a start. "What was that?" Sally blurted out, as they both were climbing out of bed.

"I don't know what it is, but I think we may have drifted into a rock." Ron was headed for the deck as he spoke. "Put something warm on and get out here, I may need your help." There was another bump and they were both heading for the door at panic speed.

Ron hit the deck first and shouted, "What the hell?"

Sally was right behind him, put her hands up to face and said, "Oh my God, where did it come from?"

Ron was holding off another boat, almost as big as theirs, away so it wouldn't bump them again. He was yelling at whoever was on it to come out on deck, but no one came. "There's no one on the dam thing, it must have broken loose from somewhere; it doesn't even have an anchor over the bow."

"Now what do we do? No one in our class told us what to do in a situation like this."

"Maybe we should have taken a longer class." said Ron.

There was a light breeze but the water was flat calm, they decided to tie the boat alongside and figure out what to do with it in the morning, when they had day light to see what they were doing. Once the fenders were in place to keep the boats from banging together, and the boat was secured, Ron made a quick check to make sure there was no one aboard. There was nothing else they could do now in the middle of the night, they went back to bed, tired and cold.

In the morning they got up and went out on deck with their coffee, climbed the stairs to the bridge and sat down to enjoy the scenery, along with their coffee, only then to discuss what to do with the wayward boat. After a short exchange of ideas, they agreed on calling the Coast Guard on channel 16 and see what they would advise them. They didn't want to get into any legal hassle with the owner of the boat.

Ron glanced down at the boat, now protruding from the side of their boat like a giant tumor, and fully exposed in the light of the morning sun. He said, "Tell me it isn't so." He stood up, went down to the deck, stepped over onto the other boat, bent down and was intently looking at something. "Hey Sally, come down here I need your opinion on something." Sally joined him on the other boat. "As my local coroner, (That was her position in the police department), tell me this isn't blood all over the back deck."

Sally was on her knees taking a close look at the spots on the deck. "I wish I could, but I can't, that is blood, maybe it's fish blood. They could have been fishing and fell overboard."

"Well one thing for certain, we're calling the Coast Guard and getting rid of this thing ASAP. Don't tell them we're retired cops; I don't want to be involved."

Ron used his VHF radio on the fly bridge to call the Coast Guard, and told them about the boat. He was talking to station Bellingham, which was the closest to his position. The station was not interested, they asked if he could tow it to the nearest marina, and turn it over to the harbor master. He said he could but that the back deck had blood smeared on it, and he thought it might be a crime scene, he thought the Coast Guard should take charge of the boat instead. They agreed and said a boat was getting underway to their location. They asked, "What is the name of your boat, and the name of the boat that was adrift?"

"Our boat is the Shiloh", said Ron, "and the other one is Poppy's Boat."

Ron told Sally, "That fish blood on the deck was a good thing for us. Now we don't have to tow the boat around, they are going to take it off our hands, and we can get on with our cruise."

The Coast guard boat was there in 40 minutes and they had checked out Ron and Sally on the computer before they arrived so they knew all about their police work. The first question they asked was if this was in any way connected with a police case? Ron explained they were retired now and just wanted to get away for some R&R on their boat before starting their new endeavor as private detectives. Ron gave them the phone number of their new office and told them if he and Sally could help in any way to give them a call, they would be back to their office in three days.

The Coast Guard had gathered all the information they needed and everything that the Steels knew, so they took charge of the boat, and let the Steels continue their cruise.

Scene 7

When Art decided to keep the money, he knew he and Karen had to move fast, their lives were at stake. He formulated a plan to use the boat as the excuse to leave the area so as not to draw attention to them, many boats were leaving now to cruise, it was boating season in the North West. Everyone with a boat was going somewhere for a few weeks, and their leaving wouldn't draw attention to them at all.

That would give them a few weeks head start with their disappearing act. They would also have to sink their boat so they would just disappear without a trace, when they didn't return. They would sink it in deep water at night and row ashore in the dingy. They could avoid Canadian customs, and staying in marinas on their way north was out of the question also, because there would be a record of where they went.

It wasn't going to be easy, but he was sure they could do it. It was worth the risk to be able to live in luxury in some exotic place for the rest of their lives, and once again, he thought he didn't have a choice.

Scene 8

Home from their cruse, Ron put the key in the lock and opened the door to the newly created Steel and Steel Detective Agency. Sally was looking at the name on the door and said, "They did a good job on the lettering."

"They should have." Ron said as he walked over to his desk. "They charged an arm and a leg for it."

"Don't be a grouch. You're in the real world now, not in the police department. We're now in the small business world. No one said it was going to be easy, or cheap."

Ron looked around the office and commented, "I think we have everything we need."

"Not quite. We could use a client or two." The phone rang and they both jumped. "Who could that be? No one has this number yet. Answer it quick Ron, before they hang up."

Ron picked up the phone and put it on speaker so Sally could hear. "Steel and Steel agency, how can we help you?" They had decided that was a good way to answer the phone, it told who they were and did it in a friendly manner.

"Mr. Steel, I'm so glad I finally caught you. I know you were out of town for a while, the Coast Guard told us that when they gave us your number. My name is Joe Dearborn, does that mean anything to you?"

Ron looked at Sally, she shook her head no. "No, it doesn't, should it?"

"No, I just thought it might, how about the name, 'Poppy's Boat'?"

"Now you have my attention." Said Ron. Sally pulled her chair closer so she could hear more clearly.

Ron continued." What is your connection with the boat? Do you own it?"

“Well, I guess I do now, my parents, Art and Karen Dearborn did. My sister and I want to talk to you about what you think might have happened to them.”

“I don’t think we can help you. We told the Coast Guard everything we know.”

“You know about the blood?”

“Yes, we saw it. There was a lot of it. It looked like something really bad had happened; or more likely that they caught some fish.”

“Did you know that it wasn’t human blood?”

“No, we didn’t know that. We thought it was probably fish blood?”

“No, it was cow blood. Do you have any answer for that?”

Ron looked at Sally, her eyes were a big as saucers, she was shaking her head and gesturing that she had no idea. Ron said, “Now you have my full attention; could you come to the office this afternoon, say at one o’clock?”

“We’ll be there. We are totally confused about this entire thing. The Police can’t give us any reasons for anything either. We don’t know if our parents are alive or dead, all we are sure of is that they are missing.”

Ron told him the agency would be willing to help if they think there is something they could do, and hung up. “I think we have our first client.” said Sally.

“At least we’re going to have a very interesting conversation.”

Joe Dearborn and his sister Mary arrived at the Steels’ office at 12:45. It was obvious that they were siblings because they looked alike. Both about six feet tall, tan from being outside, and in very good physical condition.

Sally made a mental note that they were not poor because they were both dressed in expensive Patagonia from head to toe, they were obviously out door types.

After the normal introductions, Joe asked, “What can you tell us about what happened?”

Ron said, “We really don’t know anything except their boat was adrift and bumped into ours during the night. We saw the blood in the morning and called the Coast Guard, they came and took the boat with them and we went on our way. We figured that there could have been an accident and someone fell overboard. That isn’t likely though if there were two people aboard.”

Sally spoke up, “Tell us about this cow blood.”

Mary look over to Sally and said, “Like you we thought there was an accident to, but when they said it was cow blood the police are investigating it as a possible crime scene. We don’t know what to think. They said it was bovine blood, I asked what that was and they told me it was cow blood. That’s impossible, they certainly couldn’t get a cow on the boat, and they didn’t even eat red meat anymore.”

Joe broke in, ‘If it is cow blood, where did it come from, and it means our parents could still be alive. Maybe they were kidnapped and the blood was put there to make it appear that they were dead.”

Ron and Sally were taking all this in and paying a lot of attention to the emotions of the siblings as they were telling their story. “Is there any chance that your parents just wanted to disappear and start another life somewhere?”

Joe looked at Mary and they were both silent for a moment, then Joe said, “My dad was in some kind of debt and was really worried about it. He did say that he wished he could escape to an island somewhere. To do that though you need money and that was the problem they didn’t have any. They had just spent everything they had to buy the boat.”

Sally asked, “How old were they?”

“My mom is 76, and my dad is 78”

“How is their health?” Sally continued.

Mary answered, “Mother is OK but she has to take it easy because she gets chest pains if she over does. Dad is taking medication for emphysema but he has it pretty much under control.”

Sally continued, “Do either of you have any children?”

Mary replied, "Not any more. I had a son but he was killed several years ago in a car accident. Joe isn't even married."

"Tell me about the accident." Said Ron

"What does that have to do with what we're here for? It happened three years ago." The question obviously brought back bad memories for Mary.

"It's just for background information, please, I'd like to know." Ron continued,

"Were your parents involved in the accident?"

Joe spoke up. "In a way they were, but not directly. They had Jimmy with them and were going out on a rented boat, to do some fishing. While they were putting the fishing gear on the boat Jimmy remembered he left his hat in the car. Grandma gave him the key and told him to go get it off the back seat. A pickup truck lost control in the parking lot and smashed into Dad's car on the side and pushed it into the car on the other side. Jimmy was between the two cars. He died at the scene."

"How did your Mom and Dad take it?" Sally asked.

"That's a stupid question." Was Mary's instant reply. "They bought a bottle of champagne and celebrated of course. How do you think they took it? They were devastated. Their only grandchild was dead and he was under their care when it happened. They never really recovered from it."

Joe said, "Take it easy Mary, she didn't mean anything by it."

Sally said, "I'm sorry you're right it was a stupid question, and I apologize."

Ron cut into the conversation. "I know where you're going with this line of questions Sally, and you could be right. It would be a good reason to disappear."

Mary said," Explain it to me because I don't see any logic in any of this."

"Let me run through what I was thinking and see if it makes any sense to anyone else." said Sally.

"Go ahead I want to hear it." They all wanted to hear it.

Sally started her theory. "You said your father was deep in debt. You also said that he had made the statement that he wished he could just disappear to some secluded island where they would be left alone. The loss of their grandson on their watch would have torn right to their soul and demoralized them.

They were in their seventies and both had some serious health problems. They figured that they were short timers. At your age you probably won't understand that, but when you get into your 70s or 80s, you'll understand. They had every reason to look for a place where they could live with no one to hassle them for the short time they had left. I hate to say this, but it's also the perfect situation for a double suicide."

Joe and Mary were quiet. Ron broke the silence, saying that the cow blood didn't fit a suicide and he thought they could rule that highly unlikely. He could see Joe and Mary take a deep breath and give a sigh of relief.

Joe asked, "Do you think they are still alive?"

"I don't have any idea but it is a distinct possibility."

Joe stood up and asked, "Mr. Steel, will you take our case and see if you can find out what really happened?"

Ron said, "I think we can work it in. I want to know almost as much as you do."

Ron and Sally had their first case. They stayed cool, calm, and collected on the outside but on the inside, they were a torrent of excitement.

The Dearborns left; Ron and Sally went to work. They laid out a preliminary investigation plan they hoped would produce some useful insight as to what happened to the couple.

Sally said she would take the information they had and run everything through a computer search. She would find out what the computer knew about every individual connected to the case.

Ron would do the leg work, and try to talk to everyone connected to the case. When they sat down together there should be enough information to create a profile on each one of them. They didn't know what they were looking for, were the people dead, kidnapped, or had they voluntarily just got themselves lost and wanted to stay that way.

Scene 9

Contacting the Coast Guard station in Bellingham, Ron found the boat and crew that had taken the drifting boat away was at the station and got permission from their CO to talk to them.

He left the house early; it was a bit of a drive to the station and he wanted to get there before the boat was called out for some reason. The Coast Guard station was close to the Canadian border and had the responsibility to stop the drug trade along a 100 miles of water border. They were also on standby to assist any boater in the San Juan Islands that need assistance. They were on call to respond 24/7.

Ron was relieved when he drove into the parking lot and could see the boat was still in the slip at the station.

Talking to the crew he was told, "All we did was bring the boat to the marina. The cops met us there and took charge of the boat. They were going to treat it as a crime scene instead of a missing person case because of the blood. They didn't know it was cow blood yet."

"Did you notice anything unusual about the boat while you had it in tow, and had a man aboard it?"

"The Petty officer that rode back in the boat had an hour to look everything over while we had him under tow. He did say that there was nothing out of place like you would expect if there was a struggle or someone was badly injured, like all the blood indicated might have happened."

Ron thanked him and decided to go to the police station to see what they could tell him. The officer at the desk asked him if he had an appointment. He said he didn't. All the years he worked as a police officer he didn't need an appointment. He had forgotten that he was now an outsider.

"I'm here to ask about the boat the Coast Guard brought in a few days ago that had the blood on the back deck."

"What is your interest in the boat?"

"I've been hired by the family to help find out what happened to their parents. They were the people that were supposed to be on it."

"Are you a private investigator, and if you are, can I see your ID?"

Ron got his new ID out and showed it to the officer, who said, as he got up from his desk, "Take a seat Mr. Steel, I'll see what I can do." It only took a few minutes and he was back. "The Chief will see you, he's in the second door to the right."

"Thanks." Ron got up and found the second door on the right; taking a deep breath, because he didn't know just how he was going to be received, he entered. "Hi, I'm Ron Steel. I've been hired by the Dearborn's children to see if I can help them find out what could have happened to their parents. No offence to the police intended, they are just very confused about this whole thing and are at a loss as to what they should do."

"Have a seat Steel; we actually have met before, about 15 years ago in Seattle during your investigation of the Mongo cartel. The reason I remember it, and you, is because everyone thought you had him cold. We were all pissed off when he walked. I remember you banging your fist on your desk; I thought you were going to break it. I also thought the department might send you to an anger management class" He was laughing now and so was Ron.

"No, they didn't but one of the wise asses that I worked with, told me I should just stay away from people that piss me off; fat chance of that being a cop. Not my finest moment, but someone did finally take him out for us a few years later."

"I remember that too. A sniper finally got him. Did you ever find out who did it?"

"To get the answer to that question, you'll have to get me drunk enough to tell you the truth. Incidentally, it's a good enough story to spend the money to get me drunk. They were invisible assassins; right now it's the Dearborns that I'm interested in."

"Fair enough, I'll look forward to a six pack and a good story. I can't tell you much about what happened to the people on the boat; we can't figure it out. The cow blood, you do know about that don't you? (Ron nodded his head yes), that blood messes up every scenario we have come up with so far. If you come up with anything that might make some sense out of all this, will you for old times' sake, let us know?"

"I'll add it to the story about Mongo. Don't worry, you'll know what I know as long as it isn't something that needs to be privy to my clients. Anything about solving the case belongs to both of us."

"That's good enough for me. Oh, by the way, we're not releasing the fact that the blood was cow blood to the media. That's kind of our ace in the hole to check out the information that we get, to separate the wheat from the chaff, you know how that works. Now get out of here so I can get back to work and start saving my money to buy the beer." They shook hands both laughing, and Ron left.

It had been a good meeting; he now had a friend on the inside of the case. Ron could tell by the conversation that the police were as confused about it as he was, but he knew they wouldn't be able to spend much time on it due to their heavy workload. He had Sally and they had 24 hours a day to find the answer. He was having fun and was sure that he and Sally would figure it out; after all, they had nothing else to do.

Scene 10

Sally decided to start her search with the Parents, Art and Karen. She fired up her computer and like many people, talked to it. "You and I are going to find the answer to all the questions that Ron can come up with." As a coroner she had learned to use the computer to find out about her dead clients for the police. She was going to go much deeper now than she did for them. They were mostly interested in identity, she now needed financial records and anything else she could dig up.

She found that both Art and Karen were from a town in the mountains of northern California, called Weed. They married out of high school and had been married for 57 years. There was no record of trouble of any kind in their life as far as she could tell. They were both involved in their school activities but nothing of any particular interest. Art was a member of the wrestling team and Karen was a cheerleader. Her hobby was knitting sweaters and his was target shooting in the surrounding countryside with his 22 pistol. Every once in a while, he even brought home a rabbit for dinner.

Both of them worked in the mill when they were young like most of the people in Weed, it was about the only place in town to work in those days. It was known as a 'company town' and the company even owned the houses the workers lived in. When the International Paper Company (IPC) bought the mill in the early 1950s, they sold the houses to the workers that lived in them.

Art and Karen had also worked for IPC. When the lumber industry was starting to slow down, they were concerned their jobs at IPC were in jeopardy. They decided to move to Seattle and find more secure work, they felt the need for a steady income so they could start a family.

Art was smart, a good talker and he liked people, finding a job in sales was a natural for him. He was soon working as a salesman for a boat broker on Lake Washington, where he became one of their top sales people in only four years. This was quite a feat because he knew nothing about boats when he first got the job. He was a good student, a fast learner and studied every aspect of his business, he remained on that job until he retired.

Karen became pregnant and stayed home to raise her soon to be two children. She referred to it as the hardest job she ever had, but she loved it, and was good at it.

Their financial records were easy for Sally to find. They had around $30,000.00 in the bank that had been acquired over some 20 years in small amounts, until last month. The balance had dropped to $2,000 all of a sudden. There was no record of a loan anywhere that needed to be paid off. She would have to find out from Joe or Mary what had happened to change their lives so drastically. Joe said they had been in debt and didn't have the money to disappear. He must know why.

Sally brought up Joe on her computer, he was single, no record of any marriages and was 50 years old. He had $4,000 in the bank, a loan of $6,700 to pay off on a Mustang car and seemed to live a very boring life. He had a good job at the post office and could be retiring in a couple of years if he wanted to.

He spent a lot of time camping on the Olympic Peninsula where he fished on the many streams located there. He subscribed to Field and Stream as well as Outdoor Life magazines, belonged to the NRA, a local gym, didn't appear to have any special girl he was interested in and his relationship with his parents wasn't close or strained. He saw them once or twice a month and was receiving no support from them in any way. There was simply nothing to even raise an eye brow over.

Sally found Mary was following in the footsteps of her mother; she was a happy home maker and doing a good job at it, until her son was killed. She went into severe depression to the point of needing professional help. She came out of it in a few months and from all appearances was back to normal. The one thing that changed was the frequency of visits to her parents; they went from once a week to once every month or two. Sally wondered if it was because there wasn't a grandchild to visit his grandparents or, was it because deep down she held them responsible for his death. Sally was getting most of her personal information from Mary's Face book postings and was amazed at the amount of personal information people put on the social media sights.

Mary and her husband were leading a normal mid-American life. He was a mechanic with their local Ford agency and after her son's death Mary was a volunteer in the hospital auxiliary. They had a home mortgage, a car loan and 3,000 dollars on their credit cards, all of which were up to date.

Mary went to the same gym as her brother so they were in relatively close contact. She and her husband even went on some camping trips with Joe. Sally couldn't find a smoking gun, or a bleeding cow, anywhere. The only thing Sally thought might be significant was the fact Joe and Mary were not very attentive to their parents any longer. This made her theory of voluntary disappearance even more credible. She was aware of the fact that in her head she had created the voluntary disappearance theory and that she was actively looking for evidence to prove it. She kept telling herself she had to be careful not to be prejudice in her interpretation of the facts. "This detective business is more complicated than I thought," she told her computer, then turned it off, and started dinner. Ron had sent her a text that he was on the way home.

Scene 11

Ron came in, went directly to his overstuffed chair and collapsed in it with a big sigh. "The traffic is incredible; remind me not to be on the road at five o'clock anymore.

Sally said, "Where is my 'Honey I'm home kiss?"

Ron got up and gave her a big hug, and a kiss. "Now can I sit down and have a glass of wine?"

"You're so romantic I can't believe it. What did you find out besides how heavy the traffic is?"

"Well, I have good news and bad news. The good news first; we have a friend in the Bellingham police department. He's an old timer and remembers some of our cases from years back, if we work with him, I think he will work with us too. That is big; you know how we didn't like private investigators messing around when we were on the other side.

Now the bad news; I talked to a bunch of people and found out nothing I can say is important to us in finding out what happened. The boat was in good condition on the inside, nothing out of place as far as anyone could tell."

"We already knew that from when we were on it." Sally was sipping on a glass of wine now, too.

"What did you find out on your computer? I hope you had better luck than I did."

"Come to the table, we can talk as we eat."

Ron got up, poured himself and Sally more wine, sat down at the table and said, "What did you discover that we can be excited about?"

"Nothing to get excited about, but there were a few things to think about." She told him that the information she found gave no indication of what might have happened, everyone had checked out as being normal.

Ron asked, "What do you consider normal?"

"I know you're tired, but that's no reason to get snippy. None of them did anything that caught my attention as being strange or out of place. The big question is how they got in debt; I found no hint of that."

"Well whatever it was made a big change in their life. I'm going to call Joe in the morning and pin him down on it. It had to be something drastic, and to have no paperwork whatever on it, indicates some kind of non-normal activity to me, and I'm sorry I was snippy."

"Apology accepted." Sally said, and added, "We still have our basic questions of whether or not they are dead or alive and what does the cow blood have to do with any of it."

Ron got up and poured them more wine. "I'm not sure if we are gaining on this or falling farther behind. We have nothing that applies to those questions in the mix yet. Hopefully Joe will be able to help us in the morning.

Scene 12

The two enforcers that did the job on Karbo and the boat owner reported back to their boss that they thought both of their victims were telling the truth when they said they didn't take the money. When a man is being beaten to death the truth will almost always be told. Both of them swore right to the end that they didn't know anything about where the case went. The Boss, (that was the only name they knew him by), was listening intently as they related what had taken place with both men. He finally spoke, "I waited quite a while before I had you move on that Karbo kid, because I liked him. I was looking for some other explanation but there didn't' seem to be one. Tell me, if it wasn't either of them, then who?"

"Someone could have seen him stash the case and steal it after he left the dock?" Said the taller of the two.

"Not if he put the lock on it like he said he did." his partner pointed out. "We don't have any reason to think he didn't."

"Let me think about it. I may wander down to the dock myself and look around. If I need you, I'll get in touch." The Boss turned his back to them, which meant they were dismissed.

Scene 13

Ron asked Joe to come to the office to discuss the boat and the money disappearing out of their parents' bank account, he figured there had to be connection. Ron's first question was, "How long have your parents had the boat, and why didn't Sally find any paperwork on it?"

Joe hesitated for a moment and then said, "I guess you have to know about that. I hope this is privileged information that is just between us."

Ron assured him that it was, unless it involved a murder or some other capital crime.

"Nothing that bad, it was just tax evasion. My dad was a boat broker and when he and mom decided they wanted a boat it was a surprise to Mary and me. Pop had always said, boats were too expensive for the average person to own. He was talking about big boats and that is why we were surprised when he bought the boat he did, it was a big boat. He had always defined the word BOAT as meaning, 'Break Out Another Thousand'. He frequently said he didn't need a boat to work on the rest of his life."

Ron had looked at the registration for the boat when they first encountered it to see who owned it. It said they had paid forty thousand for it. He had thought it must have been in very bad shape when they got it and they had brought it up to the good condition it was in. He was familiar with what boats cost because they had just bought theirs. He guessed the boat was at least in the $100,000.00 range. "What condition was the boat in when they bought it?"

"It was like new, that's why they decided it would be a good boat for them; my dad said there was nothing they had to do to it. The owner had died and the family was dumping the boat. When they came to the broker to list it, my dad was visiting his friends there. When he saw the boat, he loved it and asked if he could rent it for a month so he and my mom could move onto it and see if they could live on it and still be comfortable. He told Mary and me about it and that mom had agreed to try it. If they liked it, they figured they could afford it by selling their house, and living on the boat."

"Did they do that?"

"Yes, they did. My dad liked it but my mom said, after only three weeks, 'No way.' I thought it was all over. Then my dad suddenly said that he had made a deal with the family selling it, if he would pay cash and fix the paper work so they wouldn't have to pay all the taxes or commission on it. I don't know any of the details but all of a sudden, they had a boat and were off on a cruise. I don't know if they were planning to live on it or not. They left on their trip and didn't tell Mary and me anything, not even goodbye and I have no idea how he arranged to pay for it. When I asked him why he bought it, all he said was he deserved it and that he liked the name, 'Poppy's Boat'; Mary's son had called him Poppy. When I asked him how much it was and where got the money, he said it wasn't important for me to know that; we never talked about it again."

"Could that be the debt he was in, when he said he was in over his head?"

"I don't think so. He had said the boat was paid for and he seemed happy as clam."

"When did he incur the debt that he had and do you have any idea how much money was involved?"

"I have no idea. Actually I don't even know that it was money, I just assumed it was when he said, he was in over his head, unless…."

"Unless what?" asked Ron.

"Just days after they bought the boat, I think something went very wrong. He started to drink more than he always had, and mom was very solemn too. I just thought it was because of the murder that happened on the dock, down by their boat, that they might be a little scared of the marina. Dad even said he wished he had never seen the boat once, right after he bought it. I think whatever it was that was bugging him passed, because a couple of days after that, he decided he was going to take an extended trip on it. They were on that trip just a few days when the boat turned up and they had disappeared. It all happened so fast, it kind of all blurs together."

"Could the trip have anything to do with the debt?"

"He just said he had a debt he couldn't possibly pay. I asked him about it, because he always taught us to, never spend money you don't have; he hated to pay interest, to anyone. He told me to leave it alone and don't get involved. So, I did."

"What can you tell me about the murder on the dock?"

"Nothing really. Some guy that lived on his boat a couple slips past my folks, was beat to death by someone. The scuttlebutt on the dock was that he was a drug dealer and the big boys took him out. He must have done something they didn't like. I guess it doesn't take much with that bunch to get them mad and if you do, you're dead. I don't think they ever found the person that did it; at least I didn't read about it if they did."

Ron made a mental note to have Sally find out all the details about the murder that she could on the computer. He figured he was grasping at straws, but it's all he had. He was going back to his police friend in Bellingham for a chat, it was in his area of responsibility and he would know things that didn't get into the official report.

Scene 14

The Boss drove to the marina and parked his rented car behind the marina office. He got out, stood for a minute just looking at the general layout. His own men would not have recognized him in his bright sport shirt, shorts, white socks and brand-new white tennis shoes. On his head was a cap with Disney Land written across the front. The dark glasses made the outfit complete; he was a tourist.

Walking up to the man at the counter in the marina office he inquired, "I was wondering about slips in your marina. I live in southern California and was thinking of buying a boat up here and using it as my summer home. I would love to cruise your islands. Is it hard to acquire a slip?"

"You would need to get on our waiting list but we normally could get you in a temporarily vacant slip during the summer months when the renters are out cruising. You might have to move around the marina for a while until a permanent slip opens up. If you bought a boat that was already in the marina, you could keep the slip. There are at least a half a dozen boats listed for sale on the bulletin board, on the north side of the office building, that all have slips. Check them out. You might just find your dream cottage afloat right there."

"I noticed that there are boxes on the dock at each slip for storage. Does that automatically come with the slip?"

"Yes, it does. Most people just store half-empty paint cans and stuff like that in them so they don't even lock them. If you're going to store anything valuable, like things you want to leave over the winter when you are down south, I would put a lock on it. We have kids that live in the marina and I wouldn't put it pass them to check out your box if it isn't locked."

"Have you had many problems in the past with thefts?"

"No, we haven't, in fact it just the opposite. We had someone, other than the owner, put a lock on a box on F dock. I guess they thought it would be funny that the owner couldn't get in it."

"What happened when the owner couldn't get in? Did he think it was funny?"

"No, he didn't. He came up to the office and was pissed. He thought I put the lock on. I told him I didn't do it, then we called the people that were selling the boat, and they said they didn't do it – it had to be the kids. I had to lend him my bolt cutters to cut it off, he said they didn't take anything, so he told me not to call the cops

"Sounds like a good guy."

"Yeah, he is but he had us fooled. That boat is for sale and he rented it for a while to see if he and his wife could live on it comfortably. I think he liked it but his wife didn't, so he said he wasn't going to buy it. We thought he was moving off, when all of a sudden, he said he had bought it and was going on an extended cruise. Everyone was surprised. He didn't seem like an impulsive person. I guess when you are retired it's ok to be impulsive. I can hardly wait until I reach that point in my life."

"I guess he liked the name on the boat so much he couldn't leave it." The Boss said as he was laughing.

"I doubt that, 'Poppy's Boat' isn't that enrapturing." The boss quickly looked up, then smiled

"Well thank you for the info on the slips. I need to get back to the motel or my wife will be the one that is pissed." The Boss went to his car, dialed his phone and said to someone on the other end, "Get our two workers back, I've got a project for them."

Scene 15

When Ron entered the police station the officer at the desk recognized him. "You're the Private Investigator, aren't you?"

"You've got a good memory."

"Not really. You're the only PI that has ever come in here; one isn't too hard to remember. If I had a good memory, I would remember your name, and I don't."

"Steel, Ron Steel."

"I'll try to remember that for next time. You're interested in the cow blood case, aren't you? If you solve it, I promise I'll remember your name; you want to talk to the chief?"

"You got that right."

Patting himself on the back, he said "Good for me. I'll tell him you're here."

Ron and the Chief exchanged a few glib remarks, then settled down to business.

"The reason I'm here is to find out what you can tell me about the murder that took place on the same dock as the Dearborn's boat. It was just a short time before they bought it."

"Do you think it was connected in any way?"

"I have no idea, but I have nothing else to go on, so I'm grasping at straws. I don't trust coincidental events, and it happened too close to them, so I want to check it out. Their son said they changed their pattern of going to the boat when it happened. That would be a normal reaction I guess, but their buying the boat, and their disappearance not long afterward, makes me question it. What can you tell me about it that might be of help?"

"Ron, with your background I know you are familiar with how the drug cartels work. You screw up, you die. It's a very simple rule. This guy must have screwed up. The one thing that didn't make a lot of sense to me, was that he was beaten to death; the normal execution is a simple shot to the head. This guy was beaten like they were trying to get information from him. We have known about him for a long time, and he is just a low-level currier.

We track him now and then to find out who the bigger fish are, the ones he works for. They use him and his boat, to deliver money to boats in the waters between the U.S. and Canada. When the drugs are being delivered, we hit the boat as soon as it gets into U.S. waters. I don't think the drug lords could have made the connection between our victim and the busts we've done, because they happened to different boats, at different times and places. I don't know what information he could have had that would cause someone to try to beat it out of him. Even if they thought he was a snitch they would have just shot him."

“You said he delivered money?”

“That’s what we think. We were never sure, but it is the only connection we could find, because we know he never delivered the drugs.”

“Well I’m sure the Dearborns were not in the drug business, so this may be just a red herring for me.”

The Chief said he was still saving his money for the six pack as they were shaking hands goodbye. “Well back to the cow blood case.” Ron started for the door.

“Are you calling it that now too?”

“After talking to ‘Sargent Schultz’ at your front desk I am.”

The Chief said, “I will have a talk with ‘Sargent Schultz’, and remind him that, ‘He knows nothing.’”

“Don’t be too hard on him, he’s a good man.”

As Ron passed the Sargent on his way out, he put his fingers to his lips and zipped his mouth closed. The Sargent looked a little confused, as Ron left

Scene 16

When Ron arrived at his office, Sally was anxious to go over the police report she had printed and see what Ron had found out. He filled her in about the surveillance the police were doing on the victim, and what they thought he was doing, transferring money for drug deals.

“You don’t think the Dearborns could be involved in the murder and took the money, do you?” asked Sally.

“At this point, I don’t know what to think. I keep trying to think like Art would think, but I don’t know him well enough to get into his head. Let’s concentrate on the murder right now, and see if there is any logical way the Dearborns could fit into it.”

They went over the report, and made a list of items they thought might be important, or that they didn’t understand.

Facts: He was beaten to death, not just killed. What might that mean?

They thought he was a snitch: but how would they know that? He didn't even know he was under surveillance.

They thought he had information they wanted and tried to beat it out of him. What could he know?

He wanted to quit; the cartel didn't allow that, but why would they beat him?

He took the money they brought him, and delivered it by boat to another boat in the Gulf Island. No one would be stupid enough to skim money from the cartel - that would be a sure death by beating. Perhaps the people he delivered it to said he never delivered it.

It appeared that at least two people were involved in the murder. One to hold him, and the other one to beat him. There were no indications that he had been tied.

The killers were pros, there were no clues left behind, and he had a number of broken bones before he died. That would have had to been deliberate and precise.

There were just questions, no answers. They decided to head home and have dinner on the way at a family run hole-in-the-wall Mexican restaurant they both loved. They had been going there for years and felt like they were part of the family. The food was good, and the service came by way of a cheery old man and his even cheerier wife. They were stalling out on the case and could use some cheering up.

Scene 17

"Juan of the North", as he called himself, met them at the door, with a hug for each of them.

Smiling at Ron, Sally said "I feel better already."

Juan asked the couple, "The regular, or have you decided to branch out and live on the edge, and try a chili relleno tonight?"

"The regular, Juan. Mama's fish tacos are best in the world." Ron said it loud enough that Mama could hear him in the kitchen.

Sally added, "Juan, no one makes fish tacos like Mama, not even in Mexico."

Juan's smile beamed across his face, as he said, "They can't make them like Mama in Mexico, because they don't have salmon." He pushed out his chest, spun around and proudly walked back to the kitchen. The Steels went back to their discussion of the 'Cow Blood' case.

They were still talking about the case when Mama, dressed in her bright Aztec design apron, came out of the kitchen a few minutes later, and greeted them. "Juan says you think I make the best tacos in the world. Thank you, but he didn't have to tell you my secret."

"What's that Mama?"

"The salmon of course. It's the best fish in the ocean to make tacos. When we come to this country, many years ago, we fish a lot in our ponga just like in Mexico. We catch so many fish in those days that I think Papa's boat might sink. I make tacos with the salmon, and everybody loves them. I make now for over twenty years; I think you two eat most of them." She frowned at them.

"And we intend to eat 500 more in the years to come Mama." said Sally, also with a frown and look of determination. Mama broke out laughing along with Sally, but not Ron. Sally looked at Ron and could tell that he had tuned them out; he was deep in thought. "Come on Ron, lighten up don't be a sourpuss."

Ron got to his feet and said, "Thank you" to Mama, putting a twenty-dollar bill on the table and taking Sally by the hand he said, "Come on Sal, we've got work to do." She got up, looked at Mama, shrugged her shoulders, said she was sorry, but they would be back, to eat those 500 tacos, and hustled out the door after Ron.

Sally jerked her hand away from Ron and said, "Ron what is wrong with you? That was just plain rude, and I'm still hungry."

"I'm sorry; I'll apologize to Mama later, but I think she just answered one of the big questions we have on the cow blood case. It could be the key we need to find out what really happened. I need to get home and look at the police report again about the murder on the dock. Do you remember the name of the boat the murder victim owned?"

"No, I can't remember if it was even in the report."

"Yes, it was. I think I saw it. It was up in the location info at the top of the page. I saw it but didn't pay any attention to it at the time. If I'm remembering right now it could be the break we are looking for, and it was right there all the time."

When they arrived home, Sally brought up the report on the computer, and asked, "What are we looking for?"

"Two things. The name of the boat, and the exact location relative to the Dearborn's boat."

The name was up in the info section at the top like Ron had remembered. "Oh my god!" was Sally's comment, "How could we have missed that? 'Pop's Float'. It's almost the same name, and sounds like, 'Poppy's Boat'."

Ron was looking for the slip number. Finding it he said, "Look at this Sal, they were only two slips apart, and the Dearborn's boat was the first one you come to as you walk out on the dock. I think we have just found out why the victim was beaten to death and where Art Dearborn got the money to buy his boat."

Scene 18

Ron called Joe on his cell and told him he had new information and needed to get his, and Mary's, opinion on what it might mean. Joe said they both would be in his office at 5:30. He would pick Mary up after work and bring her, she didn't have any transportation.

Ron and Sally were in the office at five and set up one of their folding tables, in such a way they would all sit looking at one another." I want to watch their reaction when we tell them that their parents have a fist full of money, and that it's drug money." Sally said, as she was making a fresh pot of coffee, remembering that they both drank coffee, black, from when they were in the office before.

When Joe and Mary arrived, they got their coffee and sat down, asking what the Steels had found out. Ron and Sally told them in full detail what they knew as fact, and then what they had surmised when they put all the facts together. In brief, that their parents had found a large sum of money and bought the boat with it, in such a way that it would appear that they used their money in the bank, if anyone checked. They must have figured out that it was drug money, and that's why they decided to keep it.

When the second body was found floating in their general area, beaten to death, just like the man just two slips from them, they knew they were in deep trouble. Sooner or later, someone would figure it all out, just like they had. They had to get away as fast as they could and they would not be able to tell anyone, especially you two, where they went. You would have to think they were dead, so you wouldn't act in a way that the drug people would suspect you had any information of their where-abouts, because they would, for sure, have watched both of you for any indication that you had information they could use to find your parents.

They must have taken the boat so the name would not be there to give them away, like it did for us. They needed all the time they could get, to get as far away as possible.

"I can't believe it." Mary said. "I just won't believe it.", and she started to cry.

Joe was processing everything he had just heard." That would certainly explain a lot, and sounds reasonable to me. Buying the boat, the debt that couldn't be paid, and why they took off on an extended cruise when my mother didn't really like the boat that much. It doesn't, however, explain why the boat was adrift, and where the cow blood came from. Can you tell us that?"

"No, not yet, but I think it means they may be alive and well with the exception of being scared to death. Sally and I are going to follow this hypothesis and see where it leads. It is the most logical set of circumstances we have been able to come up with so far."

Scene 19

Art told Karen that they had to disappear fast, and completely. His plan was simple. They would take the boat north to Alaska, they wouldn't stop in any Canadian harbors or ports, they would skip customs and all the ports, on the way north, so it will be difficult, if not impossible, to trace them. Once in Alaska they will sink the boat, fly to New York, then to Dallas, and on to Los Angeles. Each time they bought a ticket, they would misspell the last name by one letter, the chances are no one would catch the error when they checked in with their ID, but if a computer check was run to try to find them, it would not bring them up. If someone did catch the miss-spelled name, they could laugh it off as being a typo.

Once in LA, they would buy a ticket to New Zealand on New Zealand Air. Art knew that New Zealand Air stopped in the Cook Islands, at Rarotonga, on the way. They would get off there, not get back on the plane when it took off, and fly out to one of the outer islands, where they would stay as long as possible. They would figure out the immigration problems as they encountered them. They both had passports, so the initial moving around shouldn't be too difficult.

"If we don't go ashore how will we get fuel and supplies?" Karen asked.

"We will go into the fuel docks to get fuel, but we will pay cash for everything and anchor out, so we won't be signing in with anyone to leave a paper trail. To get supplies we will row in to town in our dingy and just go to the store. The dingy covers the boat name when it is pulled up on the stern, so no one will see the name to remember it. I'm sure it will work." Karen looked troubled but she trusted Art and they were too deep into this to stop now, and not get killed.

Scene 20

The two 'workers' were back on the job. They both had pilot licenses for light aircraft, and were experienced in the Cessna 210 they were taking off in from the Port Townsend airport. They had rented a 210 for other jobs in the past, but never to locate a boat under way.

With the 10/50 binoculars they carried it was possible to read the boat names as they flew low around the San Juan Islands, just north of the Washington state mainland, in the Straights of Juan De Fuca. If they stayed over the water they could fly as low as they wanted, and still be legal. They were careful not to buzz right over any boats; they didn't want any complaints being called in to the Coast Guard.

It took them all day to check out the entire San Juan Island group. They had a description and name of the boat, from the advertisement on the web where it was still listed for sale. Nothing was found that matched. Tomorrow they would fly over the Canadian Gulf Islands. 'Poppy's Boat' wasn't a fast boat; they surmised that it couldn't have gone too far.

They had better luck on day two. They found the boat at anchor off of Saltspring Island in the outer part of Ganges harbor. No one appeared to be on board. They decided to land and see if they could find Art and Karen in town. They had pictures of them from Facebook.

Scene 21

Ron was sitting at his desk holding his head in his hands, when Sally came in. "What's wrong, are you OK?" She sat down in the chair in front of the desk.

"I'm fine. I keep asking myself, what I would do if I were in Art's place? Once I realized what the money was, what would I do with it? Would I call the police? No, I don't think so. Given what was going on in my life at the time, I would want to keep it. I would realize that in time someone would figure out where it was, and come after it. I couldn't just deny I had it. That is what the two that were beaten to death must have done. If they found me, I could try to give it back to them, but I would be a witness. I might not be beaten to death, but with a bullet in my head, I would still be just as dead. The only way to keep it, and stay alive, would be to disappear, and never be found or heard of again. They had the money now to do that. It's obvious that the owner of the money hasn't figured it out yet or they would already be dead.

He had to move fast. If he got the boat out of the slip, they might never figure it out. That would explain the quick decision to take a cruise. He would of course, in time, realize that moving the boat, was just a delaying tactic. He and Karen could never come back, and they would have to leave no trail as to where they ended up. A plan that involved takes time and research to pull off. He had neither and would end up leaving a trail. If this hypothesis is right, it means they are still alive and you and I needed to find them before the drug dealer does to keep them that way."

Scene 22

Art and Karen rowed their dingy into the town of Ganges. There were a number of items Karen said she needed. It took them quite a while to find everything on their list, but they had, and were on their way back to the dock, to load their bags filled with supplies into the dingy and row back to the boat. Art said, "It's hard to comprehend the reality that we are leaving the northwest, where we've lived for years and our kids, forever."

Karen started to cry. "I'm sorry Karen we have to do this; look at it as the chance we thought we would never have to leave all of our troubles behind and live like the people in the movies. I also think it's our only chance to stay alive." Karen just sat on the bench trying not to be obvious that she was crying, but she still was. Art got up, told Karen to stay put and he would get them an ice cream cone from across the street, one of their favorite things to do when they were out for an evening walk. "We'll sit here for bit and enjoy the moment, before we have to leave." He walked across the street to the ice cream store.

He ordered two double cones, one all strawberry for him, and one all chocolate for Karen. He relaxed against the counter watching the people in front of the stores across the intersection wandering around like most tourist do, when he saw them. One was very tall the other very short, Mutt and Jeff, he thought. I've seen them before, I wonder where? The clerk brought two cones over and put them in the rack. Art took out his wallet and paid for them, reached to pick up his cones, then stopped and turned to look at Mutt and Jeff again as they entered the store. "Oh my god!" He said, as he ran back across the street to Karen forgetting his cones and leaving them in the rack.

Karen had stopped crying and was shocked when she saw Art running up to her. "Where's our ice cream?"

He picked up the bags and said, "Forget the ice cream Karen, we have to get back to the boat as quick as we can."

"What's wrong now?"

"Remember when we were on the back deck of the boat having drinks with the kids? It was the day before they found the murdered guy on the boat two slips from us?"

"Yes, I remember. Why?" she said as she stood up.

"We laughed at two men that walked past us on the dock because we wondered if their names were Mutt and Jeff because one was tall and one was short. I just saw them going into the market."

"That's interesting, but so what? Why are you so upset?"

"Karen, I think they're here looking for us. They figured it out, and they must know we're on our boat. They might have even seen it anchored in the outer harbor. We've got to get back to our boat and leave before they recognize us.

We have a better chance of protecting ourselves on the boat. They don't know we know they're here, or what they look like, so we have the advantage. We know they're killers. They plan to surprise us, but we're going to be the ones that surprise them. We can't let them get close to us, they're professionals. If they do, we have to kill them first."

"Art, what have we done? What are we doing? What's going to happen to us?"

"Sweetheart, I'm not sure about the first two questions, but the answer to the last one is, we're going to stay alive."

Scene 23

Joe and Mary were now thinking that their parents might be alive. "I'm excited that they may be alive, but if they are and the Steels are right, that means they just left us without a word of goodbye or anything. It would be awful to know they didn't care anymore for us than to let us think they were dead."

"Mary, if the Steels are right, they can't contact us without putting us in a lot of danger. They would never do that, no matter how much it hurt them. If they're alive we will hear from them in some secret way that dad will figure out. In the meantime, you and I have to stay strong and keep believing they're alive. We have to keep this whole thing to ourselves. We'll just tell everyone that they are missing and presumed dead. That story should protect us, while the whole time we're praying that it isn't true."

Scene 24

Mutt and Jeff had taken the cab that was hanging out at the airport office. They asked the cab driver if he had seen these two people and showed him the picture of Art and Karen. He said he hadn't. He took them from the airport to the marina, where they rented a 22-foot fishing boat, saying that they just wanted to see the island from the water so they could look at all the beautiful water front homes. They were thinking of moving to the island. They obviously weren't fishermen so the story made sense and didn't draw undue attention to them.

After motoring out to 'Poppy's Boat' the two men went aboard and looked around, being very careful not to disturb anything. There was no sign of the case, the money or the gold bars. They didn't find Art's gun either because it was well hidden. The pistol was illegal in Canada and Art had it hidden even though he had no intention of stopping at customs; if the Canadian officials decided to board them for some reason, they wouldn't find it. Once they made it to Alaskan waters it would be ok to have the gun, but it was very illegal in Canadian waters.

Mutt said, "We need to go back to town. We may or may not see them but we need to go to the store anyway and buy a bunch of liver at the meat market. This isn't going to be simple and when we finish with them, we don't want any trace of them found. They have to disappear into thin air."

Jeff smiled, "The old liver treatment. We haven't used that for a while but your right it's the obvious solution." They climbed back into their boat and headed back to the marina.

At the marina they left the boat at the dingy dock and walked to the store. Mutt bought five pounds of calves' liver. Jeff waited twenty minutes, and then walked up and bought four more pounds. The butcher thought it was strange to have two huge liver sales in one day - usually it took him a week to sell that much. On the way back to their boat they sat down on a bench to plan their next move.

They decided to watch the Dearborn's boat from a distance with their binoculars. When Art and Karen were back on it, they would just run out to it slowly, pull up alongside, hold their boat to Arts and ask some question. When Art and Karen came out on deck, they would flash their guns and climb aboard.

They were sure if they beat Karen, Art would talk. Once they knew where the money was, they would kill them both. Then they would motor the boat out into the current, dump the bodies, get back in their little boat, and go back to the rental dock and turn their boat in. 'Poppy's Boat' would drift into the straights, be carried away by the current, and be found miles away. No connection to them, or even to the location where they were murdered. It seemed like a perfect plan. How could it fail?

Scene 25

By the time the now terrified couple rowed their dingy out to their boat, which took a while, they were a long way out, Karen had stopped crying, but now she was scared to death. They climbed onto their boat from the swim step, pulled the dingy up on the stern and tied it off, then Art saw the fishing boat coming their way. He told Karen to get inside the cabin and don't come out no matter what happens. He opened the fish box on the stern of his boat, reached up inside, pulled off some duct tape and a 22 caliber Ruger Mark II pistol fell into his hand. It had a full clip of bullets already loaded in place. Art snapped off the safety, racked a shell in the chamber, and held the gun down at his side below the side of the boat so it could not be seen as the small boat pulled up alongside.

Art was trembling. He knew he had to kill these two men, they were here to kill Karen and him. Could he pull the trigger on a human? Commit murder? He wasn't sure. The time for a decision was now. His mind went blank for a second, then he remembered the rabbits he hunted when he was young, in Weed.

"Ahoy there." Mutt said, as he reached out to grab ahold of 'Poppy's' Boat." They were only a few feet from Art. "Where's your wife?" He asked, as he dropped two packages over the gunwale onto the deck.

Scene 26

Ron was mulling over everything he knew about the case in his head, from the view point of his hypothesis. He was also thinking about the money and the Dearbornes. How could he find them if they were on the run? They had started out on the boat. Ron knew where he and Sally had found the boat, so they would start there.

Sally sat down at her computer and started checking all the marinas for any trace of their boat; she checked Canadian and US customs also and found nothing either place. She wanted to know where they might have been when what ever happened, happened.

Ron contacted the Coast Guard and asked if they had run a location scenario, based on their 'Search and Rescue' program. They needed to find out where the boat had most probably drifted from, based on the tides and currents at that time. The Coast Guard said they did, due to the fact that it appeared to be a crime scene. The police had the report and he could get it from them. The Coast Guard couldn't give out information on an active police case.

"Hello Chief, this is Ron Steel, you remember the PI you are going to get drunk."

"It sounds like you are already." was the reply.

"I always sound like that. I think it's genetic." He had the Chief laughing - a good start. "The Coast Guard told me they gave you the Search and Rescue graph on the boat involved in the cow blood case. I'm hoping you might share it with me."

"I think I can arrange that, but it didn't show much because we don't know when it started to drift. The computer showed us a 'most likely' path of the drift, but we have no idea where on that path it might have started."

"Well, it will give me more than I have now. I'd appreciate it if you could fax it to me as soon as you can." The Chief said he would, but now it was Ron that had to buy the six pack.

The fax came about an hour later. Ron got out his boating charts of that area. Sally sat down with him and they started to backtrack along the drift line the Coast Guard S&R program came up with.

"The lights were not on when the boat bumped into us, so I'm going to assume that it went adrift in the day light. It got dark about 9:00; I got up and checked everything at 11:00 and the boat got us up as I remember at 2:00 am plus or minus 15 minutes."

"That sounds close enough for government work." Sally said.

"Remember, we don't work for the government anymore." Ron kidded. "We work for Steel and Steel and they're real picky." They determined that the boat most likely had drifted for at least five hours. The high tide was at 7:30, so it was an ebb tide down the Strait of Georgia. It came either from Point Roberts or the Canadian Gulf Islands."

Sally said, "I don't think it was Point Roberts, because they would have to check in there with U.S. customs, and there was no trace of them when I checked. The Gulf Islands cover a lot more territory where they could anchor out and not be noticed. That would make more sense."

Scene 27

As the fish boat pulled alongside their boat, Art, without saying a word lifted his gun and put a bullet right into Mutts forehead; Jeff reached for his gun, but within two seconds he also had a bullet in his head. Both rabbits dropped dead in their boat. It was all over in less than 5 seconds. Art, no longer trembling, grabbed the line on the bow of the fish boat, and tied it to the stern cleat on his boat.

He went inside the cabin passed Karen, who was sitting on the couch crying again, and started the engine. He went forward, engaged the winch and pulled up the anchor. Tying it down, he looked around the harbor to see if the two shots had drawn the attention of anyone. As far as he could tell no one had noticed. They were anchored quite a way out, and the .22 wasn't very loud. Most of the boats in the harbor didn't have anyone on them anyway. He motored away from the area, towing the small boat with the two dead bodies in it.

Art was thinking about how he was going to get rid of the bodies as he maneuvered his boat out into the Strait of Georgia, away from the islands where the bodies could wash ashore in just a few hours. He decided to sink them in deep water tied to his second anchor to hold them down, at least as long as it would take for Karen and him to leave the country. The bodies would eventually decompose and fill with gas, which would tear them free from the anchor and would bring them to the surface. The cartel would figure out what happened, and continue the search for them.

As he steered through Active Pass, he was relieved that the tide was with him, because the pass is very dangerous at times. Luck was with him, at least so far. He motored out to mid channel and put the engine in neutral. Karen was still sitting on the couch in the salon as he passed by her on the way to the back deck. She wasn't crying anymore, but just sitting there staring at the other side of the cabin. He wanted to stop, hug her and tell her everything was going to be alright, but he didn't have the time now, and he wasn't convinced everything was going to be alright.

As Art stepped out onto the deck, he was startled to see blood all over the stern section. Then he saw the two packages on the deck and remembered that they were dropped there by one of the dead men in the fish boat. They were leaking blood onto the deck. Art stood still for a moment with a confused look on his face. He reached into his pocket and took out his knife. Very carefully he cut open one of the packages He stared at the liver for a full minute, and then smiled. Going back into the cabin he sat down beside Karen, put his arm around her shoulder, and said, "Were going to be ok honey. No one will ever find these two guys. They are going to disappear just like they thought we were." He then got up and went to the galley, where he pulled out four large baggies.

Scene 28

Ron was thinking again what he would do if he was Art. If I didn't want people to remember me, would I get fuel at a small out of the way marina, or a very busy one with a lot of boats coming and going? If you want to hide, the best place is in the middle of a crowd. The busiest marina would be your best bet. If you paid cash, and covered your boat name, which the dingy on the stern would do, there would be no record of you at all. The only marina that fit that description in the probable drift chart area was Ganges harbor; it was always busy with boats of all sorts. He said, "Sally let's concentrate on Ganges harbor. I think it's our best bet, until we get a better lead. See if you can get a couple of good pictures of Art and Karen off their Facebook page. We will show them around the marina and see if we can get a hit.

Scene 29

Art took the four baggies out to the deck with him. The liver just filled them, and he carefully sealed each one. He pulled the spare anchor out of the aft locker, and the 20 feet of chain that was attached to it. There was a coil of quarter inch line in the locker. He pulled that out also.

Climbing into the small boat, with the anchor and chain, he began lashing the two bodies together. When they were secured, he tied the anchor to them. Looking around to make sure they were alone out there in the straits he lifted the two bodies up on the gunwale where they could be easily pushed over. Then he pushed one of the bags of liver under the pants of each of the men. The other two bags were pushed up under their shirts. Taking his knife out again, he proceeded to poke holes through the clothes and puncture the bags a number of times. With a little push, and splash, Mutt and Jeff were gone, never to be seen or heard from again.

Scene 30

Ron and Sally took the air taxi to Saltspring Island. At the airport there was a cab waiting at the office. They hopped in and told the driver to take them to the marina. They showed the driver pictures of Art and Karen just in case they might have flown out of there on their planed escape route. The driver said he was the only one that worked the airport all the time; it was close to his house. He looked at the photos real hard and finally said, “They look familiar, but I’m sure I didn’t have them as passengers. I remember my passengers really well.”

“Could you have seen them in town?”

“I don’t think so ma’am, I avoid being in town as much as I can. That’s why I hang out at the airport.” They drove on to the marina. They didn’t ask him why he avoided the town.

They got out of the car, Ron paid the driver and they had started walking to the dock when the driver suddenly hollered at them. “I just remembered where I saw those two. I had a fare a while back. I can’t remember exactly when, but they asked me the same question, and showed me the same pictures. It was the only other time anybody has asked me about photos.”

“Who was the fare?” Ron was excited.

“I don’t know who they were, but one was really tall and the other was really short. They stood out because they were so different from each other. I brought them down here to the marina too. The people you are looking for must be on a boat. If I see them, I’ll tell them you’re looking for them.” He waved and drove off.

Ron turned to Sally and asked, “Do you realize what we just found out?’

“I sure do. Someone else has figured it out, and they’re ahead of us.”

“You got that right.”

The kid on the fuel dock didn’t remember seeing the Dearbornes. Ron asked him, “Why do people come down to the docks, if they don’t have a boat?”

“Mostly they wander on the dock and dream of owning a boat. Some come to rent a boat so they can fish. Others rent kayaks and paddle around the harbor just having fun."

"Do you remember a couple of men one short and one tall that were here a few days ago?"

"Yes, I do. They wanted to rent a boat so they could look at the water front real estate, but if they are friends of yours, you don't have any friends at the rental dock."

"What are you talking about? What happened?"

"They stole the boat they rented, that's what."

Ron was dumbfounded. "What do you mean they stole the boat?"

They never came back with it. Mac, at the rental dock has the Canadian Police and the Coast guard in both countries, yours and mine, looking for them."

"When was this?" Ron asked.

"I'm not sure, Mac could tell you exactly. I think it was five or six days ago."

Ron decided not to talk to Mac, at least not right now. He had all the information he needed. It had been five days since they found the 'Poppy's Boat', and the fish boat hadn't turned up in U.S. or Canadian waters.

Sally suggested they check the island market to see if the Dearbornes were buying a lot of supplies. The checkers didn't remember seeing them but it was a busy season with a lot of tourist and it was a while ago. They did remember Mutt and Jeff. The police had come and asked about them when they stole the boat. The butcher remembered them because they bought a whole batch of liver. He thought perhaps they were going crabbing and going to use it as bait, the locals used cat food mostly, because the liver drew more sharks than it did crabs.

Scene 31

After Art disposed of the bodies overboard, he figured they had just 12 hours to ditch the small boat and get themselves to safety. He was sure the boat rental service would report the fish boat missing and everybody would be looking for it. He didn't want to use it after sunrise the next day.

It would a be a few days at least before the cartel would figure out that their enforcers were not coming back, and start looking for them again

He gathered up just what they needed to survive until they could get to safety, and stores, where they could buy more clothes and whatever else they would need, as they ran for their lives. Karen was still sobbing when they got into the fish boat and said goodbye to 'Poppy's Boat', watching it drifting away on the current. Art decided not to sink it because the cartel already figured out he had the money; he would let it be found hoping everyone would think they were dead.

Art checked the fuel tank and found it full; the hit men hadn't used hardly any gas. Pointing the bow north he pushed the throttle to the wall and the boat jumped to 30 knots. He only had until sunrise to get as far away as possible. It was 7:00 pm so they had about 12 hours to find a safe haven and ditch the boat.

Scene 32

When after several days the workers had not reported in to the boss, he got his network to start tracking them down. It took several days more to find out that the Cesna 210 they rented was still at the Saltspring Island airport. It only made sense they had located the Dearborns. He also was informed they had rented a boat at the Ganges marina, and that they stole the boat and disappeared. The Boss thought they were hot on the trail. When he read in the newspaper, and saw on the TV news that 'Poppy's Boat' was found with blood on it, and was adrift with no sign of Art and Karen, he was enraged. "Those SOBs found my money, killed the old people, and took off with the money. I'll find them, wherever they are in the world, and gut them out; no one takes money from me." The word was put out that Mutt and Jeff were dead men walking and $100,000.00 would go to the individual that erased them.

Scene 33

Ron and Sally were able to put the same scenario together that the boss had. When the two men didn't return the boat, they checked the airport because the taxi driver said he picked them up there. The plane was still there. They contacted the rental agency at Port Townsend and found they had rented it for a week. They seemed to have abandoned the plane and taken off in the boat, it appeared almost certain they had killed the Dearbornes.

"I still can't account for the cow blood." Ron said.

"I can." Sally said so softly that Ron couldn't understand what she said.

"What's that?"

"I know where the cow blood came from; it came from the liver that our henchmen bought at the store. Remember what the butcher said about it? He said it brought in lots of sharks to the crab traps and that is why the locals don't use it. If it were tied to a body, the sharks would eat the body along with the liver and there would be no trace. Ron, what are we going to tell the kids, that their parents were eaten by sharks?"

Ron just looked her, "I don't think we have a choice. There doesn't seem to be any other reasonable explanation. Two elderly people in poor health against two professional hit men don't stand much of a chance. It all makes sense"

Scene 34

Art had the fish boat firewalled and was racing up the inland passage at maximum speed. He estimated they could make about 250 miles by dawn. If he didn't hit a log and sink the boat in the dark, they would make Port Hardy on the north end of Vancouver Island. The only spot he was concerned about was Seymour Narrows, about half way to Port Hardy.

The currents ran very heavy there and he didn't know what the conditions would be when he reached it. He had been lucky at Active Pass, maybe he would be lucky at Seymour also. If he was going with the current, he would need to hug the east shore, but if the current was against him, he would need to be on the west bank going through. He had read all about the various trouble spots in the cruising books about navigating the Inland Passage, when he was making his original planned escape route. He just hadn't planned on doing it at 30 knots in the dark.

Karen, no longer crying was now standing, silently, beside Art at the helm. She was holding onto the dash with both hands as they sped along, to keep her balance. She leaned over and kissed Art on the cheek and said, "I don't know what is ahead for us but I want you to know that whatever it is, we will handle it together. I'm going to stop crying and start helping." Art put his arm around her and gave her a hug, as they both stared ahead into the darkness, and into their future.

Scene 35

The Steels meeting with Joe and Mary was short. They laid out all the facts they knew and let Joe and Mary arrive at their own conclusion - it was the same as theirs.

Joe said, "If we are really honest about it, they were both rather frail. My dad was in fair shape for the shape he was in, he just wasn't in very good shape. They wouldn't have had a chance of getting away once they were found."

They all considered the case closed. Joe and Mary sold their parents' house and the boat; paid the Steels, split the money from the sales, and went back to living their lives. The Steels filed away the papers on the 'Cow Blood" case and found new clients.

Scene 36

Seymour Narrows came and went. The only a real scare was Karen being knocked to the deck when the boat was yanked sharply to the left as they ran into a whirlpool they couldn't see in the dark. It was common for whirlpools to form around the point as the current rushed through the narrows. It scared both of them but the speed of the boat broke them out of it in just a few seconds, and they were back on their way on calm water. There wasn't enough wind to create even a small chop, and the current was with them.

Art slowed the boat to idle speed as they entered Port Hardy harbor. He didn't want to draw any attention to them. He steered past the ferry dock to the commercial dock just south of it, and pulled in between two huge fish boats. The dock was quiet, dark and cold. Sunrise was still at least an hour away; not a person to be seen anywhere. They were lucky it wasn't fishing season or the dock would have been a frenzy of pre-dawn fishing activity.

He told Karen to take the suitcase he had packed and leave for the ferry dock. It was a short walk and the suitcase had rollers on it. "Go in and find a place to sit. I want you to appear to be a single. I will come in about an hour and will not acknowledge you. I will be a single passenger also. Buy a ticket to the last stop, as far north as you can. I will do the same thing. Anyone looking for us will be asking about a couple. We can sit together on the ferry. There will be other couples on it and we won't stand out. This early, in the terminal a couple would be noticed. I'm going to sink the boat before anyone comes down on the dock." He kissed her and said. "Stay strong, it's going to work out, I love you."

Art got busy; he cut the cooling system hose to the engine, and the water started gushing in. Hurrying to the toilet in the bow, he cut the intake hose on it too, more water was flowing in, and then going to the stern he pulled both of the drain plugs in the transom. The boat was rapidly filling with water, and he helped it by tossing five large concrete bricks that were sitting on the dock into the boat.

Standing on the dock he watched the ocean rushing into the boat with a vengeance, like an army that had flanked its enemy and was attacking from all sides, intent on destroying and disposing of the adversary that was poking a hole in its surface with its hull, Art had mental reservations; but no regrets.

The fathometer had told him the water was 60 feet deep under the boat and it was low tide. The boat would be completely out of sight. He kept watching the ramp, hoping no one was going to come down to the dock before the boat sank out of sight.

The boat was almost out of sight slowly disappearing when he saw a man coming down the ramp. Picking up the case with the money in it, Art walked along the dock towards the man. He was thinking, "I have to delay him for just a few minutes." He waved at the man and said, "Good morning." Then stumbled and fell onto the cement dock. Grabbing his knee, He moaned, "Oh my knee." The man hurried to help him.

"How bad is it?"

"I'm not sure? I seemed to have twisted my knee. Could you help me to the top of the ramp? I think I can make it once I get on flat land." The ruse worked. Together they went limping slowing down the dock and up the ramp. Art thanked the man profusely, and hobbled off towards the ferry dock. He looked back just as the man walked by where he had sunk the boat. "Thank god, it was out of sight." He said out loud and realized he was shaking again. Taking in a big breath, letting it out slowly, he walked to the ferry terminal.

Entering through the side door, he proceeded to the ticket window, passing Karen, who was seated on a bench; he winked, smiled, and gave a thumbs up as he passed her on his way to the ticket booth.

The sun was just below the horizon, starting to replace the darkness.

Scene 37

Ron and Sally were in their office, opening a bottle of champagne. Ron poured them both a glass and made a toast; "Here is to three years in business and we're still here." Sally raised her glass; they touched them together and took a drink. The phone rang, breaking into their private party. "Steel and Steel detective agency, how can we help you?"

"Mr. Steel, this is an old client. My name isn't important. I think you will recognize who I am when I tell you that my sister and I have been invited to live with our family in a much warmer climate. It seems that as they grow older, they want us near them. They were so happy we could join the family that they sent us tickets and told us that if we wanted to come live with them, we could live happy ever after, just like in the movies. They also said they don't eat liver anymore like we did when we were kids. I just wanted to let you know, you should never under estimate an old man." The phone went dead. Sally heard the conversation over the speaker phone.

Ron looked at Sally and started laughing. "I'll be dammed!" was all he said, and poured more champagne, and made another toast. *"Here is to 'Living Happily Ever After."*

They closed up the office and went out to a dinner of fish tacos - made with salmon.

THE END

The Weapon

A Steel Mystery

Ron and Sally Steel boarded the plane at 6am at SeaTac airport in Seattle, Washington, on their first trip to France. Their retirement from the police department had been good to them. The detective agency they started was doing well and they decided to take a trip to France when they had a lull in business instead of another cruise on their boat, like normal. "We need a change." Ron told Sally. "Let's get away from our job, our Puget Sound environment and do something out of our comfort zone."

They had met a police inspector from Aix, a city in France, at a global meeting of law enforcement personnel a few months earlier. They had bonded even though they were only together for a short time. Paul came to stay with them a few days, after the conference was over. He told them that if they came to France, he would show them around; they decided to take him up on his offer.

The plan was to stay three weeks in a hotel and Paul said they would not need a car. He said they could walk everywhere they needed to go. Their big concern was if there was a gym nearby. They both were fanatics about working out. Paul assured them the gym was within walking distance. They were going to stay at the Saint Christophe hotel downtown.

They arrived in Aix by bus from the Marseilles airport and were only a couple blocks from their hotel. They walked over with their luggage. Checking in they were handed a message; it was from Paul. "When you get settled, give me a call, I'll meet you for coffee."

Going to their room they were happy to find it satisfactory and comfortable. As they started unpacking their suitcases, they were excited to get involved in the culture. "I've heard about how the French go to coffee at an outdoor café; I'm anxious to get started learning to be French. Hurry up Ron, we only have three weeks."

Ron was laughing at her excitement. "I haven't seen you this excited for a long time. Maybe we should travel more often. Right now, you need to calm down a bit, we can't call Paul until we change the sim-cards in our phones to the French ones."

"I didn't forget, the man at the Verizon store went over that with us. I'm sure the people at the lobby desk can tell us where to do that. Come on, don't be a slowpoke, I want my coffee."

They got directions at the lobby desk, walked a couple of blocks and bought their new sim-cards; then Ron made his first phone call in France. "Hello Paul, I guess I should say bonjour Paul." Paul asked where they were and then gave Ron directions to a nearby side-walk café, where he said he would meet them in 20 minutes.

Finding the café, they sat down in the sunshine and ordered two coffees. Ron looked around and said, "What a beautiful day. The sun is shining, the trees all around us are glowing with the backlight from the sun and people are walking in all directions. It's sure different from Seattle."

"I love it." Sally said, just as their coffee arrived. "Oh, my gosh, it's a little cup of expresso. I'm glad we're from Seattle where expresso is common and we know what it is. I was expecting a big mug of coffee."

"We have a lot to learn," said Ron as Paul pulled up a chair and joined them. He gave them a general verbal tour of Aix, and a more specific tour of the center of town where they were staying. He pointed out where the gym was located. They said they would join the next day for the three weeks they were going to be there. Their routine was to work out every morning early before they started their work day. They wanted to kept up, except for the work part. This was a vacation.

The next morning when they went to the gym, Sally asked the manager if they had a yoga class. "Yes, we do, it meets every morning at 6:30. There is a small fee that you can pay each day if you choose to join them."

"Great, I'll be here every morning." She could keep her normal routine of yoga stretching every morning, followed by. resistant training, alternating between upper body and lower body on different days. She was one happy tourist.

Ron was just as happy. He had the same schedule of upper and lower body exercise, but instead of the yoga he spent 30 minutes working hard on the cardio machines. The gym became their anchor, so to speak, in

Aix. It was where they were every day, meeting the people that were also there every day and making new friends.

Paul spent as much time with them as he could but he was preoccupied trying to apprehend a serial rapist that murdered his victims. He talked a lot about the case when he was with Ron and Sally because he wanted to see if they could pick up on something that he might have missed. He knew that was the business they were in as private investigators. The police had good DNA evidence, but nothing matched in the data bank. The attacks seemed to be entirely at random. There was no connection the police could find between the victims.

By the end of their first week at the gym Ron had made a couple of casual friends, but Sally, being a truly social person, had made at least five new good friends. She had been invited to go for tea twice and went both times.

One of Sally's new friends had fallen and broken her arm and her friends in the yoga class were planning a party for her. Sally was right in the middle of it. Her yoga friends had totally accepted her as one of them and she was loving it.

Ron was spending more time with Paul. Paul invited Ron to spend a day at the police station the next day and he was looking forward to it. He was interested in the different procedures between his police department in Seattle, were he and Sally had retired from, and the French police department.

Eric Smout sat at his desk eating lunch as he did every day. Most of the company employees sat in the conference room at lunch time, chatting together. They used to ask Eric to join them but he never did, so finally they stopped asking. Eric was a good accountant but had less than adequate social skills. He didn't talk to anyone unless he had to and then he rarely looked them in the eye, only at the floor or the item they were discussing.

Eric oversaw the grant money the company functioned under. It was in the millions. He was perfect for the job. He had a degree in mathematics and one in accounting. He was also bored with his job. He decided that with his skills he could work out a system to beat the local casino in blackjack. Unfortunately for Eric, he was mistaken and lost a lot money. Embezzling money from his company was easy and he paid off his gambling debts.

Once he discovered how easy it was to take money from the company, he made a habit of it, helping himself to thousands of dollars over time. He started sending money to an offshore bank in the Cayman Islands as his secret retirement account.

He was also known for staring at the women he worked with when they weren't aware of it, but others were. They just considered him strange and let it go at that, but he made some of them ill-at-ease when he was around.

She was tall, close to six feet with high heels. Her long blond hair, was combed to spread evenly over her shoulders. Every part of her wardrobe was matched and coordinated to accentuate her figure. She walked with authority as she walked home after working all day at a desk. Her morning exercise and her two-mile night walk home kept her trim. She was on her way home now, thinking if she needed anything at the store, when she felt the hands that grabbed her from behind and slammed her to the ground. She put her right arm out to break the fall but felt it break instead. Her attacker, drug her into a deserted ally behind some dumpsters and leaned down to grab her.

She was so taken by surprise and in such pain in her right arm that for a moment she didn't react, except to her pain, but in the few seconds she was being dragged into the ally she became totally aware of what was happening.

As her assailant leaned down to grab her, she poked the index finger of her left hand into his eye. He jumped back with his hand to his face; she used her good left arm to get herself up onto her feet. The man was mad now and came at her snarling like a mad bear. She took a few steps backward and collided with the dumpster. Using it for support, her eyes narrowed to a squint as she leaned slightly forward in a crouch, the pain in her useless right arm being forgot, as *she* attacked the monster in front of her.

Ron went to the hotel lobby where Paul was picking him up to spend the day with the French police. Paul told Ron on the way to the station, that there had been a murder two nights ago and it was their main focus right now. Ron was pleased, it was going to be an interesting day. He asked Paul the details about the murder and Paul said he didn't know much yet. They would find out when they got to the station.

At the station they had some information but not much. They knew who the victim was from his wallet, Eric Smout. He wasn't robbed, there was a lot of money in his wallet. They didn't have a motive or a murder weapon yet. His neck had been ripped wide open severing the carotid artery on the left side as well as the jugular vein and the wind pipe. Paul said, "It reminded him of the *Murder in the Rue Morgue,* it looked as if an orangutan had ripped his neck open. The coroner said it was torn, not cut, so it wasn't a knife."

Paul told Ron, "The forensic team covered the entire area, finding nothing that could have created that kind of damage, or anything that had blood on it. Whatever it was would have been covered in blood. The coroner thinks it must have been a stick of some kind, but he found no indication of what it could be in the wound except traces of dirt. We're looking into Eric Smout's life and background now to find out who might have had a motive to kill him."

The police flooded Eric's company, interviewing everyone, asking about his life, friends, and work. They found some evidence of his gambling which led to a close look at his finances and discovered that he was stealing money from the company. Ron was impressed. They had completed all of this in just two days. The information gave them several possible motives and a team was well into investigating each one to see where it might lead.

When Ron got home that night, he related all of what he had learned to Sally. He knew she would be interested because of the wound that they didn't have a weapon for. He explained that their coroner said in his report that it was a small blunt stick that must have been jabbed into the neck with great force from a low position, to have done so much damage. The forensic team report said, "There was massive bleeding instantly from the artery that was severed."

"The murderer even stepped in the blood with one foot; there were blood splotches where he walked away, but the cement was too rough to get a foot print." Ron continued. "It was interesting that he walked away, instead of running, it's the sign of a pro; he knew exactly what he was doing. They will catch him; they're good at what they do." Sally had listened and cataloged all the information in her head, but not really paid much attention. It wasn't her case and she had a party to go to.

Sally had the address of where the party was being held but had no idea where it was. The streets were so convoluted and unfamiliar to her, she took a cab. It took her to a door in a tall wall. She saw a button to push. She pushed it and heard the door latch snap; she opened the door and entered a splendidly decorated court yard. It was the home of Jackie, the friend with the broken arm. Some of the other women from yoga, were there and were setting up chairs and card tables for the group in the court yard.

Sally jumped right in and asked where the folding chairs were. They told her there were a couple in the closet in the bedroom. She went in and was fascinated with how organized Jackie was. The closet was a large walk-in. She saw the chairs and picked up two and started to carry them out when she froze. She stood there for a minute, looked puzzled, then shrugged her shoulders and took the chairs out to the court yard. More people arrived and a good time was had by all.

The next morning Sally and Ron went out for breakfast. They ordered coffee, baguettes, and orange juice. "How was the party, Sal?" Ron asked, while they were waiting for their food.

It was fun. We sat around and laughed at each other, just the way we do at our morning yoga. Some of us are not limber enough to get into the poses and we look silly being half way there. Jackie has been doing yoga for over 20 years and just slips from one to another effortlessly. She can sit on the floor, spread her legs apart, bend at the waist and touch her nose to the floor; can you believe that?"

"She belongs in the follies with all the high kicking Rockettes." Ron joked.

Sally got serious and said, "Tell me more about the case Paul is working on, the one that they don't have a weapon for."

"I told you most of what I know. They think the motive to kill him must do with the money he was stealing from the company. Paul didn't think the company was in on the killing, but maybe he wasn't stealing enough to pay his gambling debt, and someone hired 'Big Louie from Detroit' to knock him off."

"Ron, I'm serious."

"Well so am I. France must have a 'Big Louie' or two and if you don't pay up, you're put down. It's the same all over in the gambling culture." They finished their meal and took a stroll to look at all the merchandise at the street markets.

The next morning Paul called to invite them to dinner and got Sally on the phone. He said he wanted to take them to his favorite restaurant to make sure they had some real French cuisine. She was excited again and accepted for the next night. Before they hung up Paul said, "Tell Ron there has been a huge break in the murder case we worked on the other day when he was with me."

Sally said, "You found the weapon, what was it?"

"No, we don't have the weapon yet, but it's not important to us anymore. This is much bigger than that. The routine DNA test we did on our Mr. Smout, came back and matched the DNA of our serial rapist and murderer we've been after for six months. It looks like he got in trouble with the big boys and they took him out for us. If I knew who killed him, I'd write him a thank you note."

When Ron came back from the bakery, he was carrying two baguettes. "I found the best place to get them, I asked a man on the street that had one in a bag and he pointed to a shop called Jacobs and said his were the best"

"Ron, I have news."

What, you look upset?"

"Paul called, and invited us to dinner tomorrow night and I accepted."

"That's great. I guess I just misread your expression."

"No, you didn't. I have a problem."

"What is it Sal, can I help?"

"Not right now. I may need your advice later. This is something I have to do some checking on before we talk about it."

"OK Sal, but don't tune me out if I can help."

"It has to do with my yoga group."

"You're right, that's a social problem, I'm not qualified in that area. Good luck."

"Paul had some big news about the murdered man that had his throat messed up. It seems that his DNA matches the DNA of their serial killer."

"That's great! What a break that is. It changes everything."

Sally said, "Yes, it does change everything."

The next day, at the yoga class, Sally asked Jackie to coffee after class. They talked about their lives, what they did for hobbies, how much they liked their work. A lot of other subjects came up like, just when Jackie broke her arm and where she worked. Sally told her that the reason she enjoyed being a private investigator was she always had a puzzle to solve and that was her strong area. She loved to work on puzzles of all kinds. She added, "You seem to really like the yoga class, Jackie, you're so flexible."

"Yes, I do love yoga. I started it years ago when I was in college, it was one of the PE classes. I have always like being physical and took a different physical education class each quarter to search for a lifelong exercise I could keep up after school. I took volley ball, tennis, Savate and even a basketball class. The one I enjoyed the most was the yoga, so I never stopped it."

"It's too bad everyone doesn't do that, find something that they love doing and then keep using it to keep them healthy and in good shape. I admire you for coming to yoga, even with a broken arm."

"It doesn't hurt unless I bump the cast and I can still do most of the stretches."

They talked a while longer and parted, cheek to cheek. Sally was enjoying being in France and trying to learn the customs.

At dinner that night with Paul, Sally asked him, "What is Savate? I was talking with a friend and she said she took a Savate PE class in college. I was embarrassed to ask her what that was."

"It's one of our martial arts. We normally call it kick boxing. They combine kicking with boxing, it's quite popular. They do it in the states too but it is combined with all the other martial arts and you folks call it cage fighting. It's too brutal for most people to watch; we stick with Kick Boxing here; it's a little more civilized." They all laughed.

The dinner at the Hotel de Caumont was as good as it gets. One of the best meals Ron and Sally had ever experienced. Paul said he was going to be out of town for the next couple of days on another case, but he would be back before they left. They would get together again.

Ron wanted to take the tour to "the little Saint-Tropez of Provence". It was a place he had heard about from a friend at home, in Seattle. "It's more beautiful than the San Juan Islands in Washington." Ron wanted to take an all-day tour, but Sally said she would rather stay in Aix and walk the city some more and go to the out-door flower market. She loved flowers and the open-air markets were special to her. There seemed to be one for everything. She knew Ron hated wandering around shopping. It was decided. They each were going to do their own thing tomorrow. Today, they would go back to the Hotel de Caumont and go through the museum, the current special exhibition was about Marilyn Monroe. They decided to take the day to tour the museum and a few art galleries, then have coffee in a street cafe, like the French do. They were on vacation.

In the morning, Ron caught the tour headed off to Saint-Tropez and Sally slept in till 9 am. After she got up, had her coffee and baguette for breakfast; she took out a pencil and paper and just stared at it for minute, then shook her head and started writing.

When Ron returned, he was tired and hungry. He took Sally by the hand and said, "Come-on sweetheart, let's go to the place we went to the day we got here. It is good and close."

They sat down and Ron asked, "What did you do today? Did you have a good day?" Sally just looked at him and tears came to her eyes.

"My God! What happened?"

"Well, you picked up on the fact I was bothered about something a couple of days ago. I made a list of some things that were bothering me and tried to see if they could be related. I spent my day checking it all out and wish I hadn't, but you know me, an unsolved puzzle drives me crazy."

"What on earth could you have gotten involved with that would make you cry? You never cry. You always said coroners can't get involved with our clients *and we don't even have a client.*"

"This is different. It's not part of one of our cases, in the past, most of my clients were dead and I didn't know them. I have discovered information that could destroy the life of someone that I really care for and I'm torn on what I should do about it. You know the talks we have had with each other when we left the police department and became private investigators about legal justice and poetic justice."

"I sure do. There are many times when there is a big gap between the two, but what does that have to do with your puzzle?"

"Everything. It's about the case Paul was working on - the man that was murdered in the ally."

"That's old news, they have it figured out. The cartel took him out because of his debt. They probably will never find out who did it even though they are good. It was more than likely some out of town professional."

"No, it wasn't Ron."

"What do you know that they don't, Sal?"

"I know who killed him and it wasn't Big Louie from Detroit. I know why they killed him and it had nothing to do with money. I also know what the weapon was. Is that enough?"

"Sal, I know you well enough to know you're not kidding, but I don't understand what you're saying. It doesn't make any sense. You weren't even that interested when I was telling you about it. How could you possibly have all that information?"

"Do you doubt me?" She asked with tears in her eyes.

"I know better than to do that. We've worked together too long. When you put a case together, you're almost never wrong, but this one you've got to really educate me on before we go to Paul."

"Ron, that's my dilemma. I don't want to tell Paul and I know I should."

"Why, if you have solved his case, wouldn't you want to tell him?"

“Not this time. Because I don’t want the person caught that did it.”

“Now you’re not making any sense at all, Sally.”

“Yes, I am. You’ll understand, when I tell you, but I don’t know what you will think we should do and that scares me. I don’t even want to tell you, but we’re not just partners, we’re married and in this I feel I need your counsel. It’s a decision I don’t want to make on my own.”

“Well tell me. I’m totally confused right now. I have no idea what to think.”

“Sit back, I’ll tell you as we eat.” Their food came and Ron settled in to hear her story.

“When we first arrived here Paul said they were working on a serial rapist that killed his victims. That caught my attention, like it would any woman in a strange environment. Then you came back from your day with Paul and told me about the man that had his neck tore open. That caught my attention, as an ex-coroner, because they didn’t have a weapon. Just two unrelated facts.

When I joined the yoga group, the first day, I didn’t work out because I was just new and signing up, but I talked to some of the ladies that spoke English and asked a lot of questions as they were getting dressed after their session to go to work. There was one that stood out from the others because she was just perfect. I especially was entranced by her shoes. They were fantastic, as you know, I have a shoe fetish anyway and I had never seen shoes quite like hers before.

She told me where she bought them and that they were her favorite shoes. She said she wore them every Thursday to work because they made her feel good. I know you don’t understand that but it’s a girl thing. We love our shoes. One more unrelated fact.

Then Paul told us that this Smout victim was the serial rapist. Paul even said he would send a letter of thanks to whoever killed Smout, but I couldn’t forget the unknown weapon. It would have driven me crazy when I was an active coroner. Remember the party I went to for Jackie? ”Of course, I do, it was just two days ago. Keep going this is getting interesting.”

“I went into her walk-in closet to get some chairs and saw her shoe rack.

She had about 20 pair, all neatly on the rack, but the ones I had liked, weren't there. She wasn't wearing them when I came in and I wondered where they were.

Then I remembered what Paul had said, the killer had stepped in the blood and left a foot print that showed he had walked away, instead of running as you might expect. It was interesting, but that's all.

While you were gone, I had coffee with Jackie. I found out that she broke her arm the same night Smout was killed. I went to where she worked and walked towards her house where the party was. Ron, she had to walk right by the place where Smout was killed. I think he tried to rape her and she broke her arm in a fight with him. She isn't one to submit to anyone without a fight."

"Sally, if she had a broken arm how could she have fought him off? How could she have killed him anyway? With what?"

"Well it's not obvious, but it's an easy answer. She is outstanding in our class for being the most flexible of all of us. Remember when I first told you about her, you said she belongs with Rockettes in the chorus line with all the high kickers. You were right and that's how she killed him, with a kick to the neck with the shoes I liked so much. Ron, it was Thursday, she would have been wearing those shoes I told you about, that's why they weren't in the shoe rack in her closet. One of them would have been covered in blood, she had to get rid of them.

The heels on them were four-inch spike heels, a high frontal kick like she learned in her Savate class years ago, to the throat, would have easily torn the flesh and caused a wound like Smout had. With a broken arm, she would have walked away, she couldn't run, the pain would have been too intense and Paul said there was blood only on one foot, as indicated from the foot print on the cement. Ron, I'm sure that's what happened."

"Sally, I love you. What you just told me is incredible, not only that it happened, but the way you put it together, I think you're right. Now I understand your comments earlier, about legal justice and poetic or street justice and why the tears. If we tell Paul, he will have to arrest her for murder, just like we would have done when we were cops. She will be exonerated of course as self-defense and be a hero, but her life will be changed forever because she will be on the news and the front page of the newspapers for weeks."

"Ron, I really, really care for her. I don't want to destroy her life."

"Nor do I. We have a week left before we go home. Paul is a good friend and has been a cop a long time. I'm sure he has encountered, during his time in law enforcement, where a situation needs to be bent a little to arrive at true justice. Let me chat with him off the record and feel him out."

They finished their meal which was cold now, because they forgot to eat when Sally was telling her story, but it was still good, after all it was French.

The day came when they had to board the bus for the airport in Marseilles. Paul was out of town again and they said goodbye to him two days earlier. Sally asked Ron if he talked to him about Jackie. Ron said he did.

"What did he say he was going to do?"

"He didn't. He just said, he would 'ponder' it."

"What does that mean?"

"I have no idea, but he was spellbound as I told him what you did and how you put it all together. He said they needed more women on their police force."

As they were leaving the hotel with their luggage, to walk to the bus station, Jackie entered the lobby.

"I'm glad I caught you. I wanted to say goodbye, and thank you".

They gave her a hug and Sally asked, "Thank us for what?"

"I'm not really sure. I got the nicest letter from a man named Paul. He didn't sign his last name. It thanked me for making his job easier and not to worry about the recent unpleasantries. He said the arm will heal and the memory will fade. Then he said that you were truly good friends and I should thank you. Do you know what he meant?"

"Yes, we do and I think you do to. We love you." They left to catch their bus, with big smiles on their faces.

Deja Vu

Are you a team player

He sat at the wheel, staring out over the bow, which bobbed up and down lazily, into the grayness of the fog that divulged nothing of what might lay ahead, as he steered his small outboard boat down the main channel.

The water was smooth and quiet as would be expected at Dawn in the fog. The growing light was defused by the fog so that Jim became aware of it, rather than seeing it. "Television be damned," he said out loud, as if he were arguing with someone sitting next to him. "So, what if California is playing Stanford, why should I care? Besides, I can read about it in the paper tomorrow."

He turned and waved at a boat coming back into the harbor. He turned his boat hard to starboard around the breakwater and into the open sea. "Look out fish." He said, "Here comes the winner in for the tackle. I'm no quitter."

He was a big man and had the pushed-in face and thick neck of a football player who in his day had seen many hard games. His features were perfectly set to give him a definite look of determination. He realized he was tense and tried to relax, but to no avail. He wondered for a moment what he was doing there. Why did he feel that he had to catch a marlin? Why did he have to prove to everyone he still could. Perhaps it was just himself he had to prove it to.

He fidgeted in his seat, then checked the compass again as it swung on a gimbal attached to a projecting bracket behind the wheel. Then he checked his chart which lay on the seat next to him and had a red line drawn from the harbor to a circled area.

"Right on course," he said. "Funny, I could have sworn in this fog, I was headed back to shore." He shrugged, and sat back in his seat, satisfied he hadn't lost his focus and wondered off course.

The fog was not as thick as it might have been, but it was thicker fog than he had ever been in at sea, and he was concerned about it. It would be a perfect excuse to turn back like the other boat had, but he reminded himself that he wasn't a quitter. Realizing he would have to rely on his compass, he had meticulously laid out his course on a marine chart before leaving the dock. He practiced this often, but he had never been in a position where he needed to do it for real before. The heavy fog was a whole new ballgame for him, but he didn't turn back. He had never quit anything in life.

He felt a feeling in the pit of the stomach which he was trying to analyze. He could remember a similar feeling many years ago when he was sitting in the stadium dressing room just before the Washington game. He wanted to throw up but he couldn't. The air was stale with the odor of sweat and antiseptics, as he was busy getting into his shoulder pads. Strap under each arm, strap across the back, strap across the chest, then tighten them until they became a part of you and you became a part of the team.

He also remembered, once on the field, he had done well. The stands came alive and a mighty cheer always met him as he trotted onto the field. He was a star. It seemed he could hear them now; he turned to see it was just the big red engine vibrating smoothly behind him.

The breeze blew his thinning hair, revealing a spot which had been covered by longer hair from the sides of his head. He swept it out of his eyes and peered even more intently ahead. His eyelashes, as he looked through them, were like spider webs. Each individual hair had several small glistening drops of water hanging from it.

He wiped the water from his face and checked his direction and the time again. 185°, right on course. Again, he made an effort to sit back and relax. Why was he so uptight? Was he afraid? No, of course not. He wasn't afraid of anything except failure.

He looked to the back of his boat where his rig lay on the deck. A stiff 6-foot rod of split bamboo; its shortness and girth gave it the appearance of a piece of reinforcing steel. Bolted to it was a wench like reel, 6 inches in diameter with 600 yards of 72-pound test line coiled on the spool; attached to the end of the line was a braided steel leader of 375-pound test. The hook on the end of the leader was a full 2 inches across from the point, which showed shiny file marks, to the brown colored shank, 1/8 inch in diameter. Nothing can break this rig he thought when he had put it together. No weak link on my team.

On the rear seat over the two gas tanks was the harness, which would make him and the rest of the rig a solid team when the time came.

The harness had a pocket in the center of the stomach area to secure the butt of the rod, and two strong snaps which snapped the reel to the harness so he could use his back to help pull. When he had first seen the harness, he had remarked it was, damn near the same as shoulder pads, and the thought occurred to him again. The harness was a major part of the team, and connected all parts of his team into a single unit, including Jim, giving him complete control.

He had paid a lot for it, but as a coach, he used to say "A team is only as good as its weakest player." He wanted no weak players on his team.

He squinted as he looked up and tried to make out the sun overhead. Suddenly the fog parted and the bright circle of the sun blinded him. He shut his eyes. When he opened them again, moments later he was back in the fog. He glanced at the compass once more. It made him think back to the Oregon game where near the end of the second quarter, he was carrying the ball straight down the sidelines in a magnificent run. The crowd was screaming in his ears, "Run man run". Then just before he crossed the 5-yard line, a flashbulb went off in his face. Blinded for an instant he lost his focus and stepped out of bounds, and didn't make the touchdown. The crowd started booing him. He sat down on the bench with tears running down his cheeks and watched the next play as Rusty Maas made the touchdown, and the cheers from the crowd filled the air. He leaned over and checked the compass again to make sure he hadn't drifted off course.

Picking up his binoculars. He focused them under the now thinning fog and saw nothing. The sun was trying to break through and that was good for the marlin would be rising to the surface.

There was a small speck and horizon that caught his attention. He lifted the glasses to inspect it. At first, he saw nothing. Looking again, he saw it was a lonely seagull trying to rest on a piece of drifting kelp and having a hard time keeping its balance.

His friend Max always laughed at him at the club whenever he mentioned catching a marlin. Max had said, "You're too old to tango with one of those big bruisers, especially from that little boat of yours, and Chuck, his other friend, had added, you ought to sell that thing you call a boat, settle down and be satisfied watching the games on television with the rest of us.

He laughed with them, but he wasn't satisfied with the television set. He wasn't like the rest of them. He was a star. Then last night Max had remarked, "Let old Jim talk; you don't see him going, do you? Everyone can dream." They all laughed again.

He couldn't help himself. He remembered himself saying, "I'm going tomorrow." In fact," he continued. "I was just getting ready to leave for home to get some rest." He went home, went to bed, but slept little.

The fog was almost gone now, and he smiled for the concern it had given him. Picking up his binoculars once more. He studied the horizon. The ark the glasses were taking in came to a sudden halt as a blurred image appeared. He adjusted the dial in the center of the binoculars and the image came into focus. It was a marlin feeding on a school of mackerel.

Almost dropping the binoculars, he leaned into the back and grabbed for the harness. Realizing the boat was still heading into the fish's path, he reached forward to the controls and quickly put the engine into neutral, then turning back he strapped himself into the harness. Now his team was complete and he was locked into his harness and ready for the kickoff.

Just beyond the bow, the huge fin, broad at the base and tilted in a cycle shape, cut through the water like a sharp knife cutting through a banana. He could feel his heart pounding like it was trying to get out of his chest.

He put a mackerel bait on his hook and slipped it into the water. Then he put the engine in gear. He trolled slowly letting out 75 yards of line and started a big circle pulling the bait so close to the feeding fish that he was afraid his bait might scare it. With a sudden burst of speed, and splashing water, the marlin charged and hit the bait with his mighty sword.

"Turn the engine off," he ordered himself, and he did. The bait sank slowly. Agonizing seconds ticked by. Then minutes, as Jim waited for the Marlin to return to pick up his wounded prey.

His reel slowly came alive tick, tick, tick - then faster tick tick tick tick tick tick, - and then the line started to melt off the spool, as the ticking turned into a scream. Jim set the lock lever on the reel and he, with all his strength, yanked back on the rod to drive the hook deep into flesh of fish.

The big fish responding to the sharp hook digging into its jaw bone, jumped high into the air so Jim could see it. He smiled a broad smile, it was gigantic. He was in the red zone now. There is nothing more to do now, except cross the goal line and make the extra point.

The fish jumped again, and its body flashed in the sunlight. To the right it charged, then to the left, and the line was melting off the spool and the clicker on the reel was screaming. It was the cheering of the crowd to Jim. The spool almost empty now started to slow down and then stopped.

"Reel, man, reel!" He commanded himself, and he did. When he had taken up 40 yards of line, the rod was yanked down into the water. Once again, more line roared off the spool. Straight away the fish ran, then hard left again. You're a great broken-field runner, Jim thought, but I'm' a great broken-field tackler.

Into the air the marlin leaped, not straight up as before, but at 45° angle. Is he getting tired? Jim thought. The leap covered 20 feet before it fell back into the water. Even before the spray had settled, it was up again. Then again and again until it covered over 100 feet on its tail in just a few seconds. Jim didn't have a chance to adjust his harness, reel or do anything, but just watch and hang on for dear life.

Then, like a steel blue torpedo, the huge fish headed straight for the boat. "Dammit!" Jim shouted as he watched the fish pass only 20 feet beneath the boat. It was just a blur to his sweat filled eyes.

Jim got back 50 yards of line, then down went the rod again, and he saw the spool yielding line even as he reeled the crank in the opposite direction. He set the drag tighter, and felt the added pull on his shoulder which were aching badly now.

His arms were numb, and seemed to ache from the skin clear down to the bone marrow. His shoulders were cramped by the harness and he was starting to twist and turn to avert the back ache, which was bringing tears to his eyes.

The Marlin was not ready to give up. It catapulted into the air once more to cover another hundred feet on its tail. Then it went down. Deep down. The rod tip disappeared under the surface of the water and the rod bent to its maximum angle as Jim pumped on it to regain a few feet of line at a time.

The surface water was quiet now, and the salt air smelled good to Jim as he sucked it in. He was taking large gulps of air trying to ease the lack of oxygen to his entire muscular system. He kept pumping his rod, pull up and reel, pull up and reel, over and over, have to get more line. The fish after an hour was finally back on the surface and was running straight-away as it had done earlier, but not nearly as fast.

Jim pictured himself walking up to the bar at the club and saying casually to Max, "Well, I got a marlin yesterday." He would lay the huge sword on the bar and show Chuck and the others his pictures. Chuck and Max would ask questions; how much did it weight? Were you alone? The other men would gather around and buy Jim drinks. They would tell their friends about him. "You know Jim at the club? You should see the Marlin he got!" Why, he might even have his picture in the newspaper. It would be just like old times.

The fish jumped only 40 yards off the stern and brought him back to reality. Again, it jumped, but not quite as high. I've got him now, Jim thought. He slowly reeled in. Once again, the fish turned and stripped off line. Jim braced himself as his back muscles tighten into a hard knot, but the run stopped after 30 yards.

The fish lay on top of the water exhausted, his huge eyes revolving in their cup-like sockets. Jim slowly eased in the line, and brought the fish up next to the boat. Jim's body was one large cramp, or was it 1,000 little cramps just holding hands He couldn't tell which and it didn't matter much.

He moved to the side of the boat and gently let go of the rod and let it hang on the harness. Picking up a line with a noose tide in the end of it he knew all he had to do was slip this noose around the tail of the big fish and the extra point would be made, and the game won.

Leaning over, he reached out a tired hand and tried to slip the noose around the tail, but the loop of the noose closed and slapped against the tail fin of the fish.

The fish feeling this gathered all of the strength it had gained from the rest and dove once more. The tail smashed the side of Jim's small boat, knocking him off balance. He fell against the wheel and grabbed the compass, but the bracket broke and he carried it with him over the side of the boat.

The fish dove straight down into the deep, and the line now fouled on the rod tip dragged the entire team underwater. Jim dropped the compass and struggled for the surface, but it was already out of reach.

He put his hands over his ears to try and stop the sharply increasing pain that felt like two knives being stuck into his head. Suddenly when his eardrums ruptured the pain stopped. He was being pulled down into the dark blue world beneath him. Sick to his stomach he wanted to throw up, but didn't have the time. The last thing he saw before he went unconscious was 100 flashing lights as the sun's rays reflected off a school of passing of mackerel. He had stepped out of bounds once again, and realized it was for the last time.

How Can We Stop the Wind?

The price of being a patriot

I entered the building, looked at the register and found who I wanted on the third floor. I had a few minutes before my appointment so I decided to take the stares. I told myself that it was because I needed the exercise but I think I just wanted to postpone this as long as I could. I wasn't sure I had made the right decision.

Reaching the third floor I paused for a moment to catch my breath, or was it just one more delay?

I paused once more and read the lettering on the door. *Doctor M.A. Dearborn Clinical Psychology.* Taking a deep breath, I opened the door and went in.

The waiting room was like most others. A few large prints on the wall that were far enough out of focus that you could see anything you wanted in them, several nice chairs and a receptionist at a desk in the corner.

The lady at the desk asked if I was Jim? I said I was at the moment. She gave me strange look but said nothing. In this office she had probably heard that before. She said Doctor Mary Ann would be with me momentarily and gave me some papers to fill out. When I gave them back to her, she looked at them and said I didn't fill them all out. I told her that I would talk to the Doctor about that and sat down.

I was surprised the doctor was a woman. I thought about it and figured that was probably a good thing. She might understand my dilemma better than a man. The door opened and a very tailored woman put her hand out and invited me into her office. Her appearance was so perfect that she was a little scary, but her smile and firm hand shake put me totally at ease.

"Jim, it is a pleasure to meet you. I hope you don't mind me calling you Jim, we are very informal here. You can just call me Mary Ann if you like. I generally ask questions of my clients and they tell me their answers. If I can figure out the right questions to ask we perhaps can get a better understanding of the reason you came to my office.

Why did you come to me?

I have a story to tell and I don't know who to tell it to. I don't want to tell it to my family and friends around the dinner table. I don't want it in the newspapers either. I'd like to forget it but that hasn't worked.

It happened a long time ago and it didn't bother me at all at the time, now when I am an old man, I can't seem to keep it in the back of my mind - it just keeps coming to the front when I am alone. I find myself with tears running down my cheek and not being able to suppress a feeling of guilt. You being a psychologist I hope will be someone that might help me understand my feelings. It falls into a category I think of post-traumatic stress and I am not aware of what exactly that is. Maybe it is a topic no one wants to discuss I know I haven't wanted to.

Is this a story that has a beginning and an ending?

I thought it was for around 60 years, but it has come back to haunt me. I guess I am here talking to you to see if I can find out the end.

Let's start by having you tell me the story from the very beginning to what you thought was the end. Then we will see if we can figure out why it has reinterred your life and then why it causes you to feel guilt to the point of tearing up. Before you begin your story, I have another question. The information sheet we gave you to fill out, you have turned into me almost totally blank. For your name you have just put the Salamander and no other information except your age, it says you are in your mid-80s. I can't work with someone I know nothing about. I have no frame of reference.

You're not working with me; you're working with the man in my story. He is the one who needs your help. When you hear my story you will understand more, but know even less. You will see why I am confused and need you to understand as the third party to help me understand.

I'm listening.

A news photographer took my picture during a diving competition in Laguna Beach, California, because he thought I had won the competition. He was mistaken but the picture appeared in the newspaper and caught the attention of some people that were looking for a water person to work for them.

I was offered a job by a man that told me I would be working for a company that did not exist and doing things that never happened. The things I would be doing would be for my country and I would be a covert operative - no one would ever know about my being involved. I would be trained individually and work most of the time on my own.

It sounded so exciting, to an 18-year-old, to be a covert operative and work for the good of my country, of course I said, yes, and became another person from what I had been all of my life up to that point. That person, the Salamander, is the person in my story. He no longer exists but I will call him back to tell you his story. He is the only one that knows how he survived his only mission. It is not his mission that is now haunting me, but the ripple it sent into the future that affected many lives. I thought he was dead and his mission forgotten, but I was wrong.

If the mission was for the good of the country, why would the Salamander regret it?

I didn't say he regretted it - he would do it again without hesitation. The mission may have saved thousands of lives and that is why it had to be done, but like so many things we do, it had side effects. They weren't enough to stop the mission but they now are enough to make me tear up. They didn't become obvious to me until I was old.

I'm beginning to understand. Let's start with why he was called the Salamander?

They called him the Salamander after he returned from his mission. They said it fit him because salamanders were survivors and had been on earth for millions of years. Before that he was just called a Spook, like the rest of those that didn't exist.

During World War II, the OSS (Overseas Secret Service), was created to do several things, one of which was to find and destroy selected targets. When the OSS was disbanded there were targets that had been discovered but not yet destroyed. These targets were watched for activity by the U2 spy planes the USA had flying at high altitude and taking photograph of them.

The new Central Intelligence Agency which was formed after the OSS was dissolved was not in the business of destroying targets, at least in their early years. It was decided in some back room that a small group of totally covert operatives would be formed and trained to quietly clear out the few targets that were left – thus the company that never existed was formed.

It's time now for the Salamander to tell his story. I'm going to sit back, close my eyes and let the Salamander speak through me.

I am eager to hear his story. Tell the Salamander that I am listening.

I went through personal training on Catalina Island for five months living there as a hunting guide in a cove that is called Toyon. My training was all pointed at one mission I would go on later. I was trained in survival, demolition and the best way to be invisible in different environments. One of my tests was to crawl into a group of wild pigs that were feeding in a canyon without them knowing I was there. I learned a lot and enjoyed every minute of it. It was just like when I was a little kid on my father's farm. I got to play in the dirt.

I did take out hunters a few days a week but the other days my hunters were my handler and or trainers. During those days we worked hard training me to survive and accomplish my mission. I had no idea what my mission would be. I don't know if anyone knew at that point but they at least knew what type of mission I was being trained for. I didn't even know that.

During the five months I was on the Island I was involved and trained in hand to hand combat, sniper rifle training, explosives and demolition of certain types of explosives, the best way to survive in different environments and survival training having nothing to work with except a knife. I learned to use the K-bar knife as my primary weapon, it was silent. Working alone, in a hostile environment and firing a gun would mean your detection and death. Even worse, I was told, it would mean a failed mission.

Most of my physical training was done on my own. I was told how far and how fast I had to be able to ride a bicycle and how fast I had to run 5 miles, along with other physical criteria for me to work on. I found out the directions I got for those general things were not specific to me. Although I never met another Spook, I knew that there were others – I have no idea of how many or who they were.

I worked on the training I was told to do for several years before I was sent on my mission. I rode my bike to school in college and even got into bike racing. I ran the 4 miles to work and back when I was a teacher until I could make the criteria I was given. When the time came for me to go on my mission, I wanted to be well trained and in very good condition.

I told my handler that I was as ready as I could get, and asked him when, where and what. He said soon and I would get all the information when it was time. I had just finished my bachelor degree in biology and physical science, and was getting ready to start on my masters in marine biology, when my assigned master professor for the master degree, told me he had a grant to work on the fish in the Antarctic, and wanted me to be his assistant and go to the Antarctic with him. He said it would be perfect for my master's project. Now I had a dilemma.

I was married and had a small child and I was waiting to find out what and when my mission was. I was sure I would have to say no to what was a great opportunity for a new scientist – to be a member of the first biological team sent to the Antarctic by the USA.

I contacted my handler and asked him what I should do. He said you have to go to the Antarctic. I said, I have a family now and I'll be gone for five months. He said he was sorry about that but the trip to the Antarctic was part of the mission I had been trained for and now assigned to and my wife would get money every month placed into her bank account so she would be taken care of. I was stunned.

I wanted to go to the Antarctic and go on the mission I had been working so hard to be ready for but now I had to go. I didn't want to leave my wife and son for five months but I had no choice now. It was hard for me to tell my wife that I would be gone for five months when she thought I had a choice and chose to leave her alone to raise my son.

What was her reaction to your leaving?

She was upset with me as you might imagine. There was nothing much I could do about it. I guess every wife of a military person can expect to be a single mother for a period of time during her marriage at some point, if she has children. The difference was my wife didn't expect it.

Was she OK while you were gone?

I think so, as far as I know but I wasn't there to see her struggle.

Is that why you feel guilty?

I hadn't thought it was but it fits in to why I do. It may be one of the underlying causes.

Go on with the story.

The trip to the Antarctic was by Military air-craft. It took a while because it was all prop planes in those days. We left San Francisco – refueled in Hawaii, then Canton Island and then on to New Zealand where I stayed for several weeks. I was met there by two men with all of the information on my mission.

It was basically very simple. I would be transported from the McMurdo base, in Antarctica, to a location in North-east Alaska. I would then be taken across the Bering Strait where I would swim to shore with several waterproof bags filled with clothes, food and explosives. I was given maps and contacts to help me along the way to the target. I would destroy the target with fire to make sure all of the pathogens there were killed. Then I would retrace my route back to where I was originally set ashore. I was also given a radio to contact the boat and would be picked up and transported back to McMurdo, in the Antarctic.

No one would ever know I had been gone from McMurdo because they would be told I was on the New Zealand research vessel, which I was for a while, or on a field trip to Taylor Dry Valley to study the mummy seals, which I also was for a while. If I didn't come back, I would be reported lost into a crevasse in the glacier and that would be very believable in that environment.

That's incredible. Did you complete your mission?

I did. I swam about a quarter of a mile guided by a red light on shore. I was met by an English-speaking person. I was surprised that it was a woman. She would guide me to others that would aid me to reach the target. I was to ask, "How big do the fish get here?" If I had the right person, they would answer with, "So big they have to build them in shipyards". If I didn't get the right answer, I was to kill them. Thank God, I got the right answer.

I asked about the rules of engagement I would be working with and was surprised at the answer. I was expecting at least a dozen or so pages. I got three short rules.

1. **IDENTIFY AND LOCATE THE TARGET.**
2. **DESTROY / ELIMINATE THE TARGET.**
3. **GET THE HELL OUT IF YOU CAN.**

I was also told that there is a sub-war that every country is involved in and no one ever admits, but can be very consequential in our societies.

I was working within a plan that had been worked out in great detail by someone that I will never meet. I didn't even know the real name of my handler. If I was caught, I knew absolutely nothing of value, but I did know how to destroy the entire facility which was built on an island with nothing escaping – humans or pathogens. Once again it was a simple scenario.

Nothing you have told me so far sounds like a simple scenario.

Well it is considered simple because there is just one person doing the entire job. The more people involved the more complex it becomes.

Well, I guess that makes sense. Go on.

The mission was to destroy a biological nursery for several deadly pathogens and all the paper work about the project. It was unfortunate that the microbiologist and lab people that worked on the island would have to be eliminated also. Whoever developed the plan to do all that had a lot of information to work with. I was not privy to how they got it.

How many people were on the island?

The best information I had was 10. There were six guards that worked the two ends of the foot bridge 24/7 and that was the only access point to the island. One microbiologist, two lab helpers and one maintenance man. The plan was designed so that all would be exterminated at once except the one guard on the land side of the bridge. I would have to take care of him myself. He must not be allowed to radio his base.

How far was your target from where you came ashore?

Quite a long way. They had me on a boat going up a river, riding a bike and walking. My contacts were incredible. They knew they were putting their lives and the lives of their family's in danger and were helping me anyway. I asked one of them why they were willing to do that?

She said, "Were not doing it for your country, we're doing it for our country. We love our country and are horrified at how it is changing. What you are here to do needs to be done for all of us, if the world is to survive. We can't allow thousands of people to be killed anywhere in the world just because someone in power thinks they should die. Everyone knows that and that is why it has been made internationally illegal for any country to create the capability of doing it. There is nothing we can do about it. We are in hope you can, but none of us have any understanding of what you can possibly do by yourself."

I told her I was given a plan and if it worked this particular facility would no longer be a threat to anyone. She wondered what would happen if my plan did not succeed, I told her I would be dead and life would go on like nothing had ever happened. No one would know who I was or where I came from. No one would complain because your country has said that the facility doesn't exist.

She thought for a minute and then just shook her head yes. We never spoke of that again.

The trip up the river had an interesting event. The boat was a fish boat and had a diving compressor attached to the main engine, so when the engine was running a switch could turn the compressor on or off. The compressor fed air to a fitting that was on the side of the boat. A hose was attached to what I recognized as a Kerby Morgan Band Mask. I had used one of them when I was commercial diving. I was told that when we passed the check station up river I would have to go over the side and hang on to the lines they put over for me to hold on to. The captain said we probably would not be boarded but if we were, he would cough a lot and act sick so the inspector would want to get off the boat as soon as he could. I had to stay under the boat until they gave me the signal to come up.

As we approached the station I went over the side. The water was frigid: I kept telling myself, "Don't let it bother you." We weren't boarded so I was only in the water for about fifteen minutes. The whole time I was being dragged along all I could think of was the big propeller spinning just ten feet behind me. If the line broke, I would be sliced to pieces. The line didn't break, I'm still here.

You had to have a leap of faith in the people that were helping you.

I didn't have a choice. I felt they understood the problem from the answer the lady gave me about why they were willing to help me. They were all, at least the ones I came in contact with, good hard-working people that just wanted to be left alone to live their lives. They were afraid of war just like the rest of us. It doesn't matter where you live.

I think you are right on that. There are some things that almost every one, no matter what country they live in, can agree on.

Even the politicians say they hate war, but they are the ones that create it. The rest of us just fight to protect our homeland. If you could look at it from the moon it would really look stupid, all the little conflicts going on all over the earth. We are born into a world of love but as soon as we start to learn, we are taught to fear or hate others. So, the wars continue.

Is that fear and hate part of your dilemma?

Not directly but at the base it is. I have learned to accept war as a condition of the human species. It's too bad and hard for me to understand but it is a reality, at least in my world. My quandary is much closer to the surface than that. It has to do with my individual action.

Go on with your story, about your mission.

When it was time for me to leave the boat, the captain pulled into a small indentation in the shore line, out of the main current and put me ashore. It was a black night and he said to wait and someone would come and get me when he signaled them, as he passed their house a quarter of a Kilometer up stream.

I sat down on one of my bag's and took out my map and red flashlight. I had been following our progress on my map and knew where I was and that I still had 90 kilometers to go. I wondered how I would cover them.

About 30 minutes had passed when I detected someone coming. I stood up and scared them. He told me to come with him quickly before it started to get light. We went to his house.

I met his wife and found she spoke no English but his was good enough that we could communicate. I was told that I would stay in their house that night and the next day to sleep and go on with my journey the next night.

He had a balloon tire bike for me to cover the 90 kilometers that were left and I thought I could make the distance before it got light. He said there was no traffic on that road at night but if there was, I would see them far away because of the headlights, and could leave the road and hide. I saw no one. He said there was nothing between his house and my target. I was surprised that he knew what my target was.

Were the people that helped you part of a resistance or underground of some kind?

I have no idea who they were or why they helped. I think they loved their country just like I loved mine. Someone either informed them what was going on at the facility, or perhaps they discovered what was there and they were the ones informed us what was going on – I don't know

There are intelligence networks out there in the world that the public is totally unaware of. In those days you had to go out and gather information in person. There was even a famous Hollywood actress that acted as an information gathering source for the CIA. She had access to many high-ranking officials throughout Europe in her travels. They liked to brag to the *pretty lady* and talked more than they should have. There was no one you could trust.

Now you don't have to leave your office, where ever it is in the world. You just have to have good *hacking skills*. It is a very different world than I operated in. The young people today have no concept of it and have a hard time understanding how my world worked. We did things in person, now we do them by drones and the internet.

That's true, but it was the same for you when you were young. You probably wondered how your grandparents survived without all the things that you took for granted like, telephones, television, airplane travel, and even cars. Weren't they farmers in the late 1800's?

How did you know that?

I do a computer search on all my new clients so I am better prepared to understand them.

That's what I'm talking about. It's a different world and to answer your question, yes, they were and you're right. I thought of the them as being really tough.

I think it has always been like that, however with the rapid advancement of our technology it is becoming more evident with every passing generation.

Tell me about your mission. Were you able to reach your target on the bike?

Yes, I was, with no problem. The road was dirt but smooth and well maintained. There was no traffic on it the entire way. I was told it would be like that because no one was allowed to drive on it except military cars and they very seldom drove at night.

I found a few bushes in the flat landscape which made up the area around the lake and hid behind and in them. The facility I was to destroy was on an island in the lake and I had a good view of it. I settled in and watched it through my binoculars for several days. I wanted to verify the information I had about it in the plan I was given.

According to my map the lake in front of me was two miles long and one-half mile wide. I could see ice patches along the edges but the lake had not frozen over. The small island was round, and looked like a pancake sitting in the water. It was my target.

The island was about 50 yards out into the lake. I had an aerial photo of the area taken from a U2 high altitude plane, and it helped me plan what I had to do. The island was only about 90 yards in diameter. It was the perfect location for the labs that were on it – labs that were breeding highly deadly microorganisms. The process had been internationally prohibited along with all types of biological warfare, but that didn't mean much to some countries. They just deny they are doing it. It is a very efficient way to kill many people.

The five wooden buildings that rose from the island were arranged in a circle around a large centrally located tank. All of the structures were on raised foundations, four feet off the ground, in case the lake should rise, they would always be above the overflow height of the dam. In the spring when the rains came the water was channeled off the island by cement drainage ditches that ran from the large tank in the center out under the buildings into the lake like the spokes of a wheel. It was a good system and kept the island free of any standing water that could freeze.

The most impressive structure on the island was the center tank; it was huge, an impressive twenty feet in diameter, and almost that high. It held enough fuel oil to last the complex an entire year. Everything on the island was totally dependent on having fuel to run the generators. The complete isolation of the lake and the severity of the weather at times made it mandatory they have a large reserve. Running out was not an option; if the power went down and the incubator units dropped to freezing, years of work would be lost.

The closest point on the island to shore was 50 yards, and there was a floating foot bridge connecting the two. At the shore end of the bridge was a small guard house. The uniformed guard there was in contact with his command unit, over fifty miles away, by radio and reported in every four hours. I was fortunate to have only a short swim to the island so the cold water would not be a problem.

The buildings on the island were very plain on the outside but were well insulated and state of the art lab technology on the inside. One building was living quarters for six people, two of which were medical microbiologists; three were lab technicians, and a maintenance engineer. There were six guards that rotated eight-hour shifts around the clock and lived in a separate military building at the island end of the bridge. The other three buildings were high tech labs, each specializing in a particular deadly pathogen. Our information was they had been biologically engineered, cultured, and were just waiting to be spread over some unsuspecting population to prove a political point. The potential human death could be in the millions. I updated my information from 10 people to 12.

It took me four nights of swimming to the island, crawling up the different drainage channels to plant all the explosives before I was ready for the whole island to be burned to the shore line.

On the night I ignited the explosives the sky was obscured by a layer of low hanging clouds. The only sound was the never-ending low hum of the generators I waited until 12:10am in the morning right after the shore guard called in for his midnight report. He stood up, stretched, and contacted the control center on his radio. I'm sure he called in his standard report, "Island lab, operations normal, out." He sat back down, picked up a book and went back to reading even before the reply came back.

The explosion was so great that it broke the windows out of most of the buildings and collapsed two of them. The central diesel tank had a huge hole in it. The fuel oil gushed into the drainage canals that ran under the buildings filling them to overflowing. Fifteen seconds later ten incendiary bombs simultaneously exploded at various well-placed locations so as to create fires that within minutes had the entire island a raging inferno as the fuel oil, which now saturated the island, was heated to the ignition point. The buildings were all a blaze of flames as the fire under each one burned up from below. The burning oil was spilling out into the lake and the water around the island was on fire. There was no escape for the pathogens or the people.

The sentry in the guard house at the land end of the bridge ran out staring in horror not believing what he was seeing. Reality finally came to him, I guess, and, he turned to run back to the radio and call it into the command center. He never saw the knife that cut through his carotid artery, his jugular vein, and his wind pipe; he fell to the ground in total silence, dead in only four seconds.

I think when the ops-normal report didn't come into the command center at 0400, the radio operator most likely reported to his superiors that he was having radio trouble. It would not be to uncommon to lose communication due to weather or heavy freezes in that area. If there was still no contact by 0800, they would dispatch a unit to fix whatever was wrong.

By the time the attack was discovered the next day, the ashes would be cold and I would be 90 kilometers away. The only evidence of what might have happened was a dead guard with his throat cut.

Later I found out there wasn't any mention of what happened anywhere in the news. After all, how can you complain that something you alleged you never had was destroyed?

I was told when I got back home a few months later, there had been a meeting when the new U2 photos were examined that it was decided mission 'Wee Beasty" was a success.

Was that the end of your mission?

As far as what you need to know about the details of my reason for being here it is. I still had rule number three to complete. If you remember, it was to get the hell out if you can. I did. My pathway out was similar to the one in, only faster. There was no rest time, I had a boat to catch.

It took eight days because I only traveled at night for a few hours. I would find a bush to hide under or a ditch to hide in to be completely out of sight during the day. I became tired of the salted fish I was given to eat on my journey but very glad I had a bag of It. Rain solved the water problem. There were many pools I could drink out of. I shared one of the pools with a goat. There was enough water in it for both of us.

My original contact took me out to my get-home boat in a row boat, that she could row better than most men I know that think they're good at it.

I was transferred back to the Antarctic and went on with my fish project. No one realized I had been gone. They just thought I had been in the field for a few weeks working on my project. It was the perfect cover.

I came home and went on with my life, as a student and later a school teacher. I still rode my bike with a friend for the next 20 years. We rode over 13,000 miles during that time. It was a wonderful hobby/workout. I continued my martial arts by teaching Judo and self-defense for 20 years at the college where I taught. The Salamander had faded into the past. I was no longer a split personality.

It sounds like you are having a good life. Did something happen to bring the Salamander back into your life?

Yes, it did. I wasn't even aware of it for a number of years. It took 30 some years for me to recognize/analyze and acknowledge the pain and loneliness I had caused. There is nothing I can do to change that. I don't weep for myself but for those that suffered the pain and loneliness I caused them. It isn't even guilt I feel; it is empathy with those that suffered – I feel their pain, not that I have it but I have seen it.

What do you mean, you have seen it? I would also like to know what happened to make you aware of this situation that is troubling now.

When my mother was fighting cancer, my father was her caregiver. They lived 90 miles from me and I was working six days a week. I only spent one day a week with them to give my dad a little relief, for six months. It was the first time I observed and participated in that type of situation. I learned what a caregiver was and how important loving care was to the person on their journey to death. For my mother it was a long hard journey. For the first time in my life I became aware of that last journey we all take.

Years later my father came to live with me at age 86. He was deaf and I was worried about him living alone. He developed extreme dementia and for the last four of the six years he lived with me and my wife, he didn't know who we were; just the people that took care of him. Those six years taught me what a caregiver really was. It wasn't just feeding and taking care of all the physical needs of your patient, it was giving them the loving care that comes best from your child or other family member that really loves you.

I also had the privilege of being the caregiver, along with my wife, to her mother for 20 years after my father left us. She died at 102 years old. By then I totally understood the pain of those that died in some rest home with no love ones at their side.

When my wife found herself on that final journey, she had her children and me at her side for the year the cancer allowed her to live – it was during that year that I fully realized the long-term consequences of my mission.

I don't quite understand what you mean by that.

I cry now for all the old people that had to take that journey alone without their sons or daughters to love and give them the loving care they deserved. I cry for the young wives that never saw their husbands come home from the war and I cry for all the children that never had a father to love them. I don't cry just for the ones I caused to suffer those traumas; I realize now, that I cry for all of them on *both sides* of all wars. These are the ones that didn't' start or fight the wars; these are the ones I feel empathy with. As a human that loves life and his family and his country, I feel I have a responsibility in part for taking these things away from them.

You're not responsible for what has been going on for thousands of years. Wars have been going on for all of our human history. Do you feel guilty for what you personally did?

No, not at all. I am proud of what I did because I believe that I saved many lives by doing it. My mission was just a grain of sand in the big picture and it's the big picture that is eating at me. I watch the news on TV and see the thousands of people right now that are huddled together in some camp. They are the ones that are paying the debt created by the hate and fear we teach our children.

Every human is born free of hate; society teaches them to hate and fear others. All the wars I know of through history were fought because one group was taught to hate or fear another group.

Most combatants fight either because they love their families and want to protect them and their homeland from someone they fear or because someone that controls their life wants more power. War is a game played by the politicians. They create and orchestrate it but they don't fight it – the people do and become the pawns in the game. It's the people who are not part of the game at all that pay the bill in pain and suffering.

I am beginning to realize it's not guilt I feel, I will leave the guilt there for the ones that create and keep the wars moving forward. It is their burden. They don't cry, they stay removed from the consequences and rarely feel the true pain they are responsible for in the world.

Do you think that the realization that you are not responsible for the pain suffered by the people will quiet the feelings that you have?

No, but I don't think it will bother me as much because now I realize that it is not guilt, I feel, but empathy with those who are forced to endure the pain.

Empathy is good, guilt is not, but you can't let it take over your life.

You're right. There is really nothing I can do to change the big picture. The little children are taught as they grow up to hate and fear what and who their parents do. Not on purpose most of the time but unintentionally by example. The parents don't like or trust some ethnic group. It doesn't matter who you are there is always someone to not trust or not like even if you're are not aware of why. It's not your fault, we can blame society because we humans always have to have someone or something else to blame other than ourselves for whatever is wrong. I can't change any of that, but why did it take me 70 years to realize It?

I think you are one of the lucky ones. Most people never realize what you have just said.

I wish I wasn't so lucky and never realized it either. I wouldn't have to cry at night.

What do you think I can help you with?

I think you already have. You made me look into my personal mirror of life and see how I fit into the big picture. There is a song that comes to mind that was popular years ago I think as a protest song probably against the Vietnam war. I remember the Kingston Trio sang it. I'm not sure of the name but I think it was "Where have all the flowers gone". I remember the line, "The answer my friend is blown in the wind, when will they ever learn".

I think they were right, not just about that war but for the answer to so many of society's problems. The answers seem so simple to solve many of them and every politician swears they will fix them if you just elect them. They never have and never will because the answer to many of them is just blown in the wind and no one seems to be able to grab it.

Perhaps some day the wind will stop.

I hope your right but until then we can have love in our hearts if we live in the present. The past is no longer our reality. We can not let it determine our lives today. The future won't exist until it gets here and is not yet our reality. We can not let what does not yet exist determine our actions today. It is important that we live without blame from the past and with positive goals for the future with out fears to cloud them.

It sounds like perhaps you have mitigated your problem yourself.

It took the right questions in the right order for me to look into my mirror and see it. I thank you for your guidance.

Are you at peace now?

Yes, thank you. I may still cry at night but at least I'll know it is love not guilt that makes me cry, however, if I or any of my family and friends are ever attacked, I will still kill the attacker, but without hate or guilt, just love in my heart for the person they are attacking. It's hard to break old habits.

A Dream Comes True

"Flash Fiction"
(600 words)

(There is a writing exercise called "Flash Fiction;" a written piece that tells a complete story in more than 600 words but less than 1200 words. This story is 767 words, and I'll leave it up to you if it worked or not.)

****

Kent opened his eyes when his alarm went off and looked up at the ceiling in his bedroom. Just like the rest of his life it never changed. Every morning it was get up, go to the bathroom, brush your teeth, make the coffee and watch the news on TV while you ate your oatmeal to see who was killed in the world while you slept.

He put his oatmeal in the microwave oven, got dressed in his overalls and sat down to eat his breakfast. His mind was blank. He had nothing to think about. He lived alone and never socialize, he was very hard of hearing and consequently he tried not to put himself into a position where he had to talk to people, he couldn't understand them anyway. At work in the fields digging potatoes or picking what was ripe to be picked at that particular time is where he spent most of his life.

He hurt all of the time. His back hurt, his knees hurt, he was too hot in the summer, too cold in the winter but never complained. It was his life and, he saw no way out. He didn't watch TV very much. The news depressed him and the other programs showed people being happy, and he couldn't identify with then at all.

His only dream was of being happy. "I wonder what it feels like to be happy." He had no idea. It was his only wish, his only goal to be happy at least once in his life. He saw no chance of it ever happening - only more of the same, day after day, year after year.

He walked to work in the field. His old car had died. It was only two miles and he was still able to make it. It seemed a lot longer than two miles, as he walked home after hours of, bending, digging, and carrying the containers of goods to the trucks.

"If I could just be happy once, so I would know what it felt like, it would be so wonderful," he had said to himself so many times, on the long walk home, where he would take his pain pills so he could sleep, and be able to do it all over again the next day.

One day on the walk home, he stopped to buy some more aspirin at the store in the gas station and decided to spend a dollar on a lottery ticket. He had never done that before; he knew he would never win because he had never won anything in his life, but he did it anyway.

It was two months later when he was eating his oatmeal in the morning and watching the news, when the commentator said that the person that won the lottery had not come forward yet. They gave the numbers again and said that the ticket was bought in a gas station. Then they gave the name of the gas station. He jumped up. It was his station.

He ran around looking for the ticket, finally found it and sure enough it was the winner. OH MY GOD! OH MY GOD! I'm THE WINNER! - It's wonderful - I actually won something. His whole body was shaking. He was crying, he couldn't breathe. He was laughing. I'm happy. Oh my God! I'M HAPPY. I've won the lottery. This is fantastic. He sat down in the chair, he was crying, he was laughing, *HE WAS HAPPY.*

It was a week later when his foreman wondered where Kent was, he hadn't come to work for a few days and decided to check on him. Kent was never late, and had never missed a day at work before. He was a very dependable person.

When he reached Kent's house. He found the door unlocked but nobody answered when he knocked, so he went inside, only to find Kent lying in his bed with a smile on his face. On the table next to the bed was a note.

The note said, "I have accomplished my life's goal. My impossible dream to be happy before I died has come true. I now have experienced happiness beyond belief. I could never be this happy again. The money I have won would only cause me problems, rob me of my happiness, and I would lose this feeling. After careful consideration, *I have made the choice to make my dream come true and die happy.* "

There was a hole in his forehead from the 22 pistol, on the floor beside the bed.

TRUE FRIENDS

One more "Flash Fiction" (649 words)

It was early in the morning when Johnny opened the front door of his new house and stepped out for the first time to see where he was going to be living. It had been dark when he arrived with his father last night from their farm, in the hill country of Montana.

He was a strong strapping six-year-old farm boy and this was his first trip to a big city. The family had moved here from their farm because the dry seasons had wrecked their crops and they had to sell.

He was dumbfounded by what he saw as he stood in his new front yard - which was all cement. Every house as far as he could see down the street had a cement yard and all of them looked exactly alike. He went back inside the house where his mother was finding places to put things away that the family had brought with them from the farm.

"Where are all the animals and the bushes for the rabbits to hide in? They were my friends and now I've lost them and I have no friends."

His mother explained to him that he now lived in a city not a farm, he would make new friends with the other children that live in the city.

"But the animals and all of the trees and bushes were my friends." he said, and ran into his new bedroom crying.

The next day he asked his mother if he could walk to the park, she had told him about at the end of their street only two blocks away. She said there were trees and bushes in it and that he might meet some other children to play with there. She told him he could go, but not to talk to any strangers that were adults, only to the children that he met.

Off he went excited about meeting new friends at the park. When he reached the park there was no one there. He had tears in his eyes again as he felt the starvation of loneliness creeping over him. He laid down on his back under a giant eucalyptus tree. Wiping the tears out of his eyes he looked up and saw the sunlight filtering through the leaves - hanging from the gently swaying branches - restlessly moving back and forth in the wind – he could hear the tree's song as it was orchestrated by the wind – and watched the leaves as they moved like dancers on a stage to nature's own orchestra.

"I hear you talking to me Tree, do you want to be my friend? How long have you lived here? You're so big I bet it's been a long time. I'm new here." The tree was still moving gently in the wind, so Johnny told it all about the farm he had lived on. After a while the wind stopped and the tree settled into a quiet resting mode.

"I think you want to take a nap Tree. Is it okay if I come back and talk to you every now and then? You're the only friend I have now, but I promise even if I make other friends. I will still come and visit you."

When Johnny got home, his mother had lunch ready for him and he said, "Thank you." Picking up his sandwich he started to eat with the enthusiasm of a happy six-year old.

"You seem to be in a better mood today," his mother said. "Tell me about the park."

"I found a friend that lives there and I can visit him whenever I want."

"Maybe he won't be there the next time you go, so don't be disappointed if he isn't."

Oh! He'll be there. True friends, just like daddy always told me, are the same everywhere - always there when you need them.

UNCONTRCOLLED HAPPINESS

A Drabble
(A complete story in exactly 100 words)

I am waiting by the front door with great expectations of having fun when my cousin arrives. He comes over three times a month and we really whoop it up together playing ball, I love it when he comes.

Last year we went exploring and got lost. It was cold and scary at night when it got dark, but we huddled together, slept under some bushes and managed to survive.

When a search party finally found us, we were so happy, we couldn't control ourselves and jumped up into their arms, but it was okay, because that's what dogs do.

CPSIA information can be obtained
at www.ICGtesting.com
Printed in the USA
BVHW041711011020
590105BV00010B/119

9 780999 562048